# McQUEEN'S AGENCY

Also by Maureen Reynolds

*Voices in the Street*

*The Sunday Girls*

*Towards a Dark Horizon*

*The Sun Will Shine Tomorrow*

*Teatime Tales from Dundee*

# MAUREEN REYNOLDS

# McQUEEN'S AGENCY

*To Lorraine*
*With best wishes*
*Maureen Reynolds*

BLACK & WHITE PUBLISHING

First published 2010
by Black & White Publishing Ltd
29 Ocean Drive, Edinburgh EH6 6JL

1 3 5 7 9 10 8 6 4 2     10 11 12 13

ISBN: 978 1 84502 295 2
Copyright © Maureen Reynolds 2010

A CIP catalogue record for this book is available
from the British Library.

Typeset by RefineCatch Ltd, Bungay
Printed and bound by MPG Books Ltd, Bodmin

For Molly:
a Mum who loved her mystery stories

# PROLOGUE

The gunfire was getting closer. A few minutes earlier, Colin had awoken to the sharp sound of a shell exploding and could hear the sporadic chatter of machine guns. He had no idea of the time. His watch said ten o'clock but whether it was morning or night he didn't know. The window was boarded up with planks of wood and the room was dim with just a single light bulb hanging from the high ceiling.

He thought the room had been a child's bedroom in a previous life because of the crayon marks on the walls, but now it was a dingy square box with a few items of furniture and a single iron-framed bed with a grubby pink candlewick cover. Everything had a dusty and neglected look about it, as if the former occupant had moved out years before.

He moved over to the window and tried again to cut away at the wood with a small penknife but the wood was too thick and the knife barely scratched the surface. Another shell whizzed by and his heart suddenly filled with hope. He had no idea why he was being held prisoner but surely he would be released from this locked room soon.

He moved over to the tiny bathroom with its rust-stained toilet and small washbasin and splashed water on his face. He hadn't shaved in days.

Still, he had one secret his captors knew nothing about and he smiled to himself at the thought of it. Something he had found.

He lay down on the bed and wondered if it was time for a meal. His stomach certainly thought so. He was thankful that his captors hadn't starved him and although the food was stodgy and the bread dry it was filling and the enamel mug of tea was hot and sugary, just the way he liked it.

Another shell exploded and the walls shook with the blast, Colin reckoned they must be within a mile of the house. Maybe the next shell would blow the window in and he could escape.

He heard the step on the stairs and the old door creaked open. He was going to ask about the gunfire but his captor didn't carry a tray. Instead the figure was holding a pistol.

The dim light shone on the cold grey steel and Colin, taken aback, gazed open mouthed before realising his fate.

# I

The entire city was in a festive mood. Banners and flags flew from every building and there was an air of joyful anticipation.

Molly McQueen was no exception. It was June 1953, and the coronation of the young Queen Elizabeth was tomorrow.

It was a new start for the country; a time of renewed hope after the restrictions of war and Molly was experiencing her own new beginnings. She gazed at the shop with pride. It wasn't the largest business in the busy Wellgate . . . but it was hers.

The small shop was situated on the corner of the Wellgate and Baltic Street, smartened up with a coat of glossy brown paint, the sign painted in gold lettering. McQueens Agency.

The sign was the reason she was standing impatiently on the pavement. She was scanning the busy street for the young sign writer who had promised to call back first thing this morning.

Although the war had been over for eight years there was still signs of wartime ration restrictions in the clothes of people who hurried past in their thick serviceable woollen coats although a few young girls sauntered past in summer dresses that were un-suitable for the cool unseasonable weather with its threat of rain.

Molly sighed and wished the young painter would hurry up. She had two women to interview this morning and she was keen to have her agency up and running.

She gazed at the sign, still uncertain about the name. She had toyed with dozens of names, spending hours trying to compose a catchy name, until she realised her own surname was ideal. After all the new monarch was a queen and Molly was a McQueen.

Suddenly she spotted Ronnie making his way through the crowds of pedestrians, weaving his way towards her in his paint-streaked overalls that hung from his thin body like discarded skin. A victim of severe acne, his face was a mass of red spots but he was a cheerful lad with a lovely smile.

'Morning, Miss McQueen,' he said. 'The boss said you wanted to see me.'

'Yes I did, Ronnie.' Molly gazed up at the sign. 'You left out the apostrophe in McQueen's.'

Ronnie also gazed at his handiwork. 'An apostrophe?'

'Yes,' Molly was trying hard to be patient and polite. 'It should read McQueen's with an apostrophe between the n and the s. It's only a small matter, but it is a secretarial agency and it wouldn't look good if I couldn't spell my shop title correctly, would it?'

Ronnie shook his head. 'Right then, Miss McQueen. I'll just go and get my ladder and paint pot and be back in a jiffy.'

Molly sighed. Why hadn't he brought his paint pot and ladder with him?

However, this small nuisance disappeared when she saw the woman and girl approach the shop. This must be Mary Watt, and the older woman was obviously her mother. She had answered the advert in the *Courier* for an office receptionist.

Molly ushered them into the shop, which still had the smell of fresh paint. The reception area, painted in a pale blue was furnished with a desk with a black Imperial typewriter, a telephone, a large diary and three comfortable chairs for the clients. A small table held a collection of magazines.

Molly still got a small thrill of pride at her new venture. She hoped it wasn't too noticeable as she sat behind the desk while the woman and girl sat on the chairs.

She glanced keenly at Mary Watt. The girl was fifteen years old and soon to leave school. Dressed in a navy gabardine coat, white ankle socks and black sensible school shoes, with her fair hair in two plaits tied with white ribbons, she didn't look any older than twelve.

'You know I'm looking for a young receptionist, Miss Watt. Someone to be behind this desk and deal with the telephone and take bookings. I need someone who can take messages correctly and has a pleasant manner, both here in the shop and on the telephone.'

Mary Watt nodded eagerly. 'I've done a commercial course at Rockwell School and my marks were very good in shorthand, typing and bookkeeping.'

Mrs Watt leaned forward and said. 'Mary will get her School Leaving Certificate in three weeks' time and she's also got the prize for commercial subjects.'

Molly smiled at the girl but addressed Mrs Watt. 'At the moment the job will be in the office, but when Miss Watt is a bit older she can join the agency staff if she wants to. The wage is twenty-five shillings a week but if the agency becomes successful then there will be a wage increase.' Molly turned to Mary. 'Can you sit here and pick up the telephone?'

Molly handed her a business card. 'When you answer the telephone this is what you say. "McQueen's Agency, 3435." If the caller wants to make a booking you must write all the details in the diary and make sure the name, telephone number and address are written clearly, plus the dates the agent is required to work.'

Mary sat at the desk. Molly was surprised at her manner. She may have looked like a twelve-year-old child but her voice was strong and clear.

There was just one final thing. 'Should you have two bookings for the same date and time, you must consult the diary and see if we have any spare agents. If in doubt just ask me. Now that is all I think except to say that the job is yours if you want it, but maybe you want to talk it over with your parents and let me know soon.'

Mary and her mother exchanged a look then Mary nodded. 'I'd love to work here but I can't start till the end of the month.'

'Yes, I know and that will be fine. I can stay in the office myself or get a friend to stand in till then.'

What Molly didn't say was that the diary was as pristine as the day she had bought it and no bookings had come in yet. It was early days.

Half an hour later the second applicant arrived.

She was tiny. Molly guessed she was an inch less than five feet but her height was raised by her high-heeled shoes. Edna McGill was dressed smartly in a navy blue suit and her dark hair was neatly cut. She wore little make-up apart from pale pink lipstick. So far so good.

The woman introduced herself. 'I have a ten thirty appointment.'

Molly shook hands with the woman.

'Mrs McGill, what I'm looking for is someone in the office to supplement a small list of names I already have. I'm hoping to supply secretarial staff to businesses that find themselves short of staff. This means you would have to go anywhere when needed and there may be times when I won't have any work for you.' She hurried on when she saw a flicker of worry cross the woman's face. 'Still, I have high hopes that when the agency gets off the ground that there will be loads of work.'

Edna McGill was candid and down to earth. 'I do need the work. As I explained in my letter, I have a five-year-old son and agency work will suit me fine.'

Molly knew all this. 'Who will look after your son if we have to call you out with short notice?'

'I live with my mother and she will care for Billy when I'm working.' She made no mention of a husband, but that didn't bother Molly. People's private lives were just that, private. As long as the work was done to a high standard that was all that mattered.

Edna handed over her references, which were excellent. 'I worked in Smith & Horner's office from leaving school in 1940 until Billy was born and although I was asked back, I can't work full-time. That's why I answered your advert. I thought agency work would maybe be a bit more flexible.'

Molly glanced at the references once more. She knew that Edna was twenty-seven years old, two years younger than herself. Her address was Paradise Road which was close to the Wellgate. Another plus in Edna's favour.

'The problem is this, Mrs McGill. If you are keen to start work right away then I can't guarantee this as I have just opened for business. I've placed adverts in the *Courier* and *Evening Telegraph*, plus I've mailed out business cards to quite a few large companies, but until I hear from them, my diary is empty. I can employ you on a month's trial with pay and see how it goes, but if you would rather look elsewhere for a job then I understand.'

Edna smiled and Molly suddenly realised she wanted this tiny woman to work in her agency. She held her breath.

'You've been very honest with me, Miss McQueen and I would love to be on your books if you think I'm suitable.'

Molly nodded and stood up. 'If you come in every morning at eight thirty I'll let you know what work is available and, as I said, it will be full pay for a month. Now let me show you around.'

At the back of the reception office was a tiny back shop with a staircase leading up to a small apartment with two rooms, a tiny kitchen and toilet and washbasin. 'I'm hoping to live here later but at the moment this will be a staff room,' Molly explained.

Along with Mary and Edna, she had another six names on her register; six friends who were willing to do a few hours work when necessary.

Molly watched as Edna walked away towards Dudhope Street, marvelling how well she walked in her high heels.

Ronnie reappeared at twelve o'clock with his ladder and paint pot. It took a few minutes to paint in the apostrophe in gold paint.

Molly gazed with pride at the sign. McQueen's Agency was ready for business but was business ready for McQueen's Agency?

# 2

Molly walked through the streets bright with flags, bunting and banners, which made a bright splash of colour against the grey sky. Lots of activities were planned for the next day but Molly didn't think she would see any of them. A fine drizzle soaked her hair and face and seeped through the fabric of her coat, making her blouse and skirt cold and damp. It was going to be an uncomfortable journey home.

Fortunately, when she reached Craig Pier, the ferry was just docking and she ran to catch it. The 'Fifie', as it was better known, was quiet at this time of the evening, with only three cars and one lorry making their way slowly up the ramp.

She lived with her parents in Newport and the ferry journey each day was a bit of a bind, but there was nothing she could do until she saved enough money to renovate the rooms above the shop. As she huddled on a seat on the lower deck, she thought of the Coronation the following day. According to the newspapers, London was full to bursting with people pouring in to witness the occasion, from foreign royalty and dignitaries to journalists and cameramen from the television; the new invention that had captured the interest of the nation. People were camping out overnight on the streets and, judging by the weather, they were in for a cold, wet night.

She was glad when the ferry docked and she hurried up the road to the warmth of the house. In spite of it being June, her mother had put the lights on.

The agency was worrying her. It had been open for a week but so far no work had materialised. Then there was her parents' 'holiday'. This was to be Archie and Nancy McQueen's last night at home for the next six months.

Her mother's voice called out from the kitchen as she hung her wet coat up on the back door hook. 'The tea is almost ready. It's macaroni cheese.'

Her father rose from his chair by the fire, putting his paper down and taking his off his glasses. 'Well, how did your day go, Molly?' he asked.

Molly didn't answer right away. She didn't want to worry her parents on the eve of their longed for holiday. 'I'm putting another advert in the papers and I've got another list of businesses. I'm planning to post off my cards tomorrow.'

'I wish you were coming with us to Australia to see your sister,' said her mother, spooning large portions of hot food onto plates. 'After all, this is her first baby and surely you want to be there when it's born.'

'I'm not long come back from Australia, Mum. I've only been back nine months and I was at Nell's wedding. Nell has a new husband and will be a new mother in a couple of months so she has her own life now, which doesn't include me.'

This seemed to satisfy them both because the conversation turned to the imminent Coronation.

'Isn't it lovely to have a young queen on the throne? Queen Elizabeth the second.'

'Actually she's Queen Elizabeth the first in Scotland,' said Archie.

Nancy gave him an exasperated look. 'Oh stop being political, Archie. You sound like some of those Republicans who are going on and on about her title. She's a brand new Queen and hopefully the country will forget all about the war and the rationing and let us all have a good life again.'

Molly smiled. Her mother had a good life. Archie had been a clerk in the offices at Craig Pier, from which passengers and motor vehicles bought their tickets for the paddle steamers that crossed the River Tay every day. His retirement two months ago had been a bittersweet moment for him. He loved his job and after they moved house a year ago, from Strathmartine Road to Newport, he missed the daily crossing of the river.

This long trip to the other side of the world was to celebrate his retirement. They would have a long cruise out, arrive in time for the birth of their grandchild, and spend time with Nell and Terry in sunny Queensland before sailing back again to a Scottish winter.

Later, in her bedroom, Molly took out the photographs from an old handbag and spread them on the bedcover. It was as if the hot sunshine shone out from them and Molly recalled the two years she had spent with Nell in Australia.

How exciting it had been in the beginning, going out as emigrants on the Government's £10 scheme, the luxury of the outward boat journey with food that they hadn't seen since childhood and all the fun on board ship.

In Sydney they had both worked as secretaries and shared a flat together. They had made loads of new friends, spent long hours on the beach and generally revelled in the warmth of this new country.

She had met Tom on the boat. He was another emigrant leaving Dundee, hoping for a new and better life. He was a bit older than Molly and Nell and his parents had died.

They had spent lots of time together on the journey. Then in Sydney, where he quickly found a job as an electrician with a large company, their friendship had blossomed into something more serious.

Then it had all gone wrong.

Nell had answered an advert for an office worker on a remote sheep farm in Queensland, met Terry and got married.

Molly had travelled up to the farm for the wedding. She smiled when she recalled the wedding clothes. Nell was dressed in faded jeans and a white halter-neck top, while she had worn a thin seer-sucker dress with pastel-coloured stripes, both of them wearing flat strappy sandals. She remembered how hot the sun had been and how vast the fields were. Under the wide, blue sky they seemed to stretch to the very ends of the earth.

How happy she had been that day. She vowed then that she would spend her entire life in that country and that had been her intention until arriving back in the city. A letter was waiting for her; a simple white envelope that held no warning of its contents.

Tom was dead.

He had been a passenger in a van involved in a road traffic accident. The driver, a work colleague, had escaped unharmed. Tom had often told her what a reckless driver his colleague was. Always driving too fast and taking unnecessary chances. He had been told off by the boss of the firm but he never heeded any warnings and now this accident had happened and Tom had paid the price with his life while the driver had escaped unharmed and had even been acquitted of the charge. She couldn't stop thinking if only Tom had been with someone else in another vehicle or if the boss of the firm had been more strict with this reckless driver then Tom would still be alive. Her days were filled with angry thoughts of 'If only'.

She felt ashamed now but at the time she had wished it had been the driver who died, a thought that sent her almost crazy, raging at the four walls in the flat and crying non-stop. Nell had come to see her but the joy and pleasure had all disappeared to be replaced by a deep sadness and rage.

She had carried on working for a few more months, going out and coming in but never ever leaving the flat except for work. Then she booked her passage home, bringing with her the money she had saved; the money she now hoped would finance the agency.

The trip home had been a terrible time for her. It was a complete contrast to the journey out. She stayed in the cabin for most of the day, only venturing out at night for an evening meal. Then she would walk the decks for hours until tiredness drove her to bed.

To start with some of the cabin crew had asked her if everything was all right but after the first week they stopped, apart from one kind steward who brought her meals to the cabin and checked on her periodically. No doubt they thought she was some kind of crazy woman.

She quickly gathered all the photographs and stuffed them back in the handbag. It was a pity that memories couldn't be stuffed away like that, pushed into some dark handbag and put away in the wardrobe.

It was going to be a busy day tomorrow. She would drive the family Anglia to Wormit station where her parents would catch a train on the first step of their journey to Southampton, and the ship *The Golden Empress*. Then over to the agency where hopefully there would be clients all eager for her services.

In spite of her sad memories, she slept quite well and Coronation day dawned grey, misty and drizzly.

Her mother was ready to leave. She gazed out the window at the weather.

'What a shame the sun's not shining for the Queen.' She turned to Molly. 'Now you will be all right on your own, Molly?' Her voice sounded concerned. 'This new venture is a worry to us but if it doesn't work you will go back to Woolworths, won't you?'

Molly had worked in the department store ever since arriving home. She had loved the work and the company of the other girls but had set her heart on being her own boss. Molly, who didn't want to contemplate failure, nodded.

'Of course I will, Mum. Don't worry about me.'

'If you need any help just ask Marigold next door. She said she would keep an eye on you.' Her mother stopped to load the suit-cases into the car. 'And you'll look after Sabby?'

Sabby was the large tabby cat. Her father, with his wicked sense of humour had named her after one of his favourite films, *Sabu, The Elephant Boy* but because the cat was a she, the name had been changed to Sabby.

Later, she stood on the station platform and waved her parents away until the train was half way across the Tay Bridge before driving the Anglia back to the garage.

Later, in the office, she was despondent that no enquiries had come in. Edna appeared and they sat down with a cup of tea but no clients.

Edna kept looking at the door every time someone passed by. If she could have drawn people in by the intensity of her stare then the office would have been mobbed. However no one even gave a passing glance to the shop, let alone crossed the threshold.

Later Edna's mother and son appeared and she introduced them. Billy looked like his mother. He had the same dark hair and brown eyes.

'I'm taking Billy into the town to see the celebrations,' said Edna's mum, Irene.

Molly said. 'There doesn't seem to be anyone wanting our services today Edna so go off and spend the day with your family. Maybe some work will come in tomorrow.'

# 3

Molly was tidying up the reception area when the bell above the door made a small musical sound. At first she thought Edna had come back for something which made the woman's appearance quite startling.

She looked like a film star, dressed in an expensive looking grey suit with matching black shoes, handbag and a small black hat perched on her blonde wavy hair. She was beautiful. The only thing to mar the perfection was the woman's right arm, which was in a sling. Molly saw the white bandage, just visible at her wrist.

The stranger hesitated in the doorway. Molly went over and introduced herself.

'Good morning, I'm Molly McQueen, owner of the agency. Can I help you?'

She felt quite dowdy next to this exquisite creature.

The woman seemed to make up her mind. 'My name is Mrs Lena Lamont and I'm looking for a temporary secretary for a few weeks,' she gestured towards her arm, 'until I get this plaster off. My husband, brother and I run a family antique business and I do all the paperwork, but since my accident I haven't been able to keep up with it and it's starting to pile up. It's mostly typing, filing and taking down letters. I saw your advert in the paper.'

Molly made a great show of looking at the empty diary. 'Yes, that can be arranged, Mrs Lamont. When do you want her to start?'

'Oh, as soon as possible. Perhaps next Monday.'

Molly could hardly believe her luck. This job would keep Edna employed for a while. She got all the relevant paperwork out of the desk and wrote down the details.

'We work from home most of the time and my address is Cliff Top House. It's just a few miles from Newport-on-Tay.'

Molly gave her a sharp glance, 'Can you give me the directions to the house, please?'

'Of course. It's about five miles from Newport, on the St Andrews Road.'

Molly wrote all this information down and asked, 'What time would you like our secretary to work?'

Mrs Lamont gave this a bit of thought. 'Perhaps ten o'clock in the morning till three o'clock. If we need any more I can always arrange it with her in advance. I may need help on a Saturday but not on a Sunday.'

Molly offered her client a cup of tea but she declined. 'My husband will be picking me up. We came over on the ferry. We have a shop in the Nethergate, Lamont Antiques, and I like to drop in every now and then. We also wanted to see some of the events that are planned for the Coronation celebrations but the town is so busy we might give it a miss.'

After she left, Molly kept a lookout for Edna to give her the good news and also to give her the times of the ferry and the bus that regularly ran from Newport to St Andrews.

According to Lena Lamont, the bus stop was a few hundred yards from Cliff Top House.

By four o'clock, there was no sign of Edna so Molly decided to go to her house later with the details.

She was debating about closing up at five thirty when the phone rang. Molly, who hadn't taken a message on it since it was installed, looked quite dazed at the insistent ring before picking it up.

'McQueen's Agency 3435.'

'Good afternoon. I saw your advert in the paper and I want to hire someone who can do shorthand, typing and book-keeping.' The man had a pleasant voice and sounded quite young.

Molly couldn't believe it. Two jobs in one afternoon.

He started to give his details and Molly had to lean over and grab the diary.

'My name is Mr Knox and my address is 27 Constitution Place. I'm writing a book and I need help with taking notes and typing the manuscript. Is it possible to have someone tomorrow? I'll need her for a week or two.'

Molly said that would be no problem.

After the call, she realised it was a problem. There would be no one to stay in the office next week and take messages. What a pity Mary couldn't start until the end of June.

It meant getting in touch with Jean, one of her friends who had offered to help out if needed and, if other work came in, then it would mean calling on other friends. Molly was suddenly struck with how small her workforce was but until she had built up a steady stream of clients, her finances couldn't stretch to hiring permanent staff.

Edna and her family lived two flights up in a two-roomed flat. The close was still well lit by the evening sunlight that had emerged after a day of grey drizzle. Molly thought she wouldn't like to climb these stairs in the dark but maybe it was well lit in the winter.

Billy was in bed, tired out after a busy day in the town, but Edna and her Mum were pleased that work had come in.

Molly explained about the job at Cliff Top House. 'I'll do that one, Edna, because I live on the same side of the river and also it doesn't start until next week. Another job has come in which starts tomorrow and I thought you could take that one on. Molly left the typed sheet with Mr Knox's details before leaving to make her way to Craig Pier and home. She felt tired and was glad the day was over.

Tomorrow, she would get in touch with Jean about coming into the office next week and she also wondered if Mary might like to come in after school and all day Saturday. She would write her letter tomorrow.

It had been an eventful day and hopefully the start of a successful agency.

# 4

Harry Hawkins made his way down the narrow gangplank of the cargo ship and, dodging the many obstacles that lay on the dockside like discarded rubbish, made his way towards the town.

He was in a jubilant mood and still couldn't believe his good luck. This was his first visit to Dundee and what a bonus it had turned out to be.

He put up the collar of his jacket. It may have been June, the month with the longest day coming up, he thought, but the weather wasn't summery.

Walking swiftly through the Victoria Arch, he saw the bar at the corner of Dock Street. The City Centre Bar. It was seven o'clock and the bar was very busy.

He managed to get a space and when the barman approached, ordered a double measure of navy rum, straight from the bottle with nothing added.

The alcohol hit his stomach and he felt the warmth spread through him, Aye, there was nothing to beat a nip of rum on the cold nights at sea.

An old man standing next to him noticed his drink.

'Are you a seaman then?' he said, nodding towards Harry's glass, which was almost empty.

Harry was in an expansive mood tonight. He turned to the man and nodded. 'Aye, I am.'

The old man had pale blue watery eyes that immediately became animated.

'I'm an old sailor myself. Served with the Merchant Navy for twenty-five years until I retired in 1940. I wanted to stay on but my eyesight wasn't that great so it was cheerio to the seven seas and back on dry land for me. Are you in the Merchant Navy?'

'Aye, I am. I've been at sea since I was sixteen,' said Harry. 'I've been knocking around the world ever since. Last year I got a job on some of the big ocean liners as a cabin steward, but now I'm back working on a freight ship. We docked a couple of days ago and leave tomorrow.'

Harry ordered another drink for both of them. He wanted to keep a clear head tonight so this was to be his last.

The old man was in a reminiscent mood.

'I miss the sea. There's nothing like the wide open ocean, except maybe when there's a twenty-foot wave coming towards you. It fair beats living in a wee dark single room in Gellatly Street. Still, I like to go round the docks most days and look at the ships.' He started to laugh and took a large gulp of his rum.

'I was just going to say, when I see the ships, I feel like becoming a stowaway. Now is that not a stupid thing for an old man like me? What good would I be on the deck of a ship going through a force ten gale? Let me buy you a drink.'

Harry didn't want another one but the man had caught the attention of the barman and Harry was dismayed to see it was another double measure. But he was a man who could always hold his drink and wasn't too bothered.

It was coming up for nine thirty and closing time and he reckoned he had loads of time to get back to the docks.

'You wouldn't like to come up and have some supper with me?' The man sounded hopeful.

Any other time Harry would have jumped at the chance to have a meal that wasn't cooked on the boat, but he had other plans this evening.

'I'm sorry, mate, I'm meeting someone and I have to be back

on board by eleven. Maybe we'll bump into one another tomorrow if you come to the dockside. The name's Harry Hawkins and the boat's called *The Mary Anne.*'

They were out on the pavement by this time and although it was twilight, there was a mass of dark clouds that made for a bad forecast.

The old man looked at the sky as well. 'Aye, it'll be heavy rain before the morning.' He held out his hand. 'I'm Tam Burns and it's been great meeting up with you. I'll see you tomorrow.'

Harry watched as he walked up the street. He had no idea where Gellatly Street was but it couldn't be far away if the old man had walked to this bar.

As he turned away, a small sharp stab of fear hit him. He dismissed it immediately but it still niggled him as he made his way back.

He reached the Victoria Arch when it started to rain, heavy drops that blotted out the surrounding landscape. Harry pulled up his collar and started to run towards the docks.

He muttered under his breath at this turn of events. He could well have done with it being a fine night for his business. What if the person didn't hang around and wait in this heavy downpour?

Urgency made him run faster and he was nearly out of breath as the lights of the ships came into view.

Just a hundred or so yards to go and then he could get a good night's sleep. He wasn't going to be greedy. A few hundred pounds was all he was asking. Enough to let him retire from the hard slog of the freight ships, to maybe settle down somewhere in a nice little house. Maybe here in Dundee, he thought. Then again, maybe not.

He felt the rope around his leg a split second before he plunged into the oily waters. His head hit the concrete wharf and his last thought was of Tam and how he should have taken up his offer of supper.

No one from the ships heard him fall and there were no urgent calls to help a fellow shipmate from drowning.

The ships lay at anchor as the heavy rain battered down on their decks and it looked as if the crews were all below decks. No one saw Harry fall.

One person was abroad that night however. A person who slipped from the deep shadows, peered casually over the silent water then returned the same way they had come . . .

The following morning saw some sunshine at last. The previous night's storm had passed and it was going to be a pleasant day.

Tam, along with his faithful Jack Russell terrier, made their way past the Earl Gray dock. He thought he would go and say hello to Harry before he sailed. The place was a hive of activity as cargoes were loaded and unloaded. He soon found *The Mary Anne* and seeing a young lad on deck, he called out,

'Is Harry Hawkins about?'

The young lad shook his head. 'He didn't come back last night and the captain says he'll sail without him if he isn't here by dinnertime. Must have got drunk last night and be sleeping it off somewhere.'

Tam couldn't understand this. Harry had been fine when they had parted company.

'No lad, he was with me and he left to come back to his ship. He'd had a drink but he was fine.'

The lad shrugged. 'Well he's not here now.'

Tam didn't own a watch but he reckoned it must be half past ten. He would wait here until dinnertime and hope that Harry had returned by then.

He found a vacant spot where he sat down on some discarded boxes and kept the ship in his sight.

Apart from the shouts and commands of the stevedores swarming around the freight, there didn't seem to be any sign of Harry. Tam then saw a dock official go up the gangway of *The Mary Anne*. Good, he thought, the captain has notified the proper officials about Harry's disappearance.

The man wasn't long on board when he reappeared and made

his way back along the wharf. A few minutes later the ship was ready to sail.

Tam got stiffly to his feet and made his way towards it. The young lad was overseeing the lifting of the gangway. Tam shouted up. 'Is there any news?'

The lad looked annoyed at having to stop what he was doing. 'No, he hasn't appeared and the captain has notified officials that he's a missing person.' He turned his back on Tam and *The Mary Anne* slipped from her mooring on her way back to Rotterdam.

There was nothing else he could do. Tugging gently on Rover's lead, they walked slowly back. Rover hurried over to the edge of the wharf.

'What is it?' said Tam, looking over the edge into the murky water. Rover was sniffing at a stain on the concrete.

Tam's head was too full of the mystery of Harry's disappearance to really take much notice.

'Come away, Rover, it's just rust from those heavy chains.'

# 5

Edna had difficulty finding the house. It lay back from the road, hidden by a high hedge. The garden, which had obviously been well cultivated in a previous life, was overgrown and had a neglected air. The lawn looked as if it had been cut with a pair of rusty shears.

There were some lovely rose bushes but their thorny stems had encroached onto the brick path. Edna was careful to avoid these thorns, as she didn't want to snag her good pair of nylon stockings. Nylons were very hard to find in the shops and she kept this pair strictly for work.

The house had an imposing look and a solid-looking wooden door. The windows could have done with a good wash as they were dusty and had cobwebs hanging from the frames. However, the bell was loud and clear and was answered almost at once by a youngish looking man, wearing a faded green jumper over a brown checked shirt and thick brown corduroy trousers.

Edna was surprised. She had expected him to be elderly.

He ushered her into a room whose windows overlooked the untidy garden. Edna was dismayed to see the room was every bit as neglected as the garden. There were papers everywhere; on tables, chairs, even on the lovely old grand piano which stood in front of the grimy window.

One desk was reasonably clear and held an ancient looking Imperial typewriter that amused Edna when she saw it. It looked identical to the typewriters she had used in school.

The man shook her hand. 'I'm John Knox. No relation to the guy in Edinburgh.' He smiled, 'Would you like a cup of tea?'

Edna said no, not just now but maybe later. She had brought her sandwiches with her for dinner time, but as she had no idea how long Mr Knox would want her to stay, she decided to play it by ear. This agency work was all new to her and she realised it wouldn't be like a nine to five job.

'I'm Edna MGill, from McQueen's Agency.'

'Just call me John,' said the man. 'Can I call you Edna?'

Edna said that would be fine.

He picked up some papers and put them down again. 'I'm in such a muddle. I'm writing a text book on engineering and need help with it. If you could take down notes and then type them out that would be a great help.'

Edna smiled. She thought he looked less in a muddle and more in an earthquake or volcanic eruption. She half expected the bundles of papers to topple from their perches. She sat down at the typewriter, pleasantly surprised to see it had been fitted with a new ribbon. She had visualised it all dried up and in shreds.

They soon settled into to a routine where he would dictate and she copied it in her shorthand pad. It was all double Dutch to her with all the technical terms but she was being paid to help, not understand the book.

At twelve o'clock, John said, 'I normally have something to eat at this time. Will you join me?'

They moved through to a large and airy kitchen, which was spotless, in sharp contrast to the other room.

John must have noticed her expression because he said, 'I know I've let the house go a bit, but I like to keep the kitchen and bathroom clean.'

Confused, Edna dug in her bag and produced her sandwiches while he made a pot of tea.

Now it was his turn to be surprised. 'Oh, I've made some soup, would you like some?'

Edna, who was starving, said she would love some. They sat at the big wooden table and gazed at the back garden that was even more overgrown than the front.

He noticed her gaze. 'I'm afraid the house and garden have gone a bit to seed. My wife always kept both in tiptop condition. She died a year ago. She kept the house and garden beautiful and also did my typing for me. I miss her very much.'

Edna, who was in the process of biting into a cheese sandwich, put the bread down. She didn't know what to say.

The afternoon flew by and at five o'clock John said, 'I think we'll call it a day. Can you come at the same time tomorrow? I think it might take two or three weeks to get the book finished, if that's all right with the agency?'

Edna assured him that this was fine, pleased that this job would last as long as two weeks. Hopefully by then the agency would have a lot of work on its books.

Molly was putting the final touches to the rota. Jean would be in the office during the day and Mary had said she would take over at four thirty every evening and all day Saturday. The way was now clear to start at Lamont Antiques on the Monday morning.

On Saturday, Molly watched as Mary coped with the telephone and was pleased to see the girl was proficient. Mary was a quiet, serious girl and Molly was glad she had hired her.

She hadn't recognised her when she appeared at the door. Instead of the young girl who had been interviewed a week ago, Mary had lost her schoolgirl look. She was dressed in a plain white blouse and black skirt with black court shoes and silk stockings.

The two plaits were gone and she now had a short curly style. She saw Molly's glance. 'Mum gave me a home perm last week'

'It suits you Mary. It makes you look a bit older.'

Mary was pleased. If there is one thing a fifteen-year-old girl wants then that is to look older and more grown up.

In the early afternoon, Molly said. 'I have to go out for a wee while Mary but I'll be back before we lock up. Do you think you can manage?

Mary gave her a quick look. 'Oh yes. I'll be fine.' She was full of confidence and of course she could manage.

Molly hurried down the Wellgate, which was thronged with pedestrians. The Murraygate was just as busy and she had to dodge past loads of children who were making their way into Woolworths to spend their pocket money. Sweets were now off the ration and no doubt most of the money would be spent on them.

After the long years of rationing, things were now appearing in the shop windows as the ration books were slowly being abolished.

Molly was heading to the Nethergate, making her way past the Overgate where the shops were busy with customers. She had to make sure she didn't bump into the women with their wicker shopping baskets which had colourful plastic covers over the top in order to keep the goods dry. This seemed to be the latest shopping fashion.

Some of the older women still had their sturdy message bags but the young and trendy housewives wanted something with a bit of colour. It was after all going to be a brave new world, this Elizabethan Age. And with Everest being conquered on Coronation morning by Edmund Hillary and Sherpa Tensing, Britain was leading the world in this new golden era.

The Nethergate was a bit quieter and she made her way slowly along the street, looking for Lamont Antiques. She had no idea why she was curious but she had been intrigued by Lena Lamont and wanted to see for herself what kind of business it was.

The shop, when she saw it, was something else. It wasn't a large shop but it was painted in a deep glossy green with black lettering. The window was small and simply furnished with a large vase of flowers and small desk in red and black lacquer. A swathe of expensive looking material blocked out the interior.

Molly had been hoping to view the business through the window but this was no run of the mill antique shop with all its stock on show. If she wanted to see inside then she had no option but to go in.

'I'll just say I'm browsing,' she said silently.

The glass door, which also had Lamont Antiques in black lettering, had the biggest brass doorknob she had ever seen. Everything looked as if there was no expense spared.

She pushed open the door and stood hesitantly on the threshold. The interior was as grand as the exterior. A faint but pleasant perfume was evident; a mixture of flowers and beeswax polish. The highly polished pieces of furniture looked expensive and grand but Molly's attention went straight to the collection of beautiful old rugs which hung from a rack at the back of the shop. They lay side by side with exquisite tapestries and embroidered panels.

Molly decided this shop was far too grand for her, but as she turned to leave, a man's voice called out, 'Can I help you?'

He was one of the most distinguished men Molly had ever seen. Tall and slim with grey hair and blue eyes, he looked every inch the successful businessman in his dark grey suit that she knew instinctively had not been bought at Burtons, Claude Alexander or the Fifty-Shilling Tailors.

Business must be good, she thought, if the salesman looked as posh as this. The quietness of the shop and the lack of other customers made her feel uncomfortable.

'Can I help you?' the man asked again. His voice sounded cultured and was certainly not a Scottish accent.

Molly tried not to look flustered. 'I'm just looking, if that's alright.'

He waved an elegant hand, which swept over the objets d'art and the wonderful rugs and tapestries, then returned to the papers on his desk.

'Is there anything in particular you're interested in?'

Oh my God, thought Molly, what do I say? Her mouth was dry but she returned the man's gaze with a smile. 'Not really. I'm looking for something to do with ships.'

The man gave her a sharp gaze. 'I'm afraid we've nothing like that at the moment, but do come in again. I get new stock in every month.'

A thought crossed her mind. Who had the money to buy these expensive things? After all, the shop was hardly a hive of activity. And as for her paying another visit, that was debatable.

She made her escape and walked quickly back to the Wellgate. She was shaking and couldn't understand why. It was four o'clock. She decided to spend the rest of the day at the agency and then lock up.

Mary was excited when Molly returned. Her face flushed with pleasure. 'There's been a booking Miss McQueen. The owner of a small potato firm needs a typist for next week as his regular office girl is off ill.'

Before Molly could answer, Mary continued. 'Jean came in and she said she would contact one of your friends to do it. Is that alright?'

Molly was pleased at Mary's initiative and said so. The girl blushed scarlet at this compliment.

'I've also typed out the address and Jean said she would come in later and pick it up.'

Jean did come in just before closing time. 'I've got Betty to do that job and she'll put her hours in at the end of the week.' She looked at her friend. 'Are you alright, Molly?'

'I'm fine, Jean. Just a bit tired.'

Later, as she walked through the streets towards Craig Pier, she still felt flustered by her encounter at Lamont Antiques.

The 'Fifie' was berthed as she made her way down the sloping pier. The evening had turned out warm and sunny and she settled down on one of the wooden benches. A breeze from the river swept over her and she was grateful for it's cooling effect.

She was halfway across the river when she realised she hadn't had one thought of Tom all day.

Marigold was waiting for her in the house. She had put out fresh food and water for Sabby.

'Shall I put on the kettle for a cup of tea, Molly? You look worn out.'

'Thanks Marigold,' said Molly as she sank gratefully down on the kitchen chair. The sun was still a blaze of light on the river. Sabby made for the cushion on the windowsill and pointedly turned her back to Molly, making it plain she wasn't the mistress of the house.

Marigold laughed when she saw this. 'She's a right snobby aristocrat. Pay no attention to her.'

'Mum told me you've lived here all your life, Marigold, is that right?'

Marigold, who was pouring the water into the teapot, nodded. 'That's right. Ever since I was a young child.'

As she carried the cups over to the table she gave Molly a sharp look. 'Is there something wrong?'

Molly shook her head. 'No. It's just that I have a client on Monday who lives near here. I just wondered if you knew where the house was. It's called Cliff Top House and it's on the road to St Andrews.'

'Cliff Top House?' said Marigold, looking puzzled. 'I can't think where that could be as I've never heard of a house called that. It's near here, you say?'

'Yes and I have to be there on Monday morning.'

'What's the name of your client?'

'A Mr and Mrs Lamont. Her name is Lena.'

Molly looked in her bag for the slip of paper that Lena had given her with the directions.

She handed it over to Marigold.

Marigold looked at it.

'Lamont,' said Marigold. 'There used to be a farmer here many years ago called Jock Abbott, but his house wasn't called Cliff Top House. It was called Tayport Farm and he died a few years before the start of the war. There was a daughter who used to come down now and again, but I think she may have died so I've no idea who owns the farm now. Yes that's the farm right enough. The people must have bought it from the old man's estate but as far as I know it's been lying empty for all this time. Maybe they've just moved in.'

Molly sipped her tea and scrutinised the small scrap of paper. 'It should be easy to find. It looks like I've to take a turning off the main road.'

'Actually', said Marigold, 'It's right off the beaten track. The road down to the farm is a very narrow one and isn't even marked on some maps. It's a dead end and the farm lies at the end of it.'

Molly walked over to the window and watched as the sun dipped behind the buildings of Dundee.

Although she hadn't seen this house before she arrived back from Australia, she was entranced by the ever changing views of the river.

Marigold said goodnight. 'Good luck in your new venture' she said as she went out.

Molly was amused by her neighbour's concern. However, as she got ready for bed, she was grateful to have such a caring person near at hand.

# 6

Monday morning dawned cold and grey with a thick mist that blanked out all traces of scenery. Molly carried her cup of tea through to the living room but she could hardly see the middle of the garden, let alone the river.

She had spent ages on her appearance as she wanted to portray herself as a true professional. She thought her hair looked a bit curly so she tied it back with a clasp.

She drove slowly, frightened of missing the road end and also because trying to see the edges of the road was difficult.

She strained her eyes to see the turning and the signpost but all this peering into the grey mist was giving her a headache. That would be a fine start to her career, she thought, if she fell out of the car with a blinding headache instead of being the cool person she hoped she was.

Suddenly, looming out of the mist, she saw a small white wooden sign and she stopped. It said 'Cliff Top Farm. 3 miles'. The opening was narrow and looked more like a break in the overgrown bushes, and she was dismayed to see it was more of a farm track than a proper tarred road. The trees lining the edges seemed to hang very low. She heard the faint sounds of scratching as the branches scraped across the top of the car.

'I'm not looking forward to this journey every day,' she said out loud.

The track wasn't straight and there were a few sharp bends

which almost gave her heart failure when they appeared out of the misty gloom. Also frightening was the fact she was heading for a farm on a cliff top. What if she missed the building?

'Oh, stop being silly,' she said, but the feeling of isolation still lingered.

After what took ages, a building loomed out of the mist and she drove thankfully into a small paved courtyard. It was difficult to see the entire house but it looked squat and low; like a sprawling grey, slumbering animal.

A door was flung open, its warm golden light spilling out onto the yard and Lena appeared.

'Thank goodness you've arrived. I was worried you might miss the sign at the road end,' she said. She crossed the yard and helped Molly with her typewriter bag. Molly was proud of her portable typewriter. She carried all the necessary items she needed for a job in this professional black bag.

'Come away in,' said Lena. 'I've put on a fresh pot of coffee.'

Molly let herself be led towards the door and the delicious smell of coffee wafted out. She was feeling better by the minute.

The kitchen was a huge contrast to the outside appearance. It was large with a low ceiling, covered with wooden beams. A large table with eight chairs sat in the centre of the room and it held a huge vase of roses and a tray with cups on its surface.

'Sit down, sit down,' said Lena. 'Let me take your coat. What a terrible day to have to drive somewhere strange,' she said, giving Molly a huge wide smile.

She was dressed in a black skirt with a deep blue woollen jumper and, like Molly, she had tied her hair back. Her arm in its sling made a sharp contrast to this look of perfection.

As Lena poured out the coffee, she mentioned the work that needed done.

'I normally work for five hours and I like to finish about three o'clock. Does that suit you, Miss McQueen?'

Molly was slightly surprised by the short afternoon but she nodded. 'Yes, that's fine.'

'We have a well-known antiques business in the town but we also export items to America, Canada and Europe. I do all the office work and the invoicing but I've had to stop due to my arm.'

Molly wondered if she was still in pain with her injury.

By now, the coffee cups lay empty and Lena stood up. 'I'll show you the office and perhaps you can type up some letters and invoices for me.'

When she reached the door, she stopped. 'Did I mention I only need you for four days a week? My husband and I normally go on business trips at the weekend and we like to make a start on a Friday.'

This was also news to Molly, but it would allow her to work in the agency and catch up with any backlog.

They walked down a long, narrow corridor, the walls of which were covered with oil paintings. Portraits of people from previous centuries gazed out from elaborate frames. They nearly all had a pained or arrogant expression and Molly felt quite intimidated by this gallery of dead dignitaries and their buxom wives.

Lena laughed. 'We call this our family album although we aren't related to anyone here. Thankfully we've no skeletons in our cupboards or long dead relatives on our walls.'

She threw open a door at the end of the corridor and ushered Molly into a large room which was obviously the office. One wall was filled with filing cabinets and another wall had a fitted book-case with books that looked really old.

Molly was taken aback by the size of the room. After the kitchen with its low ceiling and corridor she had been expecting some-thing similar, but this room had high ceilings and a big window with expensive looking curtains hanging in heavy folds from an ornate pelmet, decorated with large tassels.

'The front of the house has two floors and these large rooms,' said Lena. 'It's only the back of the house that's low.' She marched over to the window and gazed out. 'The view from here is superb on a good day, but not today.'

Molly agreed. The mist hadn't risen and it was difficult to see more than a foot out of the window. The room, however, was warm and a large polished desk stood in front of the window. It was extremely tidy with only a telephone and tray of pencils on its surface and Molly thought of her own desk at home, the top cluttered with paperwork.

Molly held up her bag. 'I've brought my portable typewriter.'

Lena smiled. 'Oh, we've got our own typewriter here.' She moved towards a small cupboard, took out a valuable looking typewriter and carried it over to the desk. 'Now if you sit at the desk, I'll curl up on this chair and dictate my letters.'

Molly was amused to see that the chair was a chaise longue and rather than curling up on it, Lena stretched out and gave a contented sigh.

The next couple of hours passed quite quickly and Lena then suggested a break for more coffee and biscuits.

When they reached the cosy kitchen, Molly was surprised to see a man sitting at the table.

Lean said, 'This is my husband Joe. Joe this is Miss McQueen from the agency.'

Joe stood up and shook her hand. Molly winced slightly as her hand felt as if it was gripped in a vice.

Lena was about five foot eight inches but Joe was a good three inches shorter than his wife. What he lacked in height however he made up for in breadth. He had a muscular frame with a plump face which seemed to rise out of his shoulders.

'What are you doing today, Joe?' Lena asked her husband.

'We're out in the sheds, sorting the furniture and the china. We've got to get things packed this week for that large order in America.'

Lena turned to Molly. 'We keep a lot of our stuff in sheds in the grounds here, but we also have warehouses in Holland. We buy from all over Europe and some of the large houses that had rich owners before the war now need to sell some of their treasures, which is a great shame but good business for us. I was wondering if you would like a look around our sheds. It will give you an idea of the business.'

Molly followed her out, pleased to see the mist was rising slowly. It looked like it was going to be a sunny day after all.

The sheds, which lay beyond the courtyard, were built in green corrugated iron with sturdy metal roofs and looked like they would withstand a hurricane or earthquake.

The first shed had a large door which rolled upwards and had boxes stacked on metal shelves; hundreds of them.

Molly hadn't given much thought to the antique business before but she reckoned it must be a very lucrative way to earn a living.

Two men were working inside the dim interior and as Lena walked towards them, they stopped stacking boxes and gave Molly a quizzical look. The taller one looked about twenty-five and the other one was a bit older, perhaps in his early thirties.

'This is Mike and Christie. Come and meet Miss McQueen.' She turned to Molly. 'Do you mind if we use first name terms as it seems such a mouthful saying Miss McQueen?'

Molly nodded.

The younger man, Mike, came out first and gave her a wary look. 'Hullo' he said and stood beside the door, wiping his hands on his green apron. 'I'm Mike.'

Judging from his accent, Molly thought he was English. He was thin to the point of emaciation and his shirt and trousers seemed to hang from his body. His hair, however, was black, thick and luxuriantly waved. Molly would have paid good money for waves like that. He was also very good looking and the large mole on the side of his cheek didn't detract from his looks.

The second man came over and there was no doubt about his nationality. 'Hi, I'm Christie. Welcome to Cliff Top House.'

Canadian, thought Molly.

'Are you from Canada, Christie?'

He smiled. 'Yes, I am. Originally from Toronto but I'm over here on a working holiday.'

Lena led the way back into the house. 'Well you've met our little work gang, except my brother, but he'll be back soon.'

The afternoon went in quickly and Molly was entranced by the view from the window. The mist had cleared completely and the view overlooked the river towards Broughty Ferry. The sun shimmered on the river and the grassy lawn seemed to sweep towards it before curving downwards into space. The house was truly on a clifftop.

At three o'clock, Molly was finishing her typing when Lena's brother appeared. Molly was surprised when she saw it was the elegant man from the shop.

'Ah, here is Kenneth now,' said Lena

Kenneth shook her hand and his eyes were amused.

'It's the girl looking for ships.'

Lena gave him a confused look but Molly explained.

'I was in your shop on Saturday, looking for either a picture or model of a ship. My father worked all his life on the Tay Ferries, and now that he's retired I thought I would get him a present.'

Kenneth held her hand a fraction longer than was polite and for an absurd moment Molly thought he was going to kiss it.

'Well, I must look out for something for your father,' he said.

As Molly drove away, the track didn't seem as sinister as it had done in the early morning but as she turned out of the courtyard she noticed Mike watching her. His unwavering stare made Molly shiver.

It had been a strange sort of a day and she wondered a bit about Kenneth, this elegant man dressed in his grey cashmere jumper and cream woollen suit. Everything about this place reeked of money and Molly wondered if she was in the wrong business with her agency.

Marigold was working in the garden, digging up some weeds with a hoe and Molly smiled, aware that the poor weeds didn't stand a chance. Sabby was lying on a sun-warmed bench and, as usual, she ignored Molly. Marigold came over the as soon as the car was parked in the garage.

'How did it go, Molly? Did you find the house?'

Molly said she had. 'Everything looks so expensive in the house, Marigold. There seems to be loads of money.'

She began to describe Lena, Joe and Kenneth plus the two workers.

'Joe, the husband looks so ugly compared to her but her brother Kenneth is lovely and friendly. One of the workers is Canadian and the other one sounds English.

The mail was lying behind the door but there was nothing of importance except for the postcard. Her dad had written it and obviously posted it in some port. It was difficult to make out the postmark and she didn't recognize the stamp.

Having a great trip so far. The ship is so different from the Abercraig and the BL Nairn as it's huge. Lots of things to do and the food is great. Mum was seasick as we went through the Bay of Biscay but she's much better now. She sends her love.
Dad

She showed Marigold the postcard and they sat in the sunny window, discussing Nancy's seasickness and hoping the rest of the voyage would be in calmer waters.

# 7

Edna was running late. Billy had been ill through the night and she hadn't wanted him to go to school. Her Mum thought otherwise and the discussion had taken up precious minutes from her tight timetable.

She ran down the stair and into the street. The mist was thick and she felt the droplets of water on her face. She hurried up Paradise Road, thankful that she had tied her headscarf around her hair.

It had taken her three quarters of an hour last night to put pincurls in her hair with Bobby Pins. However, the result this morning was pleasing. Now, as she faced this murky damp morning, she just knew her hair would be limp and flat by the time she reached John Knox's house.

Perhaps she should follow Mary's example and get a home perm.

She made her way up the brae towards Garland Place. It was difficult to see more than a foot in front of her with the fog. She was wary of crossing the road because she could hear the muffled sound of cars and the number 4 bus as it wound its way up towards the Royal Infirmary.

She gave herself a mental shake. All this extra time spent on her appearance and hair was out of character for her and she acknowledged the true reason for it. John Knox. She was passing the entrance to Dudhope Park when a dark shadow sprang out. Edna screamed, but even that seemed muffled by the mist. She hit her side on the stone pillar that stood at the entrance to the park and because there was nowhere to go, caught the full force of the fist that struck her face.

She screamed again and a voice called out, 'Are you all right?'

The shadow darted away into the park and Edna was left crying with the shock and the pain in her face.

A man appeared beside her. 'I heard you scream,' he said. 'Are you hurt?'

Edna tried to pull herself together, smoothing her jacket and skirt.

'I'm fine thank you. I walked into the wall and gave myself a fright.'

The man said, 'Do you want any help to get home?'

By now, Edna was mortified at all the fuss. 'No, you've been very kind. Thank you.' She turned and walked quickly back to the house, half running and stumbling on the wet pavement, thinking that the dark shadow was following her. She hurried up the stairs and almost fell into the house.

Her mother was astonished. 'What on earth has happened, Edna?' She scrutinised her face and gave a sharp gasp. 'You've got a huge bruise on your cheek and I wouldn't be surprised if you end up with a black eye.' She took hold of her elbow and ushered her gently into the warm kitchen.

Edna sank down on the chair and tears rolled down her face. She looked for Billy but he wasn't there.

'I took him to school because he said he felt a lot better,' her mother explained.

Edna stood up and looked in the mirror above the sideboard. She did look a real mess but she didn't want to worry her mother about the man. She was sure it was a man, although she hadn't been able to make out any features. She thought he had had a dark scarf over his face, but with the mist being so thick, he was only an indistinct shape. But yes, she thought, it was definitely a man.

'I walked into a lamp post, Mum.'

Irene looked dubious. 'A lamp post?'

By now, Edna had fished out her small make-up bag from the drawer and was applying a thick smear of Max Factor Pancake Stick to her bruise. It helped a little bit but didn't cover it entirely. She didn't know what to do. Should she sign off work today or go in as usual?

Irene said, 'You can't go into work looking like that, Edna. Do you want me to go to the agency?'

'No, Mum, I'll be all right.'

She brushed her skirt and jacket, then almost cried when she saw the ladder in her nylon stockings.

'Oh no, and this is my only pair,' she said.

'Wait a minute and I'll sort that out,' said Irene.

She took the small bottle of pale pink nail varnish out of the make-up bag and placed two dots, one at the top of the ladder and one at the foot. 'That'll stop it running up the entire stocking.'

Edna gave another glance in the mirror and noticed that her curls had indeed gone limp. Sighing, she wrapped the scarf around her head and went back out into the street.

'Do you want me to come with you?'

Edna wanted to say yes; that she was scared to go out into the fog, but she didn't want to give her mother any more trouble. She had enough on her plate looking after Billy.

'No, Mum, I'll be fine. I'll watch where I'm walking.'

Edna was dismayed to see the mist was still as thick and, instead of going past the park she decided to go up Constitution Road and reach John Knox's house from another direction.

She half expected her assailant to leap out again but she reached the safety of the house.

John was looking out of the window as she made her way through the garden and he had the door opened by the time she reached it.

'I was worried about you. I . . .' he stopped when he saw her face.

She tried to smile. 'I walked into a lamp post. Would you believe it?'

He ushered her into the kitchen and made her sit down. As he made a pot of tea and toast, he kept gazing at her, a worried frown on his face.

'Maybe you should see a doctor.'

Edna tried to be light-hearted about the whole episode. 'No, I'll be fine.'

They sat by the fire and she was glad of the hot tea. She felt a bit calmer now but she was sure if someone measured her heart rate it would go off the scale.

She gazed morosely at the ruined stocking. Perhaps she could pay a visit to the Sixty-Minute Cleaners in the High Street. They advertised 'Invisible Mending' for hosiery.

John was talking and she hadn't a clue what he said, she had been so fixated about her nylons. He refilled her cup.

'I was saying that I don't think we should do any work today. I'm sure you are still in shock over your accident.'

Edna thought of Molly and how she would view the whole episode. It was hardly a professional thing to do, to miss an entire day at work.

'Honestly, I'm fine.'

To emphasise this feeling of being fine, she took her shorthand pad and pencil out of her bag.

John gave her another worried look but got up and reached for his notes. He had noticed the small dots of nail varnish and he thought she must have hit the lamp post with her entire body in order to bruise her face and also damage her stocking. And she was going to gave a real humdinger of a black eye by tomorrow.

However, he said nothing and they worked away until dinner-time when they stopped for some hot soup and cheese sand-wiches.

The hot meal revived Edna's spirits and she was conscious of a feeling of well being in this cosy house. Not to mention the attrac-tiveness of her client.

They then worked on his book until the early afternoon and by the time she was ready to leave, the sun had come out.

As she put her jacket on, John surprised her by saying, 'I feel like a walk in the sunshine. Do you mind if I come a little bit of the way with you?

'No, Mr Knox, I don't mind.'

'I keep telling you to call me John,' he smiled as he locked the door.

With the sun shining and everything looking green and fresh, Edna reviewed her terror following the morning's incident. Perhaps the man had been running to catch the bus and collided with her accidentally. That would explain the collision . . . but not the fist aimed at her face.

John was chatting as they walked and she tried to put it out of her mind. It was so pleasant being with him and she was sorry his wife had died so young.

They reached the top of Paradise Road before she realised he had walked her home.

'I'll see you tomorrow,' he said. 'Do you want me to come for you in the car? It's no bother.'

She felt her face go red. 'Oh no, John. I like the walk.'

She watched as he strode away and wished she had taken up his offer. What if there were other foggy days? Was the unknown man watching her and waiting for another chance to strike her?

She was glad when she reached her front door. Billy would be doing his homework and mum would be making the tea and all would be right with the world.

Wouldn't it?

# 8

Tam put Rover's lead on him and walked the few yards to the shop. He needed bread and milk but in the passing, he picked up a newspaper.

He always made porridge for himself every morning, saving a small amount for the dog who lapped up the warm milk and oats. With them both fed he settled back in his armchair with a cup of tea and the *Courier*. There was still a lot of news about the Coronation and Hillary's victory at Everest but he skimmed over most of it.

He liked to read the intimations column to see if anyone he knew had died but there were no names that rang a bell today.

He was folding the paper to put it away when he noticed the small news item tucked away in the corner of the page.

BODY FOUND
The body of a man was found in the vicin-
ity of Broughty Ferry yesterday. The man
who was approximately forty years old was
wearing a navy duffle jacket, blue shirt and
black trousers.

Tam read the item again. It sounded like Harry he thought.

Then he left the flat quickly with Rover trotting at his side and made his way to the Police Station in Bell Street.

The constable on the reception desk looked up as the elderly man walked in.

'I've come about the man found on the beach at Broughty Ferry,' said Tam.

'Can I have your name and address, Sir?' asked the constable, pulling over a large pad and pen.

'Tam . . . I mean Thomas Burns, 23 Gellatly Street.'

The constable wrote this down and then looked at Tam. 'You say you've got information about the victim.'

'Yes. I think it's a man called Harry Hawkins who was a seaman on the ship, *The Mary Anne*.'

The constable looked up from his pad. 'Are you a relative Mr Burns?'

'No, I only met him the once, in the City Centre Bar on the corner of Dock Street.'

'So why do you think it's the same person?'

'The description in the newspaper matches, and I know he was reported missing. He was leaving Dundee the next day, but he was on his way to meet someone when he said goodbye to me.

'Did he say who this person was?'

'No, but I got the impression he was nervous about it. I went to the docks the next morning to have another chat with him but he never showed up and *The Mary Anne* sailed without him. I was worried at the time but didn't know what to do.'

'Were you drinking with him, Sir?'

'Yes, we had a couple of rums together but he wasn't drunk if that's what you're thinking. He was fine when we parted company and, as I've told you, I've been worried about him ever since.'

The constable put his pad away and told Tam to wait and someone would see him.

Tam sat down on the hard wooden bench and hoped he wouldn't have long to wait. He had left Rover outside, tied to the railings.

Tam felt apprehensive in the police surroundings but when the police officer arrived he looked friendly.

'I'm Detective Sergeant Johns, Mr Burns. Would you like to come this way.'

Tam followed him down a long corridor and was finally shown into a small office with only enough room for a desk, a couple of chairs and a filing cabinet. A small window overlooked what seemed to be a brick wall.

'Now, Mr Burns, you were saying you knew the deceased man, Harry Hawkins.'

'Yes I did . . . briefly. As I told the officer on the desk we met the night before he was due to sail. We had drinks in the City Centre Bar.'

Tam described his bewilderment the following morning when Harry had seemingly disappeared.

'Well, it is definitely Mr Hawkins. He still had his wallet in his pocket and he's been identified by the captain of *The Mary Anne*. It's a ship that docks regularly in Dundee and, as luck would have it, it's back with another cargo.'

Tam was puzzled. 'But Harry said he had never been in Dundee before. How can that be when it's a regular port of call for the boat?'

Sergeant Johns leaned back on his chair. 'No you're right. The captain said Mr Hawkins signed on before the last trip. He had been on a freight ship from Hull to Rotterdam but apparently changed ships because the Hull boat was being laid up for a few weeks for repairs.'

Tam felt sad. Harry's first trip to Dundee had turned out to be his final journey.

'How much did he have to drink in the bar?'

'He wasn't drunk if that's what you're thinking,' said Tam, annoyed that this might be classed as the cause of death. 'We had two rums each and I think he had one drink before that.'

'The post mortem shows quite a bit of alcohol in his stomach. At least six measures . . . maybe eight.'

'Well yes, we had double measures but that still doesn't account for his death. How did he die?'

'We think he got his foot entangled in a coil of rope that was lying on the wharf and hit his head when he fell into the water. He must have been unconscious because he drowned. The head wound must have knocked him out, but it wasn't the cause of death.'

Tam couldn't accept this. 'But Harry had been at sea since he was sixteen. He would never have tripped over a coil of rope. Never in a hundred years. He must have walked over hundreds of wharves.'

'Maybe,' said the sergeant. 'He was probably very careful when he was sober, but after quite a few drinks his judgement would have been impaired.'

Tam shook his head in disbelief. 'I don't believe it.'

The man stood up. 'Well, it's being recorded as an accidental death. Thank you for coming in and filling us in with his last moments, Mr Burns.'

He walked down the corridor with Tam and stood at the front door.

As Tam untied Rover, DS Johns rubbed his chin. He had a funny feeling about this case but, without a witness to the event, it would remain an accidental death.

Tam walked away with Rover. He couldn't believe Harry had tripped over a bit of rope. Not an old seadog like him.

When he reached his house he was annoyed at forgetting to ask when the funeral was and if it would be in Dundee. He would maybe go back to the police station or it might be in the death column of the paper. He would have to look out for it. Harry would have precious few mourners and Tam was determined to be one. It's the least I can do, he thought. Old sailors had to stick together.

Tam tried to recall all the conversation on that night but although he racked his brains, he couldn't think of anything else. He had told the police all he knew but they were sure it was an accident.

# 9

On Thursday afternoon, Molly was finishing a pile of invoices when Lena arrived back from the shop. The weather had turned warm and thundery and Molly was looking forward to setting off for home and having a long cool bath.

'Kenneth has had to go and see to some containers coming in. I've had to look after the shop all day.' She sounded annoyed.

'Is there anything else you would like me to do after these invoices?'

Lena gave this a bit of thought. 'I think Christie and Mike might want some help in the warehouse. Could you make a list of all the containers?'

Molly took her pad out to the warehouse. Christie was working at a small desk but there was no sign of Mike, much to her relief. She hardly knew the man but he made her feel uncomfortable.

Christie had all the information to hand and Molly copied it down.

He said. 'I'm going to make some coffee. Would you like a cup?'

Molly wasn't fussy about coffee. She much preferred tea but she nodded.

'What brought you to Dundee?' she asked him.

He fiddled with his teaspoon. 'I arrived last year on a working holiday. I came to Dundee on a visit and met Kenneth. I told him

I worked in the antique trade back in Canada and he asked me to come and work for him. So here I am. What about you?'

Molly told him about her parents going to Australia and how she had lived there for some time. She mentioned Nell and the new baby and how she had started the agency.

'With lots of hope and little money,' she laughed.

She picked up her pad. 'Well I'd better be getting back. Thanks for the coffee.'

She reached the door when a dark shadow appeared. For a moment she thought it was Mike but it was Joe. He was sweating and his face was red and shiny. Behind him was Kenneth who looked as cool and as well groomed as usual.

Kenneth was speaking to Joe. 'You should have left the boxes until tomorrow. Christie and Mike would have helped you. You don't want to end up with a heart attack.'

Joe scowled and muttered something, which Molly didn't catch. Kenneth must have heard, however, because he put a hand on Joe's shoulder before walking away.

Later, Molly left the shed and walked through the garden towards the house. The lawn was well kept and she thought she would have a quick look at the cliffs. When she reached the end of the grass she was surprised to see there was no fence and the ground fell away to a small beach which lay about twenty feet below. It was hardly a cliff but it was still a nasty drop.

There was a jetty on the shingle beach with a smart looking cabin cruiser berthed alongside. She was peering over when she heard the voices but before she could draw back, Joe and Mike appeared. They seemed to be arguing.

Suddenly, as if they sensed they were being overheard, they looked up and saw her. Molly almost fell off the edge in surprise, so intense was their gaze.

Molly was mortified. Did they think she was eavesdropping? She turned to go to the house and almost fell over Christie.

She had an irrational stab of fear at the closeness of the Canadian and although she wouldn't admit it, she felt shaken by the malicious looks from Joe and Mike.

'I'm just enjoying the view,' she said, trying to inject a non-chalant and carefree lightness in her voice as she quickly made her way back to the office.

Sitting at the desk, she was dismayed to see her hands were still shaking.

'Stop it,' she told herself. Just because the men obviously didn't like her didn't mean there was anything wrong. That was the trouble with working in a home environment. You picked up lots of domestic detritus. Maybe Joe had fallen out with his wife and was in a bad mood, As for Mike and Christie, well she hardly knew them. Perhaps they were always like that.

# 10

Mary was waiting impatiently for her dinner break. She had her wages and Mum had said she could treat herself to something to wear as a reward for passing her exams. She would soon be getting her Leaving Certificate at the school and, after that, she would be a fully-fledged working girl.

She looked over at Molly who was working out all the invoices for jobs done. It had been a busy Saturday morning and the agency was picking up a lot of new business. At this rate, perhaps Molly would get another receptionist and she could become an agency worker.

She gazed at her wristlet watch, which had been a birthday present from her parents. It was twelve o'clock.

As if noticing the movement, Molly looked up from the pile of paperwork. 'If you want to have your break now, Mary, I'll hold on here.'

Mary gathered up her jacket and handbag and hurried down the Wellgate. She had seen the dress she wanted in Levinson's shop window so she quickly made her way to the Overgate.

The assistant was very helpful and Mary stood in the fitting room, admiring her reflection in the mirror. The dress was white with blue spots and it had a red belt, which made her waist look tiny. And the best part was it had been reduced in the sale from thirty to twenty-one shillings.

Mary was almost purring when she left the shop. She was planning to wear the dress tonight when she went out dancing with her best friend, Rita. There was just the one small worry, which had been niggling her since Wednesday when she last saw Rita.

Both girls normally went to Kidd's Rooms every Saturday night but Rita had suggested going to the Palais in Tay Street.

'It'll be a change, Mary,' she had said. 'After all, you're leaving school in a week's time so it's time you mixed with the grown-up dancers, not the kids you normally see.'

Mary was uncertain but had agreed to go. The only thing was she hadn't told her Mum the change of plan. Then she thought of the new dress and made up her mind. She was going to enjoy her evening at the dancing.

When she got back to the office, Edna was sitting chatting to Molly. The injury had turned into a black eye and there was blue and yellow bruising halfway down her cheek which the pancake foundation had failed to cover up.

Mary could see that Molly looked shocked.

Edna was explaining the accident and she seemed to be embarrassed by it. 'It was so stupid. Walking into a lamp post,' she said. 'I was going to stay off work but Mr Knox was very kind and said he didn't mind having me come in every day.' She sounded hesitant and unsure of herself. 'But if you would rather I didn't work until the bruising has gone, I quite understand.'

'Well, as long as you feel all right, Edna', said Molly. 'How long do you think this job will last? Did he give you any idea?'

Mary was surprised when Edna's neck went bright red. No doubt her face would have gone the same deep red if she hadn't been wearing so much make-up, she thought.

'He wants me for another two weeks, at least if that's all right with you, Molly? He's writing an engineering book and it's all very technical.'

Molly was delighted. 'We've got some new jobs in this morning but I'll get my friends to fill in and I can always do a Friday as my clients don't need me then.'

Edna left and Mary settled back in her chair, ready for the afternoon's work.

Molly saw the bag that Mary had stuffed into the cupboard behind the desk.

'Have you been treating yourself to something nice to wear, Mary?'

'Mum said I could buy myself something to wear and I'm going dancing tonight with my pal.'

Molly smiled. How great it was to be young and fancy-free.

It was five thirty and the man was getting tired hanging around the street. As far as he knew, the agency closed at five thirty but there was no sign of anyone leaving. He looked at his watch and lit another cigarette. This was definitely where she worked but there had been no sight of her. He had been standing here since three o'clock but now he decided to call it a day and walked away.

Mike was out on the town, He loved getting into Dundee and parading his good looks around the girls. He was a bit worried about this Molly McQueen and hoped she wasn't going to poke her nose into anyone's business. Lamont Antiques had just been the four of them until Christie arrived but he didn't like this woman. Neither did Joe. In fact he had said in confidence to him that he was suspicious of her motive in being in the house 'I'd love to know a bit more about her' Joe had said to him. The only people pleased by her were Kenneth and Lena who seemed to find her good at her job.

Because he was curious about the newcomer he decided to wander up the Wellgate and see this agency for himself. It was a bit of a disappointment when he saw it. The tiny shop with a house above it looked quite neglected in spite of the fresh coat of paint.

He would have loved to get some information on the owner but he knew this wasn't possible He knew it was no business of his but he always liked to find out things about people and because Joe was suspicious of her, well he just wanted to know something about her. Then, if Joe ever mentioned again that he didn't trust her working with them, he could maybe give him a few bits of information. Also, this skulking about gave him pleasure and he had always liked to spy on people. Especially women and girls.

Suddenly the door opened and the young receptionist came out onto the pavement. According to his information her name was Mary. She stood on the pavement, looking up and down, a look of uncertainty on her face. He saw another young girl hurry down the street to meet up with Mary.

They started to walk up the Wellgate towards the tram stop on Victoria Road. He was torn between following them and keeping the shop under observation. He glanced across the road and saw that Molly was still working, busy typing at the desk.

He decided to follow the two young girls. Unaware that they were under scrutiny, he overheard their chatter.

'I don't want to go to Kidd's Rooms, Mary,' said the friend.

Mary looked unhappy. 'I don't think my Mum will want me to go to the Palais. Is it not for older people, Rita?'

'Well I think Kidd's Rooms just caters for kids, It's well named and if you don't want to go, I can always go on my own.'

Mary gave this some thought. 'All right. Come round to the house at seven o'clock and we'll go to the Palais. But remember, if I don't like it, I'm going back to Kidd's Rooms next week.'

The tramcar hovered into sight and the two girls got on board.

So that was the destination for the evening he thought, making his way past the agency. It was locked up and the blind had been pulled down at the window.

He glanced down the street but there was no sign of Molly. She must have shut up shop the minute he set off after the girls.

The whole evening stretched out in front of him. He debated about going to the pictures or the dancing. He had liked the look of the two girls so he decided on the dancing. He looked at his watch again. It was almost six o'clock. He was starting to feel hungry so he set off along the High Street towards the Palais. There was a wonderful aroma coming from the Deep Sea fish and chip shop so he decided to go and have something to eat before going to the dancing.

At seven o'clock he made his way to Tay Street, making for the Ascot Bar on the corner of the street where he decided to go for a couple of drinks. The bar was busy but he was served almost immediately and he carried his glass of whisky over to a corner of the bar counter.

At half past seven, after another two drinks, he went down the street towards the Palais.

The queue, which had formed earlier, had dispersed quickly and he was able to buy his ticket right away.

He scrutinised his reflection in the mirror of the Gents cloakroom. He was pleased with what he saw. A tall, slim man with a well-cut suit, white shirt and somewhat gaudy tie. It was a pity about the tie, he thought, but there was nothing he could now. He could hardly take it off because he knew the dancehall had a strict dress code policy. He had been here before but not for over a year.

Upstairs, he quickly scanned the crowd. The band was playing a quickstep and the floor was crowded with dancers.

He spotted Mary and Rita. They were sitting on a settee, looking wistfully at the floor. Mary was wearing a white frock with blue spots. Very demure. Rita, however, had on a low-necked sweater and black skirt.

He decided to concentrate on Rita. Sauntering over, he asked her to dance. She was so eager she almost fell over her feet and they both joined the throng on the floor.

'Do you come here a lot?' he asked.

Rita tried to appear more sophisticated.

'Oh I come here every week', she said. 'Andy Lothian's band is great'

'Does your friend come with you every week or do you come on your own?'

'No, I usually come on my own, but Mary wanted to come tonight so here we are.'

Little liar, he thought.

Just then the dance ended. He walked back with her to the settee. Mary was looking really miserable. 'I wondered if you would like a soft drink at the Soda Fountain?'

Rita was immediately on her feet again but Mary didn't get up. 'You must come as well,' he said. 'You must join us.'

Rita was shaking her head at Mary behind his back and because of this, Mary decided to go along.

He breathed a sigh of relief.

At the Soda Fountain, he bought three soft drinks and offered them a cigarette. Rita took one and proceeded to blow smoke in Mary's face.

'Where do you both work?' he asked.

Rita answered for them both. 'I've got a job in an office and Mary is in an agency.'

He looked at Mary. 'That must be very interesting. Do you get clients from different places?'

Mary nodded.

Rita snorted. 'Don't be all secretive Mary.' She turned to the man. 'It's called McQueen's Agency and the owner is Molly McQueen. Mary works with a woman called Edna and some of Molly's friends.'

'Molly McQueen,' he stopped as if giving this some thought. 'I used to know a Molly McQueen. I wonder if it's the same woman.'

Mary shrugged and Rita didn't know so she remained silent.

'Oh well maybe it's not.' He looked towards the dance floor. 'Perhaps we'd better get back to dancing.' He turned to Mary. 'Can I have the next dance?'

Rita didn't look pleased and neither did Mary but she could hardly refuse. It was a slow foxtrot and Mary wasn't sure of the steps.

'Never mind,' the man said. 'Just hold on to me.'

Before she knew it, they were in the middle of the floor. Couples were crushed up beside them and she felt uncomfortable. She didn't like this man one bit and there was the smell of alcohol on his breath.

He held her in a tight grip, trying to speak into her ear. 'Tell me all about your job. Do you like working in an agency? What's your boss like? Do you like working for her?'

Mary tried to pull away, but his grip tightened and she felt a sharp pain on her neck.

Fortunately, the music came to an end and she was able to make her escape. He grabbed at her belt but it broke and she was suddenly on the edge of the crowded floor.

She saw Rita chatting to a young man and hurried up to her. 'I'm leaving, Rita. Are you coming?'

Rita looked at her with open-mouthed surprise just as the young man started to dance with her and she was swept away amongst the dancers.

Mary hurried down to the cloakroom and quickly made her way out into the street.

Thankfully it was still light but as she made her way down Tay Street she saw the man emerge from the entrance.

She started to run, frightened to look over her shoulder in case he was chasing her. At the tram stop she saw a tramcar waiting while a few people climbed on board. With an extra spurt she reached it and jumped on board.

As it lumbered away she saw he had gone.

She was breathless and almost in tears but at least she was on her way home. She was so immersed in her own misery that she didn't notice the woman walking towards her.

'Hello, Mary, I thought it was you,' said Edna, sitting down beside her. 'Have you been dancing?'

Mary turned her frightened eyes to her. 'I've had a terrible time, Edna. This man was talking to me about the agency. He kept asking questions about Miss McQueen. And he frightened me while we were dancing.'

Edna was worried. Mary certainly looked frightened. 'Have you seen him before?'

Mary shook her head. 'He was a lot older than Rita or me. He wore a good suit and was quite handsome with lovely black wavy hair, but why would he want to know all about the agency, Edna?'

Edna didn't have the answer to that but he was going to pass on this information to Molly as soon as possible.

'I'll make sure you get home safely, Mary, and you're not to worry about this man. Perhaps he doesn't have a chat up line and concentrates on his dancing partner's work.'

Mary looked at her and although she was young, she realised Edna didn't believe that. Nor did she.

After seeing Mary into the house, Edna retraced her steps to Paradise Road. This had been her first night out in ages. She had gone to the pictures with a friend and it was just chance that had placed her on the same tram as Mary.

Edna spent a sleepless night and early on Sunday morning she made up her mind.

She looked for the slip of paper with Molly's home telephone number and after breakfast with Billy and her mother, went out to the telephone box on Constitution Road.

Edna slipped her three pennies in the slot and when Molly answered she pushed button A.

She decided to sound casual as she didn't want to alarm Molly with a call on Sunday morning.

'I don't want to alarm you, Molly,' she said, forgetting in her haste to speak, her promise to herself to sound casual. 'It's about Mary.' She went on to tell the story of the meeting with the dark-haired man.

When she stopped speaking, Molly said. 'I was coming over anyway, Edna. I'll catch the ferry at eleven o'clock. Can you meet me at the agency about twelve?'

'I'll be there, Molly.'

Afterwards, when she was in the kitchen with Billy, she felt stupid. What had made her alarm Molly like that? Was it this over-zealous young man at the dancing? Surely the town was packed with eager young men who perhaps came on a bit strong with young impressionable girls.

She had also promised to take Billy to the park to play on the swings but she could do that later on the afternoon. At the moment he was lying on the rug in front of the fire, reading his comics.

'Is it all right if we go out later to the park, Billy?' she asked him.

He looked up and nodded and returned his gaze to the antics of the comic characters.

Over in Newport, Molly was puzzled by Edna's call. What could have had triggered this alarm by some young man in a dance hall? Still it was better to get it sorted out and hopefully there would be a logical explanation.

She had planned a quick visit to the office and then have a quiet day to herself with an afternoon visit to Marigold but now she would have to make her apologies.

Edna was waiting for her at the agency and followed her into the office. She was nervous and it showed.

'What's all this about Mary and some young man?'

Edna related the story again and Molly listened without saying a word. After she finished, Molly said, 'Perhaps he was just making conversation.'

Edna shook her head. 'No, he kept quizzing Mary about the agency. He mentioned it by name but how did he know she worked here? It doesn't make sense. And he frightened her.'

Molly couldn't see what the connection was but she was still puzzled.

Edna twisted her hands oh her lap. 'There's something else, Molly. Yesterday, when I said I walked into a lamp post . . . well, I didn't.'

Molly laughed out loud. 'Oh, I never believed you for a minute but it's your own business and I didn't want to pry.'

Edna leaned forwards with a worried frown. 'No, it wasn't a private matter. As I was going to John Knox's house someone jumped out from the entrance to Dudhope Park and pushed me against the stone pillars before hitting me hard on my face.'

Molly put her cup down where it landed with a clatter on the saucer.

'Did you see who did it, Edna?'

Edna shook her head. 'It was that very misty morning and it was just a dark shape, but it was definitely a man. I'm sure of that' She looked unhappy . . . What's going on, Molly?'

'I don't know, but we'll go and see Mary at her house and see if she can add anything else to this.'

The two women made their way to Moncur Crescent on the tramcar. It was a very pleasant area with six houses to every close. The windows were especially pretty with large panes of glass in the bottom and six small panes at the top. The gardens were well kept and an area of land was landscaped with stubby bushes which swept downward towards the street. A few children were playing in the swing park across the road and their childish cries followed Molly and Edna as they made their way to Mary's house.

'What are you going to say to Mary's mum?'

Molly didn't know.

The door was opened by Mary and her dark eyes opened with shock at the sight of her employer standing on the doorstep. There was a small, nasty-looking bruise on her neck which she had tried to cover with the scarf she was wearing.

'Miss McQueen. Is there something wrong?'

'Who is it, Mary?' said a voice from the interior. Mrs Watt appeared in the lobby behind her daughter and also looked surprised when she saw the visitors.

'Come in, come in,' she said, ushering them into a comfortable looking living room. 'Mary put on the kettle and bring the tin of biscuits from the kitchen cabinet,' she said.

Mary scuttled off to the kitchen like a frightened animal. It was clear she hadn't told her mother what had happened.

Molly said, 'Don't bother with tea for us, Mrs Watt. I wondered in Mary could come down to the office, as we have some important paperwork to finish before tomorrow. I know it's a Sunday, but I would be very grateful if she could help out.'

'Of course she can. Mary, Miss McQueen would like you to go to the office to help out with paperwork. Hurry and get your coat on.'

Molly hated lying to the woman but she didn't want to get Mary into trouble. Mary appeared wearing her coat and a frightened expression.

'It'll only take an hour, Mrs Watt, and I'll make sure Mary gets her fare back home.'

Before they reached the tram stop, a tall, pretty girl shouted over, 'Hullo Mary, where did you get to last night? I had to come home on my own.'

Mary went over. 'I'm never going back with you to the Palais, Rita, I'm going to Kidd's Rooms next week where I know nearly everyone.' She then turned and walked away, leaving Rita with an astonished look.

Edna couldn't resist a parting shot at the girl. 'Close your mouth, love, you might swallow a wasp.'

Back in the office, Molly put Mary at her ease. 'Now Mary, Edna has told me about your meeting last night with a stranger who seemed to want to know all about me and the agency. Can you tell me any more details?'

Mary shook her head. 'I didn't know him. I usually go to Kidd's Rooms with Rita but she's a wee bit older than me and she finds it a bit juvenile for her liking. That's her words, not mine. So she suggested we should go to the Palais, which is a great place, but filled with lots more people and most of them were older than me.' She looked at Molly.

'I never mentioned to Mum about going there as she would be mad. She doesn't care too much for Rita.'

Mary recounted the tale and then said, 'When I tried to get away from him, he grabbed my belt and he's torn my new dress. The belt tabs are torn and it's made holes in the side seams. I only bought it yesterday.' She sounded sad and Molly thought she was going to cry.

'I'll give you some extra money next week, Mary, to replace the dress. How did you get the bruise on your neck?'

Mary went red with embarrassment and pulled her scarf tighter around her neck. After a few moments she whispered. 'When I didn't tell him what he wanted to know, he grabbed my neck and squeezed it really tight. I couldn't breathe.'

The two women looked at one another in shock.

'Can you describe him?'

'He was very well dressed and much older than me. I thought he looked the same age as Rita's brother who's thirty. He had a thin face and lovely dark wavy hair. And he had been drinking because I could smell the alcohol on his breath He also had a large mole at the side of his cheek.'

Molly felt a sharp shock. It sounded like Mike, but why would he question a young girl about the agency. Molly stood up. 'You've been a great help, Mary, and we'll see you tomorrow after school. It won't be long till you leave and it'll be such a relief to have you here every day.'

Molly added, 'Be careful about who you meet on Saturday nights, Mary. If he comes near you again, go to the nearest policeman for help.'

As she was going out the door, she turned. Her face was puzzled. 'There's one thing I've remembered. Although I didn't know him I have the funniest feeling I've seen him before but I can't remember where.'

When she was gone, Edna said. 'What do you make of that?'

'I don't know, Edna, but I think I know who he is. He works for the couple I'm working for at Cliff Top House. His name's Mike and I don't like him. I can't prove it's him but I'll be keeping a look out for him in the future.'

Edna went to take her son to the park while Molly locked the door and set off for the ferry. She sat on the top deck and let the wind blow through her hair. Her mind was in turmoil about the latest developments. As Edna said, what was going on?

The difficult thing was, Molly didn't know.

# II

Tam was finishing his breakfast and was on the point of taking Rover out for his morning walk when there was a loud knock on the door.

Tam was puzzled as he normally didn't have many visitors, and was astonished to see DS Johns standing in the dark lobby and he wasn't in uniform.

'Can I come in, Mr Burns?'

Tam stood aside. 'Aye, in you come. What's brought you here?'

The detective seemed to fill the small kitchen with his bulky figure while Rover did an agitated dance of disapproval around his size twelve boots.

'Would you like a cup of tea?' said Tam, chastising Rover for his barking.

'No, thank you. Can I sit down?'

Tam pulled the newspaper from the fireside chair and sat down with a sigh.

'I swear my legs are getting worse every year,' he said and pointed to the paper. 'I've been looking for more news of Harry but there hasn't been a word except for that very first wee bit when his body was found and a small item about me knowing him.'

'No, that's why I'm here. He doesn't seem to have any family and his last address was in Hull. The police down there went to investigate but according to a neighbour he lived alone. This neighbour had a key and the police didn't discover very much. He lived in the flat on the odd occasion when he was ashore and he didn't have very much money. He paid his rent on time and his bills but other than that he only appeared to have enough to live on, but not much more.'

'Aye he told me he had no family and that he had been all round the world on various ships. He had been a crew member on the liners for a short time but worked mainly on the cargo ships. It was his first trip to Dundee and it's such a shame that he met his death here. I was wondering what the arrangements are for his funeral.'

'Well yes, that's another reason for this visit. The police found an insurance policy in his name and there will be enough money to bury him. The neighbour, when asked his opinion about a burial site, said it wouldn't matter where he was laid to rest because the sea was his life and he was never at home on dry land. So that's why I'm here. The burial takes place today at ten thirty at Balgay Cemetery and I'd like you to come, if that's possible.'

Tam jumped up from his seat. 'I'll just get my coat and cap.'

'I've got a car outside to take us there and I'll bring you back home.'

Rover didn't look too happy at being left alone, especially as his morning walk had been curtailed to a quick trip down the street where he managed to leave his mark behind on every lamp post.

There was a young police constable driving the black car and the two men got into the back seat. It didn't take long to reach the cemetery and they had to walk a few hundred yards to the grave site.

Two cemetery gravediggers and a church minister stood by the open grave as the black hearse drew slowly to a stop. The solemn-faced undertaker and two pall bearers carried the plain wooden coffin slowly, which had one wreath of carnations on top

Tam felt tears spring to his eyes at the sadness of Harry's death. He was a man with no family and very few friends by the look of it. He wished he had brought some flowers.

The minister said a moving little service and then it was all over. The two gravediggers covered the grave with a green board and no doubt would fill the hole in later, shovelling earth on Harry who loved the sea and the wild elements of gigantic waves and the feel of a force eight gale in his face. Not this small plot of earth amongst hundreds of other graves.

What kind of life had he lived? thought Tam. Had it been a happy one?

Then they were back in the car. When they reached the centre of town, the detective sergeant got out with Tam and told the constable to take the police car back.

'Let's go and have a drink Tam. Where do you recommend?'

'The City Centre Bar . . . where I met Harry the night he died.'

The bar was quiet as it had only opened for business less than an hour earlier. The policeman bought Tam a double rum and a pint of beer for himself and they sat at a table.

They both had their own thoughts.

Suddenly Tam said 'Harry didn't fall into the water accidentally. Someone must have pushed him. Harry was too much of a seaman to trip over something lying on the dock.'

The DS Johns stroked his chin. 'Well, Tam, that's the official cause of death. There were no marks or bruises on his body except for the head wound which he got when he struck his head after falling. And, of course, he had been drinking.'

'But he wasn't drunk'

DS Johns took a pack of cigarettes from his pocket, offered one to Tam who shook his head.

After he lit up, he leaned back in his seat. 'Let's look at this from another angle, Tam. Why would anyone want to push Harry into the river? He was a stranger in the town. He'd never been in Dundee before. Who could have wanted him dead? He wasn't a rich man. The insurance money will cover his funeral costs but there will be hardly anything left over.'

'What about one of his shipmates on *The Mary Anne*?'

'They were all questioned when the body was found. The same men were on board then as on the trip made by Harry. He was a stranger to them. They had all done this trip before except for him and they all say they liked him but he kept himself very much to himself. The captain said he was private man. A stranger on the boat and a stranger in the city.'

'Then why are you bothering about him? This man who is a stranger to both of us?'

DS Johns stubbed out his cigarette and gazed at Tam. A shrewd old man, he thought. Yes, why am I bothering myself with a dead stranger?

'I just didn't want him to have a lonely burial I suppose.'

The two men parted outside the bar. 'Keep in touch, Tam. Maybe we can have another drink together.'

Later that afternoon Tam took Rover for his walk and made his way to the docks.

Quite a few ships were being unloaded and the place was busy. Tam kept out of the stevedores' way as they loaded and unloaded cargoes in and out of the ships' holds.

He walked over to the spot where Rover had sniffed the rusty stain. It was faint now due to the weather. Rain had swept the concrete wharves in the time since Harry had last walked here.

Tam had a good look around. This part of the dock wasn't as wide as the rest, due to a small crane taking up part of the walkway. Harry would have had to skirt around this crane which would have taken him near the edge.

A thick, oily rope lay coiled on the ground. One end attached to a hook on the crane. Tam bent down and inspected the rope. There was no way Harry would have got entangled with it, yet this was supposed to be the cause of his death. Lying near the edge of the dock was a metal ring inserted into the concrete. There were shreds of hemp attached to it.

Tam was excited. What if someone had tied the rope on the night Harry died, hoping to trip him up and send him into the dark, oil-slicked water?

Suddenly he became afraid. He looked towards the boats but no one seemed to be taking any notice of him, yet Tam was aware that there were hundreds of pairs of eyes perhaps watching him.

He pretended to tie his shoelaces then straightened up. 'Come on, Rover.'

As he walked away he didn't know that someone had seen him, and that person was now very worried.

Tam crossed over Dock Street towards his house and as he reached the end of his close he looked back. He had the strangest feeling someone was following him but there was hardly anyone on the street.

Two men came out of the Dole office at the corner of Gellatly Street and there was a woman doing her shopping.

A man suddenly turned the corner but he also made for the Dole office. Tam climbed the stair with Rover, glad to be back home as he wanted to mull over the rope fragments on the ring.

As he made a cup of tea, he decided it was just a coincidence and resolved to put the matter out of his mind.

DS Johns was probably right when he said it was an accident.

# 12

Molly had decided to find out the truth behind Mary's dancing partner and his strange behaviour.

As she drove slowly into the courtyard, she heard raised voices coming from the house. She let herself into the office and saw a huge pile of invoices to be dealt with.

The voices were coming from the kitchen and she recognised Lena and Joe's raised tones.

'I'm telling you, Lena, that consignment never arrived. I checked it all over twice.'

'Well, it should have arrived last week along with the other crates, so where is it?'

Suddenly the door opened and Lena came in. She looked tired and pale. Her hair hung in waves on her shoulders, almost as if the hair was too heavy for her head.

'Oh, Molly, I didn't hear you come in. As you see we've had a busy weekend with deliveries, but one crate is missing. Can you phone the harbour master and get him to check if it's still lying about the docks?'

Molly got through right away to the harbour master and yes, the missing crate was waiting to be picked up.

'Thank goodness for that,' said Lena. 'I'll get Joe or Mike to go and pick it up.'

That was interesting thought Molly. Was that why Mike had been in Dundee on Saturday?

'Has the crate been missing for long?' she asked, trying to keep her voice neutral.

'Yes, since last weekend.'

Well that let Mike off the hook for this Saturday.

Lena sat down and sighed. 'I'm not sleeping very well with the pain in my arm. It seems to be getting worse instead of better.'

Molly didn't know what to say but nodded sympathetically.

After the invoices were finished, she had to go out to the sheds to check the new arrivals.

Joe, Mike and Christie were all there, checking crates against a list in Joe's hand.

'Well that's everything checked except the missing box, but we'll collect that later.'

'Do you want me to go over for it?' said Christie.

Joe gave this a bit of thought. 'No, you went on Saturday to the shop. Mike can go. He hasn't been over to the docks for a while.'

Molly almost tripped over a box when she heard this. So Mary's assailant couldn't have been Mike. She looked at Christie and wondered if he was the man Mary had met. His hair was thick and brown, not as luxuriant as Mike's but in a dark dance hall would Mary have noticed the colour? But why hadn't she recognised the Canadian accent? Could he perhaps change his voice when it suited him?

After Joe and Mike left, Molly tried to start a conversation. 'Do you like Dundee, Christie?'

'It's all right. I like the people, they are really friendly.'

'Do you do anything special when you go out?' Molly thought she sounded like the inquisition and tried to keep her voice light.

'No, I helped out at the shop till the afternoon then had something to eat, a couple of drinks and back here. It was hardly a fun day out.'

Christie gave her a sharp glance so Molly decided to stop her probing. If Christie had been at the Palais he was hardly going to admit it.

Molly made her way back to the house, She needed to go to the bathroom, which was on the first floor. She climbed the stair silently but before she reached the bathroom door, Lena and Kenneth came out of one of the rooms. She hadn't seen Kenneth since the middle of last week.

Lena saw her. 'Molly, Kenneth is going to collect the crate. Can you let Joe know the change of plan?'

Kenneth passed her on the stair and gave her one of his devastating smiles. God, he is handsome, Molly thought.

Joe took the news with bad grace. 'I'll have to tell Mike her ladyship's changed her plans.'

Molly was taken aback by the description of his wife but maybe it was a term of endearment. She was barely back in the office when Christie appeared with another batch of invoices and a cup of coffee in his hand.

'Can I bring you a coffee, Molly?'

'I'd rather have a cup of tea. No milk or sugar.'

'Oh a lady who likes her drinks strong and black.' He smiled but Molly was aware of an undertone in his voice.

'No, Christie. Weak and amber.'

He saluted and went off to the kitchen. The staff seemed to have the run of the house, she thought.

When he appeared with her tea and a plate of biscuits, he perched himself on the chaise longue, not stretched out like Lena but seated on the edge as if ready to run off.

She found his presence slightly intimidating but she was determined to find out if he was the man with Mary and Rita.

She smiled at him. 'Do you go over to Dundee a lot?'

'Not regularly but yes, I go over every now and then.' He waved his hand in the air. 'I mean, there's not a lot happening here, is there? This small corner is quiet and a bit dull if you ask me.'

Molly nodded as if agreeing with him. 'But you have to be back before the last ferry leaves. Doesn't that curtail your night's entertainment?'

'No it doesn't. I get the use of the work's van. I go to Wormit and catch the train and then get the late train back. It gives me ample time to see a movie or whatever else is on offer.' He looked at her and gave her a huge smile. She decided to end the conversation as he must be suspicious about the questioning. In fact it was more like a third degree interrogation.

She put the empty cup down on the desk and picked up the invoices. 'Well it was pleasant chatting to you but I'd better get back to work.'

He didn't move but gave her an appraising glance. 'I would like to take you out next Saturday if you would like to come. We can have a meal somewhere or go to a movie.'

Molly almost fell of her chair and she felt her face go red with embarrassment. Christie must have thought she was angling for a date with him.

'I'm sorry but I can't manage it. I'm busy next Saturday.' She was mortified that she had given him the impression she was desperate for a man's company.

He looked dejected but said, 'Maybe another time then.'

Molly nodded, but he was halfway across the room and he didn't notice the gesture.

It took ages to focus again on her work and she was annoyed at herself for giving him the wrong impression. So much for her sleuthing. She obviously wasn't a female Sherlock Holmes.

As she sorted out the various invoices she noted there had been a large delivery of rugs and furniture from Denmark. Lena had said they had an agent in Europe who bought up antiques from large houses that had fallen on hard times.

Molly got up to put the invoices in the filing cabinet. When she turned round, Lena was standing at the desk.

'Molly, I was wondering if you could help us out on Saturday evening. I'm putting on a small party for some of our best customers and I wondered if you could work that evening?' She paused when she saw the surprised look on Molly's face. 'Oh, I don't mean work in the domestic sense. I do the cooking and serving. It's more as a help to me on the business side. We normally show them around our latest stock and then have dinner and drinks and hopefully we sell our goods. It's a soft approach but we are in the business of selling our antiques.' She smiled and the tiredness left her face.

Molly thought, Lena loves her work and likes to sell her treasures to other connoisseurs.

'Yes I'd love to help out, Lena.'

'We normally meet around six thirty for the tour of the sheds and the evening is usually over by eleven o'clock. I'll get Mike to run you home afterwards.'

Molly tried not to show her distaste at the thought of sharing a car with Mike.

'There's no need. I can drive myself.'

'Well, if you're sure, then that's settled. I'm so glad to have you here. You are such a big help to me.' She sounded like a small wistful child.

Then Joe came into the room and the wistful look disappeared to be replaced by another emotion.

# 13

Edna sat at the desk in the untidy lounge. John had been dictating for over two hours and she was planning to get the shorthand script typed up by afternoon. Her bruise was fading fast and she didn't need to put on so much make-up. She had also managed to buy another pair of nylons and she felt really smart again. Her mum had repaired the torn pair and she was going to keep them for wearing around the house.

Although John hadn't commented on her black eye since the day it happened, he was glad to see she was almost back to normal.

'I think we'll stop for some dinner, Edna,' he said.

Edna put her shorthand notebook on the table and followed him into the kitchen, She had stopped bringing her own sandwiches now as John liked her to keep him company. He had made a large shepherd's pie and Edna realised she was hungry when he brought it out of the oven.

She felt comfortable in this large, untidy house and she liked working with John. He was so passionate about his book and Edna hoped he would manage to get it published.

She gazed out of the window. The garden was a bit tidier because he had brought in a gardener who worked two days a week. The man was slowly getting on top of the overgrown grass and the weeds that choked the flowerbeds.

In a way, Edna felt sorry for John, living in this large house alone.

'Are you having a holiday later?' he asked.

'I haven't asked Molly yet about having a few days off, but Mum is taking Billy to my aunt's house in Arbroath. I'd love to spend some time with them.' She didn't mention it that it all depended on the work being completed here.

'Arbroath?' he said. 'What a coincidence. I'm planning to go and see my brother who lives there. Why don't we transfer the work there for a week or two? We can work in the morning and you can spend the rest of the day with your family.'

Edna said she wasn't sure. 'I don't know what Molly will say to that.'

'Well, she will still be getting paid so what can she say?'

Edna was unsure. She said, 'Well, I'll ask her. It will be next week or the week after when we go, as Billy will be on his school holiday then.'

'That's settled then' he said. 'That's why I asked if you were having a holiday because I always go to see my brother at this time of year, but I also want to get on with my book. This is the ideal solution.'


Mary was excited. It was prize-giving day at the school and she sat in the assembly hall with all her classmates. She was dressed in her white school blouse and black skirt. She knew her mum and dad were seated at the back of the hall, along with her friends' parents.

It was a big day for them all. The last day at school before going out into the world of work.

When their names were called, they would go up the steps to the stage and collect their leaving certificates and, in Mary's case, the first prize for commercial subjects.

Nearly all her classmates had jobs to go to but some of them were envious of Mary's position in an agency.

Most of the girls had their autograph books and they giggled as they put in witty little poems.' Jane wrote 'Your job is so glam, I wish it were mine. But never mind Mary, we'll meet up sometime.'

On Monday she would start full time at the agency where she was now a valued member of Molly's staff.

She was still a bit nervous after Saturday night but she had told Rita she wouldn't be going back with her, so hopefully she would never meet up with that man again.

It was strange, she thought, that Molly should take the time and trouble to come and see her. Especially on a Sunday.

Then she put the episode to the back of her mind.

On Saturday morning, Molly dithered about what to wear that night. She knew she wasn't a guest at this party but she wanted to appear smart and professional. Perhaps this party would lead to other assignments coming to the agency.

She considered her grey suit then discarded it and settled for a dress she had bought in Australia. It was a blue and green print with tiny cap sleeves and a full skirt.

She hadn't worn it for ages but as she studied herself in the mirror, she had second thoughts. Over in Australia, with the bright sunshine, the colours had seemed subdued but now, under the electric light of her bedroom, it looked a bit garish.

She hunted through her wardrobe and found a plain grey frock with a white collar and red bow. She had pinned her hair up and she knew she looked bookish and dull but she made her mind up. It would be the grey frock and a pair of high heeled black shoes.

She was going into the agency later to see Edna and Mary. She had sent a congratulation card to Mary and was relieved to have her coming in every day. It was a big weight off her mind, knowing that the office would be covered for any calls that may come in.

She was pleasantly surprised by the work so far and she had three of her friends doing temporary work at the moment. Of course, the biggest money earners were Edna's job and her own. How long both would last was uncertain but she hoped for another week or so for both.

Mary was on the phone when Molly appeared and she was taking down the particulars of a job. 'Yes, Mr Oswald, we'll have a secretary there next Wednesday, Thursday and Friday. Thank you for choosing McQueen's Agency.'

Mary looked up a sheet of paper. 'It's Sheila's turn to work. Will I phone her?'

Molly said yes. She was conscious of the fact that all these friends were now married and had little time to spare for helping out. However, it gave them some extra money to spend on themselves.

Edna appeared later and she seemed to be anxious. Molly hoped there was nothing wrong.

'It's Mr Knox,' she explained. 'He's going away for two weeks to his brother's in Arbroath and he wondered if I could work from there. I was hoping to have a fortnight off with Mum and Billy at my auntie's house, as she also lives there. Do you think that's possible, Molly?'

Well, well, thought Molly, the plot thickens. Mr Knox and Edna. However none of this emotion showed on her face. 'I don't mind if that's all right with you, Edna. When will you be going?'

Edna looked relieved. 'I thought the week after next. I want Billy to have a wee holiday by the seaside and we usually go to Mum's sister for a break.'

Molly made up the wages and handed them to Edna and Mary. The look of delight on Mary's face was a picture. It was the start of her full-time employment.

When Molly was leaving, she said, 'You will take care tonight, Mary? Stay with your friends and if you see that man again, get a policeman.'

When she got back to the house on Saturday afternoon, Molly had another look at the clothes from her wardrobe but, after laying six or seven outfits on the bed, she decided on her initial choice of the grey dress.

She was ready by five thirty. Initially, she had pinned her hair up but then decided to leave it loose where it hung in blonde waves on her shoulders. After another quick look in the mirror she was ready.

It was a pleasant drive along the country road. Parts of the road skirted the river and it looked steely grey under the cloudy sky. The sun had shone earlier but it was now overcast.

When she reached Cliff Top House, she found a scene of organised chaos. Lena was organising the layout of the table in the dining room and Joe, Mike and Ritchie were busy in the sheds. Molly popped her head around the dining room door. 'Can I help with anything?' she said.

Lena swept her hair back from her face. 'No thanks, Molly, everything is under control.' Then she sighed. 'At least I hope it is. We have this dinner every month and it's always the same. I'm running around at the last moment like a demented banshee.'

Molly didn't think she looked demented. In fact, she looked supremely calm. There was no sign of Kenneth.

As if reading her mind, Lena said. 'Kenneth has not long arrived. He's had a busy day at the shop. But he'll want to put on the style for his dinner companion, Mrs Marten. She married a very wealthy Dutch businessman but he died some years ago. Now she's a rich widow with designs on my brother.'

Molly was amazed that anyone had the kind of money required to buy anything from the shop but now she understood. If everyone tonight was as rich as Mrs Marten then that would explain the success of the Lamont's antique business. She thought about at the widow's designs on Kenneth but she quite understood it. He was a great looking man with a lovely manner and an elegant dress sense.

The dining table looked magnificent. A white table cloth was covered with crystal glasses, silver dishes and cutlery. It was hard to believe that the wartime rationing was only now being relaxed.

Lena said, 'I've put a desk out in the shed, Molly, and you can sit there and take any orders that may come in tonight but before that, perhaps you can join the men for a meal in the kitchen.'

Molly said she had already eaten, which was untrue, but she didn't relish the idea of sitting with Christie and Mike.

'Well if you're sure. I'll get Joe to bring out something later.'

Molly went out to the shed and the transformation was unbelievable. What had been full of large packing cases earlier in the week was now transformed with beautiful pieces of furniture. Over in the corner were six or seven oil paintings that had an expensive patina about them.

The desk held a large notebook and pen, no doubt to take down the details of any purchases made tonight.

She heard the cars arriving and saw Lena, Joe and Kenneth walk out to greet their guests.

Lena was dressed in a dress of blue taffeta and Kenneth was in a dark suit. Joe looked more casual in a sports jacket and fawn trousers.

Three couples got out of their cars but none looked as well dressed as their hosts.

Then the last car drew up and Widow Marten came out. She looked about fifty years old, quite plump, wearing a frock unsuitable for her ample figure. It was a cross between brown and bronze satin and the fabric was pulled tight over her large bust and hips.

However, it was her jewellery that took Molly's breath away. She wore three diamond rings on her fingers, all sparkling in the sunlight, and her necklace of red stones, which hung from her neck seemed to glow with a brilliance that Molly had never seen before. They looked like rubies but it was a pity they clashed with the brown frock.

Mike and Christie were standing by the entrance to the shed and also looked smart in their green overalls. Lena brought the guests over and introduced them.

'You've all met Mike and Christie before, but this is Molly who will take any order you care to place tonight.'

Molly was then introduced to Bill and Marlene Farley, James and Laura Small, Ronald and Betty White and Mrs Marten.

The three couples didn't look rich enough to buy any of the goods displayed here but maybe Molly was wrong. Perhaps they were like the widow and were all filthy rich.

As she was turning back to her desk she caught Mrs Marten

staring at her and Molly gave her a smile. The woman turned on her heel and marched into the house.

An hour later, Mike and Christie came back to the shed. Christie perched on the edge of the desk. 'You didn't come in for something to eat.'

Molly said no, she hadn't.

'You missed a super meal,' he said. 'We had soup, Coronation chicken and chocolate mousse.'

Molly was starving but she hoped her stomach wouldn't rumble at the thought of this great meal. Why hadn't she gone in? However, she was pleasantly surprised when Joe brought out a plate of sandwiches and a coffee.

Christie stood up. 'I'd better let you drink your coffee while it's hot,' he said, making his way to the far end of the shed.

He switched on the lights to highlight the paintings. Molly was no expert but these paintings looked like old masterpieces.

Half an hour later, Lena led her guests into the shed. They admired the pieces of furniture and the paintings while Kenneth and Joe quietly mentioned the prices.

Laura Small sat down beside Molly. 'My husband has an antique shop in Edinburgh and we buy some stock from the Lamonts twice a year. They have such lovely things.'

Molly agreed. 'Do you run the shop with your husband?'

Laura laughed. 'Oh no, I've got my three children to look after. James is the brains behind our business.'

'Do you all own an antique shop?' Molly asked.

'Bill and Marlene do but they're based in Glasgow. Ronald and Betty are American and he's working over here. They've been married less than a year and they've bought a large house in Fife and are furnishing it. Seemingly, they only want the best and are willing to pay for it.'

Lucky Ronald and Betty, thought Molly cynically.

Mrs Marten was bending over one of the paintings. 'I like this one, Kenneth,' she said.

'You've a good eye Nelly. It's by Fergusson, one of the Scottish Colourists.'

'I'll take it,' she said.

'I'll bring it over to the shop on Monday and you can pay for it then,' he said.

The rest of the guests mingled amongst the furniture and Mike and Christie were busy showing off the workmanship. They pulled drawers out and lifted small items to show the undersides and backs.

'There's no Utility mark with those pieces,' said Kenneth.

Ronald and Betty laughed. 'Isn't the Utility furniture just too ugly for words?. There's no decoration. Everything is so basic. Just like the clothes, but now that rationing is almost over maybe we'll get some great designers again.'

'Nothing matches the true quality of really old antiques. They were made to last,' said Lena. She walked over to the desk with a paper list and Molly was surprised to see how much money had been made in one night.

'Molly, can you make up the invoices for each of the sales and the customers will take them away with them? Don't make out an invoice for Mrs Marten's painting as Kenneth will deal with that himself.'

Molly was busy for the next hour while Christie and Mike tied nametags to the pieces that had been sold. The customers were also busy making arrangements for the uplifting of their purchases.

'My van will come and collect as usual on Monday,' said James.

Bill nodded. 'I can't manage till Tuesday but it'll be in the morning.'

However, Betty and Ronald couldn't wait that long. 'Do you mind if we turn up tomorrow?'

Lena smiled. 'Not at all. We'll be here all day so just come when it suits you.' She turned to her guests. 'Now let's all go back to the house and have a drink, or coffee if you prefer it.'

Molly wasn't sure what she had to do but Lena said, 'Leave the copies of the invoices in the office and come into the lounge and have a drink.'

Molly wasn't keen on this but it seemed bad manners to refuse.

She hadn't been in the lounge before and was totally taken with the view. A large window overlooked the river and lights from the opposite shore twinkled like fairy lights

The room was furnished with exquisite items and there were three large squashy sofas grouped around the fireplace. Lena had placed a large silver tray with coffee and tea plus a bottle of whisky and sherry.

Molly settled for coffee as did most of the women. Mrs Marten, however, had joined the men and held a large glass of whisky in her chubby fingers, the diamonds glittering brightly.

The guests then said their goodbyes.

'Safe journey,' said Kenneth and, as soon as the three cars were gone, Joe muttered something and made his way to the sheds.

Mrs Marten hadn't left and gave Lena a resigned look. It was obvious Joe was well known for his churlishness.

Lena smiled at her. 'Come in and have another drink, Nelly.'

Molly stood inside the lounge door, unsure what to do but Lena said, 'That will be all for tonight, Molly. Thank you for working and we'll see you on Monday.'

Kenneth came out with her to the car. 'You're a big help to us, Molly. Lena has a lot of pain with her broken arm and she could never have got through tonight without you.'

Molly felt her face go red but thankfully it was getting dark so she hoped he hadn't noticed.

'I wanted to say . . .' he said but a voice called out from the front door. It was Nelly.

'We've poured out your whisky, Kenneth.'

He gave Molly a grin. 'My mistress calls,' he said and strode back into the house.

Molly drove through the gathering darkness and she was glad when she reached the house. Marigold's light was still on and Molly saw the curtain twitch as the car went past.

Marigold appeared. 'How did it all go?' she asked. 'Come in and tell me all about it.'

Molly was tired but she didn't want to hurt her neighbour's feelings.

Molly described the people present and all the lovely paintings and furniture. She left Mrs Marten to the last. 'She's a widow but when her husband was alive, they lived in Holland for many years.'

'She must be very rich to afford all that jewellery,' said Marigold.

Molly said she had the impression she had inherited it from either her own family or her husband's, but added, 'She bought one of the paintings. A Fergusson, I believe, and Kenneth said she had a good eye for quality.'

Molly stood up. 'I'd better get off to bed. I must go over to the office tomorrow and catch up with some office work.'

Later, as she lay awake in bed, she thought she heard a car stopping on the street and then the sound of it driving off again.

Maybe someone is lost she thought or picking up a passenger from one of the other houses.

She didn't hear the car come back and park a few yards away from the garden or see the figure emerge to stand in the deep shadows of the large holly tree at the foot of the garden.

# 14

Tam was on his way with Rover to see his friend who had an allotment on the slopes of the Law. He was going to get some flowers to take to Harry's grave.

It was a damp, drizzly morning and, because it was a Sunday, most people seemed to be having a long lie in bed. The streets were quiet as they made their way along Byron Street and up towards the allotments. Tam knew Bert would be in his plot at this early hour. He loved his allotment where he could potter about, get dirt under his fingernails and enjoy growing his flowers and vegetables. Rover also loved this place as there were rabbits to chase and lots of space to run around.

Bert was surprised to have an early morning visitor. 'Hullo, Tam. What brings you out so early?' He put down his hoe and sat down on the bench beside the wooden shed. He took out his pipe and tobacco. This was one pleasure he wasn't allowed to do at home.

Tam mentioned the flowers. 'You know I told you about that chap who was drowned? Well I thought of taking a walk to Balgay cemetery later and leaving a wee bunch of dahlias.'

'That was the chap that you didn't think had an accident?'

Tam nodded. 'Aye, it was, but the police said everything points to an unfortunate accident so I'll have to accept that.'

Bert gathered a bunch of dahlias, gave them to his friend and as Tam made his way back with Rover, he took his spade and began turning over the rich brown loamy soil.

Once back at Gellatly Street, Tam climbed the two flights of stairs and let himself into his small flat. He placed the flowers in the basin of cold water before opening a tin of dog food, which he put into Rover's bowl.

He then opened a small tin of tomato soup and cut two slices of bread for himself.

'When I've had my dinner, I'll go to the cemetery,' he said to the dog. 'But I'll leave you here, Rover, because I'll be getting the bus.'

It was still grey and misty with a fine drizzle when Tam set off for Shore Terrace and the bus stances. Luckily there was a number 17 bus already waiting.

The bus meandered slowly up Lochee Road towards Tullidelph Road and Glamis Road. Tam got off at this stop as it was the nearest to the gates of the cemetery.

Quite a few other passengers also got off here and they made their way to the rows of pre-fab houses that had been built beside Balgay Park. Tam would have liked to have one of these pre-fabs. He'd heard all about their labour saving kitchens and bathrooms. The stairs at Gellatly Street were becoming a trial to his tired old legs as well.

Also, Rover would love the park to run around in.

The cemetery was busy as people tended the graves of loved ones, changing the flowers and generally tidying up the ground. Tam made his way to Harry's grave and was pleased when he saw a small headstone had been erected over the small plot.

DS Johns had said there was money left over from Harry's insurance policy for this headstone and Tam had chosen the epitaph.

*Harry Hawkins. Home is the sailor home from the sea.*

Tam went to get water from the cold tap which was situated a few yards away and he arranged the bunch of dahlias as best he could. Flower arranging wasn't his strong point but the dahlias made a colourful splash against the wet grass.

He sat for a while on the wooden bench. He liked to sit and watch the world go by and breathe in the fresh country air. He missed the sea and the ships; the salty tang of the ocean and the height of the wild waves which sometimes threatened to overturn some of the old boats he had sailed on.

He thought of Harry and all the adventures he must have experienced as a sailor. Coming through the horrors of wartime, only to drown in the harbour at Dundee. Life could be so cruel.

Tam rose slowly to his feet. It was time to get back and take Rover out for his evening walk. He would then have a boiled egg with toast for his tea.

The bus was quieter on the return journey and Tam was glad to make his way back to the house. He never locked his door. For one thing, none of his neighbours did and he didn't have anything valuable to steal.

As always he took delight in his large nameplate, which he kept shining with a daily clean of Brasso. It had come from one of the ships he had been on and he had acquired it when the old vessel went to the scrapyard.

He had just turned the door handle when he became aware of a shadow behind him. It was reflected in the brass plate and he turned his head to see who was coming down the stair from the top flats.

A sharp pain exploded in his shoulder and he was vaguely aware of an arm with some kind of cosh. The arm was raised up high and was about to come down on his head when a white blur rushed past him. Snarling and baring his teeth, Rover grabbed the assailant's arm and wouldn't let go. Tam heard some muffled cries as the dog's teeth bit into someone's flesh.

Suddenly there was sharp yelp of pain followed by whimpering. Tam tried to stand up but couldn't. Rover was obviously hurt.

Tam began to shout for help and he heard the sound of footsteps running down the stairs.

After a few minutes he heard the door across the landing open and his neighbour, Mrs Kidd, hurried over.

'What happened, Tam? Did you fall down?'

Tam said. 'Can you see if Rover's all right, Mrs Kidd.'

The dog was silent now and he heard the woman gently talking to it. She hurried back up the stairs. 'He's been hit with something, Tam, and it doesn't look too good. I'm going to get the Bobby.'

The young constable on the beat helped Tam into his house and said he had called the doctor.

'What about Rover? Will he be all right?'

The policeman didn't reply.

The doctor arrived within the hour and examined Tam's shoulder. 'It's not dislocated and I don't think it's broken but you might have to go to the DRI for an X-Ray tomorrow. You've got very bad bruising but I'll have a better idea tomorrow when I come back to see you.'

After the doctor and policeman had left, Mrs Kidd made Tam a strong cup of tea and placed a hot water bottle in his bed. 'Would you like me to make you some supper, Tam?'

Tam shook his head. 'What about Rover. Have you heard how he is?'

'The policeman took him to the People's Dispensary in Dock Street for emergency treatment and you'll hear tomorrow how he is. What happened? I didn't hear what you told the policeman.'

'Somebody hit me with a cosh or a truncheon. Rover saved my life by biting them and now it looks like I've lost him.' He tried hard not to cry but tears formed in his eyes. He wiped them away with his handkerchief.

Mrs Kidd said, 'Now, now, Tam, let's get you to your bed. The doctor left these pills and I've to give you two before you go to sleep. They'll help the pain.'

She bustled over to the sink and filled a cup with water. 'Here, swallow them and you'll get a good night's sleep.'

Tam did as he was told but after the departure of his neighbour, he did something he had never done before. He hobbled over and locked the door.

The pills did make him sleep but when he woke in the morning, all the horror of the previous night came flooding back along with his anguish over his dog. He had heard Rover yelp in agony and it seemed like the assailant had used his cosh on him.

There was a knock on the door and Tam almost called out to come in before he remembered he had locked the door.

Mrs Kidd was standing in the lobby but Tam was surprised to see DS Johns behind her.

As the woman set about making some tea and toast, the policeman settled himself on Tam's chair. 'What all this I'm hearing about you being attacked, Tam?'

Tam, who was thinking about the episode, was beginning to doubt his first reactions.

'Maybe it was just somebody in a hurry. You know, he came rushing down from the top floor and banged into me and then knocked Rover down the stair because he was barking at him. I thought he was carrying a truncheon or something like it but maybe it's just my imagination.'

Charlie Johns didn't think this was the reason. He had the doctor's report and Tam had certainly suffered a heavy blow to his shoulder; a blow that had been aimed at his head, if he hadn't been forewarned by the shadow. He had also seen the report on Rover and it didn't make good reading.

Tam was asking about his dog. 'Will I get Rover back from the Dispensary today? Is he going to be all right?'

Charlie Johns said he was in good hands. He was going to see the vet after questioning Tam's neighbours.

Mrs Kidd hadn't heard anything to start with. 'I was listening to the wireless as I like the programmes on a Sunday. It was the high-pitched yelping from Rover that made me open the door and poor Tam was lying there in a heap. I thought I heard footsteps running out of the close but I'm not sure.'

Charlie went round all the neighbours but he had no joy until he saw old Mrs Rice who lived on the downstairs landing. She had been putting out her milk bottle when a figure ran by but she hadn't been able to give any description.

'It's my glasses, son. They're cracked.'

Charlie saw that was an understatement. One lens had a deep crack across the surface and the other lens was totally covered with a mesh of fine lines.

'I dropped then the other day and stood on them,' she said ruefully. 'I'm waiting to see the optician later today to get another pair on the National Health.'

He turned to go but Mrs Rice added, 'The man was wearing one of those coats with a hood. You ken the ones I mean. Sailors wear them but I can't remember what they're called.'

'A duffle coat, Mrs Rice?'

Her face lit up. 'That's right, son. Those coats with the toggles and the hood. I've seen them at the pictures in one of those John Mills films about ships and submarines.'

Charlie was puzzled. Here was another incident with a seaman. First Harry and now Tam. There had to be a connection.

He made his way round the corner to the Dock Street Dispensary for Sick Animals. Rover was lying in a cage. He seemed to be asleep. There was dried blood on his head and stitches covered the deep gash on his back. His back leg was in a splint. The vet came out and examined him.

'Poor wee dog. He got a good beating with something heavy. I'm not sure if the leg will heal. We might have to amputate it but I'll give it another day or two. Just to see how it goes.'

'What about that deep cut on his back?'

'That should heal all right. Luckily for him he was well fed and had a bit of fat about him. Otherwise it could have been much worse.'

Charlie made his way back to Gellatly Street. He was filled with anger at the thought of someone trying to kill a harmless old man and his dog.

Charlie sat by the side of the bed and told Tam about Mrs Rice's statement. 'Everything seems to come back to Harry Hawkins Are you sure you've never met him before? Maybe you were both on the same ship at some time.'

Tam shook his head. 'No, I never saw him till I met him in the pub the night he died. I'm much older than him and I've been retired for almost thirteen years. I never saw any action during the war. Not like Harry. He said he had been all over the world since going to sea at sixteen.'

'I checked up on Harry's work record. He was with the Hull

firm for four years and he did a year on the emigrant ships going out to Australia, as a steward. I'm not sure why he left that job but he went straight back to work on the ship from Hull to Rotterdam, then *The Mary Anne* afterwards.'

Tam gave Charlie a direct look. 'You've not mentioned Rover. He's dead. Isn't he?'

Charlie shook his head. 'No Tam, I've just left the vet. Rover has a deep gash on his back that needed stitches. He was sleeping when I left him.'

Charlie felt awful not telling Tam the entire truth but the vet had said to give the Rover's leg another couple of days. Why worry the old man until then?

# 15

Cliff Top House was a hive of activity on the Monday morning. Joe, Mike and Christie were busy loading the van with Ronald's furniture.

Lena appeared in her housecoat. She looked tired and had black shadows under her eyes.

'What a weekend we've had. Ronald's van has broken down so he wants his furniture delivered today. Actually, he wanted it yesterday but Joe fell on the beach and cut his arm badly. He won't go to the infirmary or the doctor. He says it'll heal in a couple of days.

'And as you can see, Molly, I've overslept. My arm was very painful last night and I didn't get much sleep and I have to be with Kenneth in the shop today. Can you and Christie deal with the delivery for Edinburgh? James's van is coming this morning.'

Molly said she would help Christie with the loading.

'Now don't you do any heavy lifting, Molly. Christie and the van driver will do that.' She gave a final glance towards her husband who had finished loading his van and gave a little wave as he drove away with Mike. Joe didn't return her wave nor did he say anything to his wife as he drove out of the courtyard, even though he passed within a few feet of the two women.

After a few minutes Lena headed back indoors, saying, 'I'd better get dressed or Kenneth will be waiting for me.'

Molly headed for the office where there was a huge pile of invoices waiting to be filed, plus another batch of brochures to be posted.

Molly could hardly believe the amounts of money people were spending on antique furniture, rugs and paintings. Perhaps it was as Betty said. People were tired of Utility furniture and clothes.

Glancing through some of the brochures that were sent out regularly to the Lamont's favoured customers, she saw some lovely pieces; tables with beautiful inlaid work and chairs covered in fabulous fabrics.

She heard the van before she saw it; its slow lumbering whine as it drew up at the back door.

Christie appeared as Lena and Kenneth were getting into their car. 'We'll be back about five o'clock, Christie.'

The two van drivers were standing at the side of their vehicle. Christie said to drive it to the entrance of the shed.

Molly had to go to the shed with the delivery book and note everything that was put on the van, but the three men lifted the goods and placed them gently into the interior, wrapping cloths around the furniture to protect it from bumps. Molly didn't like to be morbid but everything looked as if it were covered in shrouds. It all looked quite ghostly.

It had been cool and misty earlier on but now, by mid morning, the sun had come out and the office was warm and stuffy. Molly went to open the window but when she returned to her desk she heard a faint creak like a footstep above her head, in Joe and Lena's bedroom.

She held her breath and listened hard. There was another soft footstep.

Molly went out quietly into the hall and stood by the foot of the stair. Everything seemed peaceful. The clock in the hall chimed eleven.

Perhaps she had imagined the noise. After all, it was an old house and full of creaks and groans.

She went back to her desk and soon the only sound was the sharp tapping of the typewriter as she typed letters to accompany the brochures. Fifteen minutes later she decided to make a cup of tea.

She was sitting at the kitchen table when she heard another creak from upstairs. Someone was definitely prowling around. She made her way back out to the hall and climbed the stairs. Her footsteps muffled by the thick carpet, she reached the landing without making a noise.

She didn't like the idea that she was snooping so she called out, 'Who's there?'

There was no sound. She opened the bathroom door but the room was deserted.

She didn't like to check the bedrooms as they were personal and off limits to her and her sense of common decency.

She moved to the end of the landing and was surprised to see another small staircase which seemed to lead to the back of the house. She stood looking down this stair but all was silent. There were four doors on the landing. Lena and Joe's bedroom, Kenneth's room, the bathroom and probably another bedroom.

She opened this door and was surprised to find it full of pictures, rugs and antique vases and ornaments. There were also lots of silver items ranging from tea services and picture frames to large ornamental bowls.

As she was shutting the door she noticed one of the paintings. It was the one bought by Nelly Marten on Saturday evening. Kenneth and Lena had obviously left it behind by mistake.

Feeling like a criminal she hurried downstairs. There was a small window on the stairs that overlooked the garden and, to her surprise, she saw Christie heading towards the sheds.

Surely he couldn't be the prowler? He worked in the business and had every right to be around. So why creep around like a thief?

Molly decided to go out and see Christie. She could always make up some sort of tale to explain her visit.

Christie was checking a sheet of paper when she went in. She called out. 'Hullo, I hope I'm not disturbing you?'

Christie looked alarmed and thrust the sheet of paper into his pocket. 'You gave me a fright,' he said, giving her a big smile. 'What can I do for you?'

'I've got letters to post and wondered how far the nearest post box is,' she said.

He gave her a quick glance. 'I think Lena likes to post the mail when they go to the shop. Or else she takes it to the post office in Newport.'

Molly put on a disappointed face. 'Thanks. It's just my own private letters but I'll post them later.'

She turned to go but he said. 'I'm making some coffee. Do you want to join me?'

'I'll have some tea if you have any.'

He grinned. 'We have everything here. Even a tin of biscuits.'

He bustled about in the tiny kitchen and Molly heard the rattle of cups and the sound of the kettle boiling. She poked her head around the door. The room was compact but well fitted out. A wide bench ran along one side of the wall and a small gas cooker sat beside the other wall, next to a sink and draining board. There were three chairs grouped around a wooden table and it felt warm and comfy.

Joe and Lena were certainly thoughtful employers. Christie placed the two cups and some biscuits on the table and sat down in one of the chairs. He waved an arm towards the other chair. 'Take the weight off your feet.'

Molly sat down on the edge of her seat. She wasn't sure of this man. As she sipped her tea, Christie chatted about the previous Saturday evening.

'I bet they were pleased with the sales they got. I mean that picture must be worth a fortune.'

Molly remained silent. She wasn't going to discuss her employer's business with a worker.

'You got home safely?' he asked. 'It's a narrow road especially in the dark.'

'It wasn't too dark. The summer nights are something I had forgotten when I was in Australia.'

'That's right, I remember you said you had emigrated to Australia with your sister. Your parents are going out there now, you said. What brought you back from the land of opportunity?'

Molly froze. There was no way she was going to tell him about Tom and all the heartache his death had caused.

'My sister got married and I got homesick.'

'I know the feeling,' he said. 'I miss Canada a lot but I'll be going back sometime. Maybe you'll go back to Australia, Molly.'

Never, she thought, but she smiled. 'Maybe. Who knows where we'll all end up?'

She decided to mention the footsteps. Just to see what he said. 'When I was in the office I thought I heard someone upstairs.'

He gave her a blank look. 'When was this?'

'It was about an hour ago. I went up to check and saw you heading back to the sheds. Did you see anyone?'

He shook his head then suddenly said. 'You must have heard me. I had to go upstairs to the bathroom.'

Molly made herself look relieved. 'Oh that's all right. I thought it was a burglar.' She stood up. 'Thanks for the tea. I'd better get back and start earning my wages.'

She walked quickly back to the house and by the time she reached her desk, she was shaking. Christie was obviously lying, but why?

On Saturday evening during the dinner, she had been in the sheds and during that time she had noticed Mike going into a small cloakroom next to the kitchen.

Why, she wondered, did Christie have to go into the house to use the bathroom when there was a perfectly adequate toilet and washbasin a few yards from his work?

She gave herself a shake. 'Stop making a mystery out of nothing,' she scolded herself mentally. 'You're here to do a job of work and the running of the business is nothing to do with you. If Christie is a thief then Joe and Lena will deal with him.'

She picked up the brochures and letters and placed them in their envelopes, leaving them in a neat pile by the side of the desk, ready for Lena to deal with on her return.

# 16

Edna was enjoying working at the seaside. John's brother lived in a small house at the end of a narrow street. Ten years older than John, James was an artist. Several of his paintings, mostly seascapes and paintings of tiny villages perched on the top of cliffs hung on the walls of the house. Edna thought they were very well done and picturesque.

She had arrived the day before with her mum, Irene, and Billy and although they were a bit cramped in her Auntie Betty's house, the excitement of being on holiday eclipsed any discomfort.

Betty lived in a council house ten minutes away from the centre of town. The three of them shared a small bedroom with Edna sharing a bed with her mum while Billy slept on a folding bed that was put away in the cupboard every morning.

Billy was so excited about this bed that every morning he watched the ritual of folding the sheets and putting everything away in fascination.

The routine was simple. Edna worked from nine o'clock till twelve then had the rest of the day to spend with her family.

The weather was sunny but there was a brisk breeze with meant, on her visits to the beach with Billy, she had to wear a cardigan over her summer frock. Irene came with them on the first day but decided it was too cold and said she would stay at home with Betty or maybe go to the shops.

John came with them one day. Sitting on a rug on the sand, they had a picnic of cheese sandwiches and a flask of tea. Billy had some milk, which Edna had carried in an old cough mixture bottle.

Afterwards, Billy wanted to go swimming in the outdoor pool and ran to join the crowds of children who were leaping gleefully into the cold water.

John seemed quite content to sit with her and watch Billy splash around in the shallow end.

Edna wasn't sure how long John wanted to stay with his brother. 'We can only stay another week with my auntie,' she said. 'She puts us up for the holiday fortnight but doesn't have the room to accommodate us any longer.'

John was relieved. He had made up the pretext of coming here just to be with Edna. At night he would lie awake and try to determine his feelings for this very attractive woman who had come into his life.

'Another week will suit me as well, Edna,' he said, hoping his voice sounded steady. The fact was his book was almost three-quarters written and he was dreading the day when he would no longer have an excuse to see her.

They sat in companionable silence and watched a beauty contest taking place on the fringes of the pool About twenty or so young girls paraded in their swimsuits in front of three judges.

Edna thought they must be cold as the wind had sharpened and now blew in from the North Sea. The overhead sun was warm but the wind seemed to go right through you. As her mum would say, 'a wind that went through you rather than around you.'

John smiled. 'Heavens I can see goose pimples on those lassies legs, and that one in the blue swimsuit has blue arms to match her costume.'

Edna laughed. 'She's not the only one.' Billy had joined them and was shivering with the cold. Edna wrapped him in a towel.

The girls paraded once more around the edge of the pool and a round of applause went to the winner; a very pretty girl with long dark hair and a bright pink costume.

'That's another "Miss Arbroath,"' said Edna. 'It's always an attraction for the holidaymakers. There's great competition between the girls.'

Billy looked at his mum. 'Did you win, Mum?'

Edna laughed. 'Oh I'm not pretty enough to enter a beauty contest, Billy.'

They sat in silence for a few moments then John spoke.

'I wondered if you would like to come out for a meal tonight, Edna. Just to say thank you for all your hard work?'

'I'd love to. What time will you pick me up?'

'About seven, if that's all right?'

Edna gave this some thought. 'Make it half past seven. I should have Billy ready for his bed by then.' She told him about the folding bed and Billy's attachment to it. 'He lies in it and reads his comics for ages while we listen to the wireless. I think I'll have to ask Betty if we can take it home with us.'

Later, Edna spent ages getting ready. She rejected one frock because she thought it looked too plain but her wardrobe wasn't a huge one and she didn't really have a lot of choice.

Finally, she settled for her white dress that had red cherries printed all over the skirt and a pair of white sandals. Her mum watched as she scurried around and hoped Edna wouldn't get hurt by this man's attention. He seemed nice enough but you couldn't tell someone's nature with a few meetings.

John came dead on seven thirty and arrived in a car. 'I borrowed my brother's vehicle,' he said. He had left his own car behind in Dundee and had arrived by train.

Billy came running downstairs when he heard the car stopping, his eyes like saucers. He was torn between watching the car take off and returning to the folding bed.

The car won and he stood on the doorstep as Edna was whisked away towards the hotel where John said he had booked a meal.

The hotel lay a few miles outside the town and was really posh. Edna wasn't sure if she was dressed properly but most of the guests were dressed in summer clothes so she soon settled down and began to enjoy the evening.

He was full of stories about his time at sea. 'I've been in the navy since I was sixteen,' he said. 'Then, during the war, I was on the Arctic convoys. I got married a few years before the war but I was always away from home. It was a lonely life for Kathleen but I loved my job and I thought our times together made up for all the times I was away.' He sipped his coffee and Edna thought he looked sad. 'Then five years ago, Kathleen became ill. I was away but when I got home she told me she had received treatment and I wasn't to worry. I went back to my ship and she took a heart attack. By the time I got home she was gone.'

Edna reached for his hand and gave it a squeeze. 'That's terrible John. How did you cope?'

'I gave up my job and stayed at home. Perhaps if I had done that earlier, Kathleen might have had a longer life. Now I'm writing my book.' He gave a harsh laugh. 'Talk about closing the stable after the horse has bolted.'

'We never know what life is going to throw at us John so you mustn't blame yourself. I think if Kathleen had wanted you to stay at home she would have said so.'

'That's enough about me,' he said. 'Now tell my all about you. Where is your husband? Does he work away from home?'

Edna withdrew her hand and put it in her lap. 'He's dead,' she said quietly.

John looked shocked. 'Oh, I'm so sorry, Edna. I had no idea. Trust me to ask a personal question like that.'

'No, no it's all right. I don't mind talking about it. He died in an accident. He was a regular soldier who stayed on in the army after the war ended. He was stationed abroad and was killed in an attack on a hotel when he was inside having a drink. William never knew I was expecting Billy.'

John felt so sorry to be bringing back this painful episode in Edna's life. He leaned over towards her and took her hand in his. 'I'm sorry. What a tragedy and a waste of life. And to die without knowing he had a son.'

They made their way back to the car. Dusk had fallen but there had been a beautiful sunset earlier on. The sky was tinged with deep mauve and crimson bands. The hotel overlooked the town and it seemed to sparkle under the evening light. The sea stretched to the far horizon where the grey colours merged with one another and it was as if you could see forever.

They spoke very little on the homeward journey but when they reached the house, Edna thanked him for a great evening.

John said, 'I'm sorry I asked personal questions, Edna. I hope I haven't upset you.'

'No you haven't, John. It's all in the past.'

He smiled with relief. 'Good. The last thing I want is to see you unhappy.'

Edna opened the car door. 'I'll see you tomorrow morning.'

'There's one thing I wanted to say.' His words came out in a rush. 'My brother usually puts on a display of his paintings every summer and I wondered if you would like to come with me. It's on Tuesday night in a local gallery. It's not a big event but I like to give James my support.'

'I would love to come and thanks again for a great evening.'

As he drove home, he was elated. Oh he was sorry for Edna's husband's death but he now felt he could perhaps keep seeing her . . . even after his book was finished.

On the Tuesday afternoon, Edna and Billy made their way to the beach. Billy carried his bucket and spade and was soon digging a huge trench in the sand.

'Can I go down to the sea and fill my bucket with water, Mum?' he asked.

'Well, make sure you come straight back, Billy,' she warned.

He ran down to the water's edge and filled his little bucket before running back to his sandcastle. This went on for a few times. Edna had paid a few pence for the rent of a deckchair and she lay back in it, watching the antics of her son.

It was a very warm day and the sun shone from a near perfect blue sky. Edna hadn't realised how tired she was and soon fell asleep. Waking suddenly, she realised she had slept for ten minutes and there was no sign of Billy.

She leapt to her feet and almost tripped over his large sandcastle. The bucket and spade were missing so she ran down to the sea. Some people were swimming and there were a few boats skimming along the waves, but no sign of Billy.

Frantic with worry she ran along the beach, calling his name. Although there were lots of families spread out over the sand with loads of children running out and in the water, she couldn't see him.

'Please, please don't let him be in the water,' she prayed. At the far edge of the sand was a first aid building and she ran inside. 'You haven't seen my little boy, have you?' she asked the attendant. 'He's five year's old with dark hair and he's wearing a pair of blue shorts.'

The man shook his head. 'We've had a few lost kiddies in today but they've all been reunited with their parents. We haven't had anyone in since dinnertime.'

By now Edna was in tears and the man said he would get someone to help her search for him. A large woman appeared and said she would search one end of the beach while Edna concentrated on the other side.

Edna ran between the legs of snoozing sunbathers and capering children. The sand tugged at her sandals and she felt she was wading in treacle. She got as far as her vacant deckchair and the sandcastle now looked forlorn.

Beyond the beach lay the sand dunes; large patches of windblown grass that punctuated the sandy stretches. The grass was sharp against her bare legs but she barely felt it.

She kept calling out Billy's name but no one answered. There was no one on this part of the beach, nothing but isolation and the vast sea which could easily swallow a little boy.

Suddenly she heard her name being called and when she turned, the helper came towards her, holding Billy's hand tightly.

He ran up to her. 'You got lost, Mummy. The man tried to find you.'

Edna dropped to her knees. 'What man, Billy?'

'He took my hand and said we had to look for you but you weren't there.'

Edna looked at the woman. 'There was no one with him when I found him. He was up on the road that runs alongside the beach,' she said.

'The man wanted to buy me an ice cream but I said no. I told him I had to find you so we started to look for you.'

Edna didn't know what to think. Perhaps someone's father had found him and was only being helpful.

'Billy, why did you go up onto the road?'

Billy shrugged. 'I thought that's where you were.'

Edna could see that it was no good questioning him any longer. 'Come on, it's time to go home. Where're your bucket and spade.'

Billy's face crumpled and he began to cry. 'I don't know.'

'Thank you for helping me. You've been very kind,' she said as the woman walked away.

Back in the house, Irene tried to make light of the incident but Edna was worried.

'I shouldn't have fallen asleep, Mum, but Billy should have known to stay beside me. I've told him often enough never to stray when we're out.'

Irene had put him to bed with his comics. 'Well he's fine now so don't punish yourself.'

She looked at the clock. 'What time are you going to this gallery.'

Edna groaned aloud. 'I'd forgotten about that. Can you give John a message and tell him I can't go?'

Irene was firm. 'Don't be daft. Away you go and have a night out. Billy is fine and Betty and I will be here with him.'

Edna wasn't in the mood for a night out and hoped it wouldn't be a late event.

John arrived on the dot of seven thirty and they made their way to the small gallery which was situated on one of the quiet side streets of the town. The seafront was busy with holiday-makers and it seemed as if the entire town was out on this lovely evening.

The wonderful smell of fish and chips wafted out from the chip shop, which had a large queue snaking out the door.

The gallery was quite full when they arrived and there was a small glass of sherry for each visitor. Edna felt quite light-headed as she sipped her sherry. She hadn't eaten much at teatime because of the trauma of the afternoon.

The paintings hung on the walls and they brightened up the room. James mingled with his guests but when he saw them, he came over. 'What do you think, John? I've sold four paintings.'

They both congratulated him. After half an hour of wandering around the room, John suggested they have a seat on one of the benches by the window.

'Are you all right, Edna?'

She shook her head and told him about the drama of the afternoon.

'Did he say who the man was?'

'No he didn't know him, and he wasn't with Billy when the woman who was helping me look for him, found him.'

John said, 'I think you should get off home. You look tired.'

Edna didn't disagree and they said their farewells to James who had sold another two paintings and was exuberant with success.

At the house, John said, 'Do you want to leave and go back to Dundee?'

'Yes I think we should.'

'Have a rest Edna and we'll meet up back at my house on Friday. Will that we fine with you?'

She watched as the car slowly made its way down the road.

Betty's house lay up a quiet cul-de-sac. The neighbouring houses had large gardens and the one nearest her house had thick bushes all around the garden.

She was just opening the gate when she heard the voice. It was more of a growl actually, as if the person had laryngitis.

'You better stop seeing this man, Edna, or you'll lose your son. This is a warning.'

Her hand was rigid on the gate latch and she was frightened to look at the garden. Suddenly she marched over to the bushes but there was no sign of anyone. A small pile of cigarette butts lay under one of the thickest bushes but the garden was empty. Then she saw Billy's colourful bucket and spade.

She put the key in the lock and almost fell into the lobby. Irene and Betty were listening to a comedy show on the wireless and Betty's loud laughter filtered through the closed door. Edna made her way quietly up the stairs and lay down on the bed. Her heart was racing and she felt sick.

Not only was the warning explicit but she recognised the voice.

# 17

Kenneth was a man with a lot on his mind. He normally went to Dundee by train but on this dull and cold Friday morning he decided to take the 'Fifie.' He watched as it docked and the line of cars juggled slowly into the spaces on the lower deck.

He had left his car on one of Newport's side roads and stood beside a small group of passengers who were waiting patiently to board the ferry, pulling his overcoat tight against his body in an effort to keep out the cold wind that swept in from the river. It was hardly summer weather and it was only the first week in July.

He found a sheltered spot and settled down as the ferry slipped away from the pier and headed across the Tay to Dundee. He was at a crossroads in his personal and business life and at that moment he had no idea how he would cope.

The problem was Nelly Marten. She wanted to get married and, as she so bluntly put it, 'To make a man out of him with his own home and wife and away from his sister and her husband.'

He had known for years that she was in love with him but he had always fobbed her off. He was always charming to her but personally he found her repulsive. She was at least ten years older than him but that wasn't his biggest problem. He didn't like her coarse manner and her fleshy face and her bloated body was a turn off.

He had to make her understand that he wasn't in love with her but she already knew this and it hadn't cooled her ardour. In fact, he suspected it made it more of a challenge for her.

If only he hadn't met Molly. He had been entranced with her since the first time he saw her and the longer she worked in the house, the more he found he couldn't get her out of his mind.

He suspected that Nelly knew this and this was the reason for the urgency in her asking him to marry her. Trust Nelly, he thought. Usually it was the man who did the proposing but not with the mighty Mrs Marten on the marital path.

He planned to pay a visit to the agency this morning in the hope of seeing Molly. He had tried to talk to her yesterday before she left the house but Lena was with her for most of the afternoon. He knew he wouldn't see her till Monday.

That was the reason for his early start. Joe and Mike had given him a strange look as he drove away. Lena was still in bed and it was unusual for him to leave until he had breakfast with them all.

Joe and Mike were going fishing with the boat.

He could have got them to drop him off in Dundee but he didn't like the cabin cruiser and although it was large enough for the three men, it was still a bit tight for space. Joe and Mike loved the boat and took every opportunity to use it.

When the ferry docked at Craig Pier, he made his way quickly to the Wellgate. He wasn't sure what time the agency opened but he reckoned Molly would be an early riser and she would like to get started as soon as she could.

He thought he would catch her before any other staff arrived so his surprise was so much greater when he walked in and saw Molly with two other women. Molly was speaking but stopped when she saw him, a look of surprise on her face.

'Oh, I'm sorry, I didn't realise you were busy, Molly. I'll come back later.'

'Kenneth, how lovely to see you', she turned to the two women and said. 'This is Mr Drummond. Edna and Mary work with me but if you give me a moment I'll finish up here.'

'No, it's all right. I just wanted to say could you come round to the shop later?'

Molly looked puzzled but she said she would come before dinnertime.

Kenneth smiled at Edna and Mary before turning and walking out the door.

Mary's wide eyed gaze followed him then she looked at Molly. 'What a great looking man.'

Molly smiled but she had a problem on her hands and Kenneth was the least of her worries.

Edna was upset and the tears weren't far away. 'I can't work with Mr Knox anymore, Molly. I understand it'll cause you problems and I'm willing to leave.'

'Don't be silly, Edna. Of course I don't want you to leave but what's caused all this? Has he been a very difficult person to work for?'

Edna almost smiled. 'Oh no, he's been great and he's a lovely man but I can't work with him. It's personal and I don't want to say anymore. I wondered if I could maybe take over Jean's duties and she can finish Mr Knox's book with him. He thought it would take another week.'

Molly picked up the diary and was pleased to see it was almost full. Unfortunately, Jean was on holiday with her husband and they planned to be away another week.

Molly could have done without this added worry but she could see Edna was upset about something. She knew it had to be something serious and hoped the man hadn't made an unwelcome pass at her.

Suddenly she made up her mind. 'Do you mind staying in the office, Edna? I could send Mary out to Mr Knox and that would solve the problem. As you say, it'll only be for a week.'

If Mary could have leapt in the air she would have. Instead she simply beamed with pleasure.

Edna said that would suit her so Molly planned to phone him and give him the change of plan.

'Right then,' said Molly. 'Can you get your shorthand book, Mary, and go along to this address and work the same hours as Edna did. I'll try and phone him beforehand because he'll be wondering where you are, Edna.' She glanced at the clock and saw it was ten thirty.

The two women sat at the desk while Mary put on her coat and hurried out of the office, gazing at the slip of paper with the address.

'When did you get back from Arbroath, Edna? I thought you would be there until Saturday or Sunday.'

'No, we came home earlier than planned and I'm sure my Auntie Betty will be pleased to get the house to herself. Billy had a great time and I got a lot of work done every morning with John . . . I mean Mr Knox. I was booked to go and work for him today.'

Molly noticed the slight flush that accompanied the mention of his name and this reaffirmed her first notion that something had happened; something that wasn't to Edna's liking. Was she worried that her husband would find out and make a fuss? Perhaps it was better that Mary finished the job she thought. After all it was an agency and a client couldn't always get the same person every day.

'I'd better phone Mr Knox first then go off and see what Kenneth wants. He's the brother of the woman I'm working with.'

However, the phone kept ringing and after twelve rings, Molly put the receiver down.

'He's not answering. I hope he's in the house because Mary won't know what to do if he isn't.'

Suddenly the phone rang. Edna looked at it like it was a time bomb ready to explode. Molly went and picked up the receiver. 'Good morning. McQueen's Agency'

There was silence on the other end then a voice cut in quickly. 'My name is John Knox. I usually have one of your secretaries every morning but she hasn't turned up today. I'm a bit worried. Is she ill?'

Molly put on her professional voice. 'Mr Knox, I phoned a few minutes ago but there was no answer . . .'

'No, I was at the garden gate looking for Mrs McGill and the phone rang off before I could pick it up.' He sounded agitated.

'Mrs McGill won't manage to finish her contract with you but I've sent another secretary to finish the work. Her name is Mary Watt and she should be with you any minute now.'

'I don't want another woman. I've got used to Edna . . . I mean Mrs McGill. If you don't mind, I would like her to finish my book with me.'

Molly's heart sank. This was going to be more difficult than she first thought.

'I'm afraid Mrs McGill has been put onto another job, Mr Knox, but you'll find all our staff are qualified secretaries.'

There was silence at the other end. Then he said, 'I think that's the woman now at the door I'll phone you back soon.'

Edna sat silent at the desk as Molly put the phone down. Then she said, 'I've caused you a lot of bother, Molly. I'm sorry.'

'No you haven't, Edna. Just wait till Mr Knox sees the fair and competent Mary.'

The kettle was boiling but Molly had forgotten about the tea. 'I'd better go and see what Kenneth wants.' She sounded unconcerned but she was tense with worry. What a day it was turning out to be!

She made her way quickly to the Nethergate shop. The window display had been changed but it still had the quiet air of isolation, as if no customers ever crossed the threshold. But that couldn't be, she thought. Judging by the opulence and apparent wealth of the Lamont house, business had to be booming.

She pushed the door open and saw Kenneth sitting behind the grand desk. It was a feeling of déjà vu. Exactly like the first time she had seen him.

He gave her a wonderful smile. 'Ah, you're the best thing that's happened to me today. Come into the office.'

The office turned out to be a large area with boxes and rugs and various pieces of furniture but a small corner had been turned into a cosy enclave with a small gas cooker, a sink and two chairs.

Molly didn't have time to sit and chat but she felt she had to make some time for her client's brother. She gave a quick glance at her watch and it was eleven thirty. She had so much work to do back in the agency but she tried to relax.

'You'll be wondering why I asked you here, Molly?'

She smiled. 'Yes I'm a bit puzzled, Kenneth.'

He went into the shop and reappeared with a small painting and handed it to her. It was a lovely atmospheric painting of the *Abercraig*, sailing on a stormy River Tay.

'The artist is unknown and it's pretty much an amateur painting but I thought you might like it as that gift for your father.'

Molly was touched by his kindness. 'Oh, you remembered.'

'Yes, I've been keeping my expert eye out for something for you.'

Molly opened her handbag to pay for it. 'I think it's lovely and my dad will love it. How much is it?'

'It's a gift. A sort of thank you for all the hard work you've done. You've been a great help to Lena and I hope we can count on you helping us out for a while yet. It seems her arm isn't mending as well as it should.'

Molly was mortified. 'I can't accept it for nothing, Kenneth.'

He held up his hand. 'Yes you can. Take it with my pleasure.' He smiled. 'In fact there is a string attached to it. We have another of our dinners next Saturday and I know Lena wants you to help out. Apart from Ronald and Betty, it'll be another two couples and Mrs Marten.' The smile died on his lips at the mention of her name but Molly missed it as she was looking at the painting.

'Thank you, Kenneth. My dad will love a memento of his days with the Fifies.'

They chatted for another half an hour then she stood up to go. 'I'd better be off then. I'll see you on Monday.'

Kenneth had wrapped the painting in brown paper and string and as she picked up her bag, the doorbell pinged to announce a well dressed couple, and Molly was able to slip away. The couple were looking around and Kenneth treated them like he knew them and he gave them a huge smile.

As she hurried back to the agency she wondered how Mary had fared. She knew the girl was competent in shorthand and typing but there was an undercurrent between John Knox and Edna and she wished their working partnership hadn't been spoiled by personal reasons.

Edna had taken a few more bookings and one in particular would suit her, she said. That was if Molly didn't mind. It was a couple of week's work in the small office of a grocer's shop in Arbroath Road.

'It'll mean getting someone to do the desk, Molly.'

Molly gave it some thought. Heavens, the day was getting worse. 'Edna, you take this job and I'll phone Margaret. She said she would help out if needed.'

Although she said nothing, Edna was relieved. She didn't want to be in the office because she knew John would be down to the agency to see what was wrong. She should have given him some explanation but the warning had been explicit. She suddenly felt cold and she was desperate to get home to check on Billy.

At three thirty, Mary appeared, still beaming. Edna and Molly were eager to hear how she had got on.

'He was very nice and I soon got the hang of some of the technical terms he used. He asked if I would be back on Monday and I said yes.' She looked anxiously at Molly. 'I hope that's all right.'

Molly said that was fine. Edna hadn't realised she was holding her breath but now she was in two minds about the situation. Of course, she was relieved Mary had done well but it now looked like she wasn't going to be missed by John.

How could she have got it all so wrong? She felt stupid about all this unnecessary drama. John wouldn't bother who was sent to help him, but she had prided herself on thinking that she was indispensable.

# 18

Charlie Johns had been busy making some enquiries. He had managed to get Harry Hawkins maritime records from the shipping office. It wasn't a complete record because he seemed to have moved around a lot and there were gaps. Could that have been when he wasn't at sea? His Merchant Service record went back to before the war and Charlie saw that one of the ships he had served on had been torpedoed in 1944. He had survived that. From 1938 to 1940 he had been on a small freighter, which went regularly on the Rotterdam to Hull run.

In 1952, he had served as a steward on one of the liners which took British emigrants out to Australia, but he seemed to have suddenly given up that job and returned to the smaller ships.

Charlie made a note to find out the names of any emigrants from Dundee who had travelled over to Australia during that crucial time. It was a long shot, but if he had been murdered then there must be some connection to the city. Could it have been someone on one of the emigrant ships who had now returned home?

But first of all he had a pleasant task to complete. He made his way to the animal dispensary where he met the young vet. Rover was sitting in a wire cage and wagged his tail when he saw Charlie. He still looked a sorry sight. The wound on his back was healing up, the stitches had been removed a couple of days previously, and the leg was encased in a white Plaster of Paris cast.

The news from the vet was encouraging. 'The leg fracture is healing and the plaster can come off in a week or so. Rover will be able to hobble along and hopefully the bald patch on his back will also grow back in time.'

Charlie held the dog in his arms. 'There's someone who's going to be over the moon at seeing you again, Rover.' He turned to the vet, 'You're sure he managed to bite the intruder?'

'Well, he had blood in his mouth and on his teeth when he was brought in, so I would say yes, and a deep bite at that. Whoever it was will be suffering unless they've gone to a doctor.'

Mrs Kidd was heating up a large pan of soup on Tam's cooker. 'This scotch broth will fill you up Tam and I've got two Vienna rolls from Andrew G. Kidd to have with it. "Eat up,"' she said.

Tam was grateful for all the help she had given him over the last few days and although he didn't want to tell her, he was a bit frightened to go out to the shops. Whoever had attacked him was still out there. And he was missing Rover.

Mrs Kidd was putting his messages in the cupboard. 'I've got you a half loaf and four tea breads, a quarter of butter, a pint of milk, a packet of Lipton's tea and a packet of Rich Tea biscuits. Is there anything else you need?'

Tam had to eat his soup with his left hand because of the bandage on his shoulder which extended down to his right elbow

'No, you've got everything I need,' he said.

'Is there any more word about the person that attacked you, Tam?' she asked.

Tam said there wasn't.

'The woman down the stair got a quick look at him and she thought he might be a sailor. He was wearing one of those brown duffle coats and she said it smelled fusty. Like it had been lying in some damp cupboard or boat.'

By now Tam had finished his soup and Mrs Kidd placed a plate of Creamola custard in front of him.

'I've got the kettle on to make us both a cup of tea and for a treat I've got two Banbury cakes from Andrew G. Kidd. I must keep supporting my namesake,' she said with a laugh.

Tam was concerned at all the work Mrs Kidd was doing for him. 'What about your husband Jock, will he no be needing you?'

'No, Jock comes in at half past five.'

'Well I'm very grateful to you and I've never eaten so well in my life'

They were both enjoying their tea and Banbury cakes when Charlie arrived. Rover went frantic at the sight of his master and Tam had tears in his eyes when he took him from the policeman.

Then they all laughed as Rover tried to run around the floor, it was so comical. After a few tries he settled in his basket by the side of the fireplace and promptly fell asleep.

Mrs Kidd stood up. 'Well I'll be on my way. Tam. You'll both be wanting a chat with one another.'

'How are you, Tam?' asked Charlie Johns.

'A bittie sore still and I can't use my right arm, but the doctor says it'll heal soon.'

'When you were talking to Harry did he mention being a steward on one of the liners that takes emigrants to Australia?'

Tam gave it a moment's thought. 'Now I come to think about it, he did say that. He said he did a stint on the ships going to Australia with emigrants. He also said he had knocked around the world on ships since he was a youngster.'

Tam gave Charlie a questioning look.

'I'm just trying to find out any connection with Dundee.'

'Mrs Kidd says the woman down the stairs thinks it was a sailor she saw.'

'Yes, she did, but that mainly because he wore a brown duffle coat and she's seen war films at the pictures where the seamen all wear these kinds of jackets. And her specs were cracked so I'm not sure how reliable her statement is.'

Rover suddenly made some whimpering noises in his sleep. 'How will you manage to take him for his walks, Tam?'

This was something Tam was dreading, 'I'll not go far. Just up and down the street and I'll not go out at night. I was going to ask Mrs Kidd's man, Jock, if he would maybe take him for a wee turn before bedtime.'

'Well, watch out for yourself. Get Mrs Kidd to keep her door open when you come back up the stairs and check out the street before you leave the close.'

Tam said he would.

Charlie said, 'The vet thinks Rover bit your attacker and they'll be suffering from a bad wound that will need a doctor to treat it.'

'Good,' said Tam. 'That's the best bit of news I've had all week.'

Rover stirred in his basket again.

Tam wiped his eyes with a large white handkerchief. 'I thought I'd lost him the other day. He looked dead when the young policeman arrived and carried him to the vet.'

'I thought so myself but the vet has done wonders, Tam. He thought the blow to Rover's back was much worse than it was and also the leg wound has healed up great. The vet thinks the fact that he bit your attacker made him miss his aim and that saved his life . . . and yours.'

Charlie put on his coat to leave. 'I'll let you know how I get on with my enquiries, Tam,' he said as he opened the door.

Edna wasn't sure about this new placement at Albert's Stores. The shop was quite large with two glass windows that overlooked the street and although it had retained some of its old-fashioned style, it was trying slowly to modernise.

It was a very busy shop and Edna's job was as a cashier. She also had to do the books in the miniscule office which was a glassed partition at the back of the shop.

She had turned up in her navy blue suit but the owner of the shop had laughed and produced a sparkling white cotton coat for her to wear.

'It's a bit big for you, lass. The girl who normally works here is much bigger than you, but it'll keep your lovely suit nice and clean.'

Albert Smith was a big man with a cheery red face and a protruding stomach that a long white apron failed to hide.

On the first morning everything was new to her and she spent ages trying to master the old fashioned cash register but as the day progressed she became faster with ringing up the message slips that the customers produced at the little window of the office.

There was another assistant working in the shop, a young man called Eddie.

She had tried to keep her mind off the man's threat, but she also wondered how John was getting on with Mary. She missed him dreadfully and she missed the large, quiet house with its piles of books and papers and its dusty shelves.

A woman's voice brought her back from her thoughts. 'I've got half a pound of biscuits and a quarter pound of tea,' she said, handing over the money which Edna rang up. 'Are you going to be here all the time? Is Nancy no coming back?'

Edna smiled at her. 'No, I'm just temporary till she comes back.'

The woman made a noise as she left the shop and Edna wasn't sure if it was a vote of confidence in her handling of the biscuits and tea or a plea for Nancy to be back as soon as possible.

The morning soon went in and Edna was pleased that it was so busy because it left her with little time to think about her worries.

She was due her dinner break from twelve to one o'clock and the shop shut for this hour.

The last customer of the morning introduced herself. 'My name is Mrs Pirie and I live up the next close to here. It's nice meeting you and I have to say that you're much better than yon sour-faced Nancy who normally works here. She never looks at you when she's handing over your change. It's as if you don't exist. I mean . . . I don't buy a lot of food because I live on my own now that I'm a widow, but it's grand to be able to buy what you want now that the rationing is over. Well, it's no officially over but you know what I mean.'

Mrs Pirie made her way out as Mr Smith shut the door. 'What are your plans for dinner time, Edna?'

'I'm going home if that's all right,' said Edna.

She knew it would be a bit of a rush, but if she caught the tram which was bound for the city centre then she could hurry up to Paradise Road and have a quick snack. Anything rather than sit in the empty shop alone with her thoughts.

She was in luck as she left the shop. A tram appeared and she was soon getting off at the Wellgate where she hurried up to the house. She didn't want to pass the agency so instead she made her way along Bell Street until she came to Irvine Place, a narrow pend and lane, which led with Dudhope Street, then home.

There was a wonderful smell coming from the kitchen when she entered. Her mum was standing at the cooker, stirring a pan full of strawberry jam. A dozen jars were spread out on the thick cover that protected the dining table from spills and hot cups and plates.

'I've put the kettle on, Edna, and I'll make a pot of tea as soon as I fill these jars.'

'No, don't you bother Mum. I'll make it. She looked around the room. 'Where's Billy?'

'He downstairs playing with Brian's Meccano set but I told him to come up for his dinner. I expect they're engrossed in building things.'

Edna tried hard not to panic. 'I'll go downstairs for him now and tell him it's time for his meal.'

She hurried down the one flight of stairs to Brian's house and knocked on the door. The knock sounded loudly against the wooden door but Edna was worried.

Brian opened the door. He was the same age as Billy and they were good pals but after the warning, Edna was afraid to let Billy go anywhere. She would have to warn her mother about this, she thought.

Billy came reluctantly to the door. 'I'm not hungry, Mum. Can I play a wee while longer?'

'No, Billy. Brian will be having his dinner soon but maybe he can come upstairs to play with you in the afternoon.'

Then she thought, I should have asked Mum if this arrangement as all right. A feeling of helplessness washed over her. If only she didn't have to work but she had no option so there was no point in feeling otherwise.

'I said Brian could come up here this afternoon, Mum, is that all right?' Irene gave her a questioning look but Edna pretended not to notice. 'It's just that I worry about him when he isn't in the house.'

Irene said nothing as Edna hurried down the stairs.

The shop was very busy that afternoon and she didn't have time to think too much about her worries. Albert and Eddie were busy with a queue of shoppers, cutting cheese and weighing fruit and vegetables and wrapping bacon and cold meat. After the years of wartime rationing it was great to be able to buy food again without the restrictions of coupons.

By five thirty Edna was tired from the constant noise and chatter in the shop with customers wanting a gossip and the good-natured laughter from the grocers. It was certainly a happy shop but Edna had become used to the quietness of John's house with the view of the garden and the steady slow ticking of the pendulum clock on the lounge wall.

She tried not to think about him and, as she hurried up the close, she made up her mind to forget all about him.

That was why she was so surprised to see him sitting by the unlit fire. There was a large bunch of flowers in a vase on the table and a small box of Dairy Box chocolates lying beside it.

Billy was playing with Brian. They had abandoned the Meccano set and were now playing with the little garage and some Dinky cars.

Irene had been chatting to him when she entered but when she saw her daughter, she said, 'Come on, boys, I'll take you down to the ice cream shop and buy you a cone.

After they had gone, there was an uncomfortable silence. Then John said, 'What a great lad you have, Edna.'

'Yes I know, John.'

He looked down at his hands as if scrutinising his fingers. 'I just wanted to come round and say I'm sorry if I've upset you. Maybe I shouldn't have taken you out to dinner in Arbroath. Perhaps you thought I was pushing our friendship too far or too fast.'

Edna almost leapt from her chair. 'Oh no, John, I don't think that for one minute but I have to go to whatever job is needed at the time. That's what the agency is all about and Molly doesn't have such a large staff that she can let us pick and choose our jobs. Mary would have been no use in this job. That's why I had to go and you have Mary to help you finish the book.'

John gave her a look, which said he didn't understand but was willing to believe her. 'Well, I just wanted to wish you well in whatever you do, Edna. I miss you and all our little chats and I thought our time in Arbroath was wonderful.'

Edna felt miserable. She wished she could tell him the truth but she had to think of Billy. 'I thought so too, John.'

He stood up. 'I'd better be on my way.'

Edna sat in her chair as he left and felt the tears start. Why oh why did her past history have to rear its ugly head again? Just when she thought it was all over.

Irene appeared with Billy. He had ice cream down the front of his shirt and Edna went to get a facecloth to clean him up.

'That was nice of Mr Knox to come and visit you with flowers and chocolates. Will you be going to work with him again?'

'No mum, I don't think so.'

# 19

Marigold was heading to the village hall for a coffee morning. She had decided to take along some of the flowers from her garden for the sales table. There was always some sort of fund-raising going on. The hall seemed to need so many repairs these days, but Marigold had forgotten what part of the hall this particular sales table was for. Her friend Peggy had told her but she had been busy at the time, weeding the garden and tying back all the stray branches of the rambler rose bush, which threatened to engulf the front of the house.

There was quite a crowd when she arrived with her flowers in a large wicker basket. She was immediately approached by the president of the Womens' Institute. A very small lady with loads of energy and full of big ideas.

'Marigold, how lovely to see you and I see you've brought some lovely roses for the sale of work.'

Peggy came out from the kitchen area, wearing a flowery apron and carrying a large teapot. She sat down, out of breath. 'That teapot has a lot to answer for,' she grumbled. 'It's like carrying an elephant around.'

Peggy filled up her cup and another woman appeared with a plate of anaemic looking biscuits that looked as if they had seen better days. Against her better judgement, Marigold selected one and immediately regretted it. She abandoned it in her saucer. The tea was weak, it was like drinking hot coloured water.

Marigold was eager to talk to Peggy. In fact this was the reason she had ventured out this morning. When she awoke this morning it had been misty with a fine drizzle and she would sooner have stayed at home with Sabby.

'Peggy, you live near Cliff Top House. Who owns it now?'

Peggy was taken aback. 'Cliff Top House? I think it's someone called Lamont. They have an antique business in Dundee and seemingly are doing very well. Now that the war is over, people are getting fed up of Utility furniture and they are looking for something with a bit of quality and design.'

'Is the owner related to old Mr Abbot who used to farm there years ago?'

Peggy gave this a bit of thought. 'I don't know. Mr Abbot had a daughter who got married when she was about seventeen. There was some rumour that she had a child but she had moved away from the farm by then and I never heard anymore about her.'

The war split families up, especially if the men were away fighting but I suppose she eventually moved somewhere else with her husband. I don't know if she ever came back to see her father but I certainly never saw her again. Why are you interested?'

Marigold said it was just curiosity. 'Molly from next door is working there at the moment and I just wondered who the people are. There's a brother and sister and her husband. Then there are two men who also work there; a man called Mike and another man called Christie. He's a Canadian.'

'That's right,' said Peggy. 'They've got a lovely cabin cruiser which regularly goes out to sea. Sailing must be a hobby for them.'

Marigold realised she wouldn't get any more information from her friend so she stood up.

'Well, I'd better go and inspect the sales table.'

The two women joined the large crowd milling around the pots of jam, garden produce and some home baking. Marigold bought two pounds of potatoes and a jar of strawberry jam which she reckoned she would have to pour onto the bread, owing to its runny mixture.

When she arrived home, she went out the back door and saw Molly in the back garden, hanging out her washing. A weak looking sun had appeared and the mist was lifting slowly. However, there was still a scattering of raindrops on the windows and she recalled her late mother telling her that this was a sign of more rain to come.

Still she didn't say this to Molly.

'Have you got time to come in for a cup of tea?' she called over.

Molly said she would be over in a minute and was as good as her word. Sabby ignored her but Molly just laughed. 'She doesn't like me, does she?'

Marigold scowled at the cat. 'Oh just ignore her. She's completely spoilt.'

Marigold thought Molly was looking really nice today. She wasn't wearing her working suit, which, although neat and business-like, was a bit severe. She was dressed in a simple floral cotton frock and her blonde hair was shining and swept back with a plastic Alice band which were all the rage at the moment.

'What are you planning to do today, Molly?' asked Marigold, pouring out a nice strong up of tea, which was the opposite to the weak stuff she had just endured at the hall.

'I'm doing some housework then it's over to the office for some work. I've promised Mary I'll look after the desk this afternoon to give her a wee while off. She's done a great job with Edna's client, Mr Knox, but she'll be back in the office again next week because that job is finished.'

Later, Molly made her way to the pier to catch the ferry. The sun hadn't managed to make much headway with the mist and although it wasn't cold, she wished she had worn her woollen jumper and skirt instead of this thin frock.

The 'Fifie' was already docked when she arrived and she hurried aboard. She watched as the boat set off from the pier, its paddles churning up the water into a frenzy of white foam as it headed over the river to Dundee.

Normally, she would stand or sit on the upper deck to catch the sea air and the wind in her hair, but she felt cold this morning and decided to pay the extra money to sit in the saloon.

There were just three other women sitting in this glassed cabin, all quite old and wearing thick tweed coats and felt hats. Molly was amused to be sitting in the domain of the elderly, which was who this saloon normally catered for.

The ferry was extremely busy as it was a Saturday and lots of folk used it to go shopping in Dundee or to meet friends. Craig Pier hovered into view but she decided to wait till most of the passengers had alighted. She heard the large gangplank being lowered as metal hit the concrete of the pier with a loud clang.

She was making her way to the exit when there was an uproar ahead of her. A woman started screaming. A large crowd gathered around her as she lay on the wet stones of the sloping pier. She was shouting, 'My handbag's been stolen.'

Some of the passengers helped her to her feet and Molly saw that her face was bruised and her frock torn.

One of the passengers shouted that a man had made off with the woman's handbag but he was nowhere to be seen.

A policeman arrived and the woman, who was now on the verge of hysteria and crying, said someone had pushed her and grabbed her bag. She said she almost fell into the water and if she had been nearer the edge, then she would have.

Molly hovered on the edge of the crowd.

'I saw him,' said one burly man who had his shirtsleeves rolled up to reveal two large, colourful tattoos on his arms. 'He was quite young, I thought, thin with dark hair.'

Another woman thought he was older and quite plump and there was this large variance in descriptions from the witnesses. Suddenly an ambulance appeared and the woman was put on board, protesting that she wasn't hurt, but the policeman said it was just a precaution in case she had suffered from something more serious.

'What was in your bag?' he asked, as she made her way into the interior of the vehicle.

'All my money,' she cried. 'Four pounds which is all I had left from my housekeeping money.' I don't know what my husband will say when he finds out. He'll go mad.'

The policeman assured her he wouldn't and this statement seemed to mollify the woman.

After the ambulance left, the small knot of people thinned out and made their way towards the street. One of the elderly women who had been in the saloon, but had moved right up to the action to watch all the drama, walked beside Molly.

She had shrewd grey eyes under a beige felt hat. 'You know, it could have been you, my dear, who had her handbag stolen.'

Molly looked at her with surprise. 'Me? Why do you say that?'

'Well she was wearing a frock very similar to yours and her fair hair had one of those bands just like you're wearing. And she is about the same size as you and the same age I would guess.'

Molly was shocked but she didn't really believe this old woman's theory. Why would anyone want to steal her handbag. She said this to the woman.

'Yes, well why would anyone want to steal that woman's bag? It didn't have a fortune in it.'

'Perhaps the thief thought it had.'

The woman gave her a shrewd glance. 'Aye maybe he did, but just watch yourself, my dear.'

Molly didn't think she was upset till she sat down in the office. Her hands were shaking and she found she couldn't put the sheet of paper in the typewriter. What a strange thing to happen, she thought but, on the other hand, why should she have been the target?

Then she realised that normally she would have been in the same spot as the woman if she hadn't gone into the saloon, and she had hung back until the ferry docked which was unlike her. She always made her way to the exit before the ferry docked.

Mary was getting ready to leave.

'Are you planning anything special this afternoon?' Molly asked.

'Yes, I'm going swimming with Rita at the swimming baths then we'll maybe have our tea in a café before going home.'

Molly smiled at her. 'Well, have a pleasant day out.'

Rita was waiting for her outside. She was carrying the two rolled up towels with the swimsuits neatly tucked up inside.

Molly watched as the two girls made their way down the Wellgate. Mary must have made it up with Rita, she thought.

As they walked along the Murraygate, Rita was grumbling. 'I thought you would never get finished today. I stood outside for ages.'

Mary said she hadn't. 'I saw you when you arrived and you were only waiting for two minutes at least so don't exaggerate, Rita.'

They reached the Victoria Arch and they joined a crowd of people who were all heading for the swimming baths. After walking over the narrow swing bridge they made their way into the building.

The cubicles had small half-sized doors and Mary, who was really modest about undressing in public, squeezed into her blue seersucker swimsuit and pushed her hair under the swimming cap.

Rita was already in the pool when she came out and she made her way into the water, which was freezing.

'I'm sure my legs have turned blue,' she said but once they were in the water it didn't feel so bad. The girls slowly swam a few lengths of the pool then Rita went and stood on the diving board. Mary sighed. Rita always did this because she liked to show off her new black swimsuit with the polka dot panel around the waistline. But it was a wasted effort today because there was no one in the pool that they knew.

Mary came out of the pool and climbed to the middle section of the board and dived into the water. She was an excellent swimmer and Rita, who had walked back to the water's edge, looked on with envy.

She thought Mary looked babyish in her blue swimsuit. It wasn't like the fashionable one she was wearing.

The girls swam for another hour and then made their way back to the cubicles. Mary was drying her hair with the towel while Rita started munching on her 'shivery bite'; a small snack that they always ate after a swim.

A cool wind had sprung up when they reached the swing bridge. Mary was glad she had her short jacket with her. Rita, however, was wearing a thin dress and had sandals on her bare feet.

'Where will we go for our tea?' asked Mary.

Rita shrugged her shoulders. 'I don't mind. Any place where it's a bit warmer than this.'

'Let's go to Keiller's restaurant and have a high tea.'

They were almost at Shore Terrace when Rita saw the handbag. 'Somebody's lost her handbag,' she said, picking it up and opening it.

Mary didn't think she should have done this and warned her. 'You'd better hand it over to the police, Rita.'

'Nonsense,' she said, 'I'm just looking to see if there's a name and address in it.'

The handbag was a cheap-looking plastic affair with a heavy chrome clasp and the contents were sparse. There was a purse with some money in it. Rita counted it.

'Two pound notes, three ten bob notes and some coins,' she said out loud. 'There's also a door key and a white handkerchief but that's all.'

'Do you see a policeman around that we can give it to?' asked Mary, but although there were crowds of people waiting at the bus stances at Shore Terrace, there was no Bobby to be seen. 'Let's take it to the police station in Bell Street,' she suggested.

'I'm not going all the way to Bell Street. We'll look for a Bobby on our way to Keiller's.'

When Mary scanned the road looking for a policeman, she suddenly saw the man from the Palais. Drawing back into the shadow of the Arch, she said, 'It's that man who was at the Palais. You know, the one who frightened me.'

Rita looked excited. 'Where?'

Mary pointed to the dock where boats could be seen bobbing on the water. 'He's in a boat over there, but don't let him see you.'

Rita stepped out from the shadows and looked at the boats. She saw him standing on a lovely white cabin cruiser. Her eyes were

121

shining. 'Have you seen the boat he's got? He must be loaded with money and he's really very handsome.'

Mary suddenly became frightened for her friend's sake. 'Please don't let him see you, Rita. He's a horrible man.'

Rita was still holding the handbag. 'I think I'll forget about the high tea, Mary, if you don't mind. I'm really cold in this thin frock so I'll just catch the bus back home.' She handed over the bag. 'Maybe you can take this to Bell Street and hand it in. I'm sure the poor wifie will be goings nuts over losing it.'

Mary was suspicious. 'Promise me that you'll not contact that man, Rita.'

Rita looked outraged. 'Of course. I just want to get home.'

Reluctantly Mary took the handbag and made her way to the police station, but at the top of Reform Street she saw a policeman on the beat. She walked up to him and explained about finding the bag. The policeman took note of her name and address and said he would hand it in at the lost property department.

When Mary was out of sight, Rita sauntered up to the edge of the wharf and gazed at the boat and the young man in it.

'Are you admiring my boat?' he asked.

Rita tossed her dark hair out of her eyes and said, 'I might be.'

'Well then, hop on board.' He placed a wooden walkway over the side that reached the a small set of steps. 'You'll have to come down the steps to get on.'

Rita stepped daintily on the boat's deck and admired the all the expensive fittings, before placing her towel and handbag on the deck.

'I wanted my friend to come with me but she went home.' Rita knew this was a lie but she wanted to portray herself as an intrepid traveller. 'You met us at the Palais a few weeks ago and you were asking her loads of questions about where she worked.'

Rita was gazing at the cabin and didn't see his eyes narrow. 'Oh yes, I remember you both.' He smiled. 'Do you want a sail round the dock?'

Rita tried to look nonchalant, as if she was a passenger on a boat like this every day of the week. 'That would be great. My name is Rita. What's yours?'

'No names, no pack drill. Right?'

Rita was taken aback by his attitude but was determined to make the most of being aboard this lovely boat.

He guided the boat expertly around the dock then out into the river. Rita was slightly shocked but tried hard not to show it. Then just as she was about to tell him to take her back, another man appeared from the cabin. He was older, with a stocky build, and was wearing a navy blue jumper and waterproof trousers.

'What the blazes are you doing, Mike?' he sounded angry.

'I'm taking a young lady for a trip, Joe, but I hope she doesn't drown. You know how easy it is to do that.'

The river was choppy with a cool wind and grey waves slapped against the sides of the boat, rocking it as it moved into the deeper water. Rita was frightened now and she sat on one of the seats on deck with tears rolling down her cheeks. How stupid she had been. Mary was right. This was a dangerous man and she had stepped into his zone.

The older man, the one called Joe, went back into the cabin while the other one leered at her.

'Where are we going? I should be home by now,' she cried.

'Well you shouldn't have come on board, should you? I thought we could stop somewhere and have a wee party.'

Rita stood up and looked all around her. The boat was now in the middle of the river and the waves were really big out here. The boat rose with a wave then dropped into the trough and Rita was thrown off balance and almost fell on the deck.

'I want to go home,' she cried. The man ignored her.

She could see a house on the headland with a jetty jutting out into the water. It looked as if they were going to land there but Rita had no idea where she was.

She made her way into the cabin. The man was sitting, reading a newspaper and drinking a beer. 'I want to go home, please.'

By now she was in tears and the mascara she had so carefully applied after her swim was running down her cheeks in long black streaks.

He glanced at her and got to his feet. They both moved out of the cabin and he said, 'The lassie wants to go home.'

Mike narrowed his eyes and Rita wondered how she had ever thought he was good looking.

'Well she's been for a swim. That's her swimsuit and towel there, so let her swim home.'

Rita was so distraught that she stepped back and almost slipped on the wet deck. Joe went up to the wheel and pushed Mike out of the way, 'Get in the cabin and stay there,' he told him.

Turning the boat around, he headed back to Dundee and within ten minutes Rita was getting off at the same place she had got on. Her legs felt like jelly and she knew she looked a right mess but she didn't care. She was back on dry land.

As she stepped off the boat, Joe came over and said, 'Keep away from that guy. He's not the person for a young lassie like you.' He handed her the towel and her handbag. 'Have you got your bus fare?' He put his hand in his pocket and took out a shilling. 'Here, take this and get yourself home.'

She tried to thank him but the boat was already making it's way back out onto the river with a surly looking Mike glaring at her through the window.

She knew her face was a mess and she couldn't go on the bus looking like this. When she got home her mother would ask all kinds of awkward questions not to mention the curious stares from the passengers

She suddenly remembered the wet swimsuit. Thankfully it was black and she wiped her face with the wet fabric. Taking care not to smear mascara onto the white spotted insert. The chlorine from the pool made her eyes sting but once she was sure her face was clean, she made for the bus stance and got on board a bus just as it was leaving.

Luckily she had the man's shilling because when she looked in her bag for her purse, it was gone. That horrible Mike must have stolen it, which meant she would have had to walk home. The conductor took her fare and she sank back in her seat.

She started thinking how silly she had been to have acted so dramatically. There was no way he would have put her overboard and made her swim. Then she remembered his look and she wasn't so sure.

Meanwhile, Mary had returned to the Victoria Arch and seen the cabin cruiser making its way across the river.

She waited for the next bus with a feeling of relief.

After she had her tea, she decided to go and see Rita and tell her about meeting the policeman. Rita's mum opened the door.

'I'm sorry, Mary, you can't see Rita. She said she didn't feel very well after her swim and she's gone to bed. She didn't even want her tea.'

Mary was puzzled by this sudden illness. When she returned home she mentioned this to her mother, who said,

'I hope she's not coming down with a summer cold.'

# 20

Charlie Johns had been busy. He had managed to get the relevant documents from Australia House and the shipping company, regarding the emigrants who had travelled out to Australia during Harry Hawkins' year long employment on the liner.

Thankfully, there weren't too many people from Dundee and the surrounding areas to check up on. He had managed to trace most of the names and was now left with the last two. He was now on his way to see the parents of a young couple who had left Dundee in the autumn of 1952.

They lived in Cochrane Street; a dark, dismal street lined with tenement houses which was part of the Crescent area of the city. Their flat was three floors up a narrow spiral staircase and a neat brass nameplate was screwed to the brown painted door. P. MacDuff.

A tall woman came to the door and it was obvious that she wasn't long back from her work. She wore a colourful overall and her hair was covered with a floral turban. She gave him a wary look.

'I'm sorry to bother you but can I come in and ask you some questions?' he said, after showing her his warrant card.

By now the woman looked apprehensive and she called out. 'Pat, it's the police.'

Pat was a large man who was quickly going to fat. He wore a pair of blue dungarees over a checked shirt and his hands were covered in a grey film

'Sorry, I haven't washed my hands yet. I'm a bricklayer.' He looked at his wife and said. 'What's this all about, Ella?'

She shook her head.

Charlie said. 'I'm making inquiries about people who emigrated to Australia last year and your son and his wife are on the list.'

Ella jumped up from her hair. 'Has something happened to Pat and Jane?

Charlie calmed her down. 'No, it's just that I'm working on an accident case concerning a steward who worked on the liner that took your family out to their new life, and I wondered if they had come back home again so I could speak to them.'

Pat, who had moved to the sink and was washing his hands, laughed. 'Come back? To this?' He swept a large hand around the tiny room with the small window which hardly let in any sunlight. 'Of course they haven't come back. They've both got good jobs in Melbourne and are hoping to buy their own house soon. Their letters are full of the great lifestyle over there, not to mention the warmth and the sunshine.'

Ella brought out some snaps. 'These were taken a few months ago.' There was pride in her voice. The small black and white photos showed a young couple standing on a beach, wearing big smiles and shorts and short-sleeved tops.

Charlie made a few correct noises about how well they looked and thanked them for their help.

He wasn't getting anywhere and the last name on his list was his only hope. He glanced at it. Molly McQueen, Strathmartine Road.

He decided to have a quick meal then go to see this woman. She hadn't travelled out with the liner but had returned to Scotland during the relevant time.

The house turned out to be a neat bungalow with a garden full of flowers. The path was made up of crazy paving stones and there were floral boxes on the windowsills. A very pretty house Charlie thought.

The doorbell made a pleasant chiming sound and the door was opened by a young woman.

'Miss McQueen?' Charlie held out his warrant card.

'No, I'm Mrs Whyte.' She looked slightly alarmed by the sight of a policeman on her doorstep and gave a quick look up and down the street to make sure none of the neighbours saw him but apart from a few people in their gardens, no one took any notice of him. After all he wasn't in uniform so he could just be a visitor to the house.

After a minute the woman said, 'You had better come in.'

She ushered him into a neat lounge. The three-piece suite looked as if it had never been sat on and the sideboard was well polished. There were a few photographs in wooden frames on the mantelpiece and a lovely handmade rag rug in front of the unlit fire.

She sat on the edge of the chair and asked what it was all about.

'I'm looking for a Molly McQueen who used to live at this address. Do you know where she went?'

Mrs Whyte shook her head. 'We bought this house from a Mr and Mrs McQueen over a year ago. They went to live in Newport-on-Tay, but I don't remember a daughter living here. It was just the two of them. He was retiring, he said. They had always fancied living near the river and that was why they were selling the house.'

'Do you have their address?'

She shook her head. 'They never said where they were moving to, just that it was in Newport.'

Charlie thanked her and stood up.

'Is it something criminal?' Her voice had a breathless, trembling sound.

'No. it's just a question of identifying someone.'

As he was leaving, he noticed the phone in the hall. 'I don't suppose they gave you their phone number by any chance?'

She shook her head again. 'We didn't really have much to do with them. We bought this house through an agent as we were coming back from Hong Kong where my husband worked. He did most of the dealings with the McQueen's. I'm sorry I can't help you, there wasn't a phone in the house when we bought it.'

Charlie smiled. 'It was just an off chance that I would find Miss McQueen but thank you for your time.'

She saw him to the door and watched as he walked away.

Charlie had come to the end of his inquiries here. He would have to search for the McQueens in Newport but until then he decided to pay a visit to Tam.

Tam had just finished his tea. Mrs Kidd was washing the dishes and she called out when she opened the door. 'It's Detective Johns to see you, Tam.'

Charlie got a shock when he saw the old man. He seemed frailer than ever and even Rover wasn't so bouncy. If Charlie could have got his hands on the person responsible for this change in the man and his dog he would have gladly locked him up and thrown away the key.

Instead he said, 'How are you today, Tam?'

Tam cheered up at the sight of his friend and Rover wagged his tail 'Oh, I'm keeping fine but my shoulder is still a bit sore, but Rover's back has healed up and he isn't limping as much. Jock was saying he can walk a bit faster now.'

Mrs Kidd bustled across to the table with the teapot, two cups and saucers and a plate holding two cakes which she placed on the table. She took off her apron. 'Now that you've got company, I'll be off. Jock will be in later to take Rover for his wee dander.'

Tam sighed. 'I don't know what I'd do without the Kidds. They're so good to me.'

'Have you any more news about Harry?'

'Well there's another lead I'm following up, Tam, so we'll see how it goes.'

He stood up and Rover hobbled to the door with him.

Tam called him 'No, Rover, you'll get your walk later.'

Charlie was amused by the expression on the dog's face as it hobbled back to the fireplace.

As he walked down the stairs, he wondered why he was spending his own time on this case. His intuition said there was something more than an accident and hopefully when he managed to track down this Molly McQueen, everything would maybe be a bit clearer.

Edna was on her last week at Albert's Stores. Nancy was seemingly feeling much better and was due back the following Monday. She was going to miss this cheery shop, she thought.

Mrs Pirie was a customer who normally came into the shop every day and she usually came in with her friend and neighbour, Sally. Although she didn't know it, Sally's nickname in the shop was 'Snappy Sal', because she was always complaining in a loud voice about everything she bought.

Albert had warned Edna to always address her as Mrs Little. She hadn't married until she was almost fifty and she was so grateful to be a married woman she insisted on being called missus. 'Poor Mr Little never lasted the year after getting married. I think he gave up the ghost and died just to spite her.'

Today, Sally was complaining about her groceries from the day before. 'Now listen to me, Albert. My Rich Tea biscuits were broken, I had two chipped eggs and my half loaf was all squashed.'

Albert smiled at her. 'Well, give me your message bag, Mrs Little, and I'll pack it.' He deftly placed the three pounds of potatoes on the bottom and put the lighter things on top. He always knew that items would get damaged with her because she would put things like biscuits, eggs and bread on the bottom of her bag and the heavier items on top,

Mollified, she came to the window to pay for her goods 'Good morning, Mrs Little,' said Edna.

Sally suddenly sneezed loudly.

'Bless you Sal . . . Mrs Little,' said Albert in his usual jovial manner.'

Dolly Pirie came in later. Although Snappy Sally was a neighbour, Albert said Dolly got a bit fed up with her friend's complaining. Dolly bought a quarter pound of boiled ham and a small white loaf.

She handed over her money at the till and she liked to linger if the shop was quiet. 'Are you married, Edna?'

Albert called over. 'Stop quizzing my assistant, Mrs Pirie. This is no *Twenty Questions* on the wireless and you're no another Anona Winn.' Still this was said with a laugh so the woman didn't take offence at the remarks.

'I'm just asking Edna if she's married. Where's the harm in being friendly Albert?'

Edna smiled. 'No, Mrs Pirie, I'm a widow.'

'Well that makes two of us,' she said, smiling at the shared misfortune of losing their husbands.

'I never had any bairns. Have you any?'

'Yes, I've got a five-year-old son called Billy.'

'Have you got him in one of the nurseries that's springing up all over the place?'

'No, my mum looks after him.'

This seemed to please her. 'Well that's what mums are for, to look after their grandchildren and help out.'

With all this information safely tucked under her floral head square, she made for her house, which lay in the close beside the shop.

Albert shook his head. 'She likes to know everything does Mrs Pirie but there's no harm in her. She gets a wee bit lonely living on her own.'

Edna smiled. 'I don't mind. I like her a lot because there's nothing subtle about her. If she wants to know something, she just comes right out with it and asks.'

Edna was aware that Eddie was looking at her during this conversation but when she smiled at him, he blushed. He was about the same age as her. A tall, thin man with red hair slicked down with Brylcreem.

A quiet man, she thought. Edna had hardly spoken to him during her time at the shop. Albert was chatty and he did most of the talking, not to mention the customers and Mrs Pirie in particular.

Later that morning, Mrs Pirie turned up again. 'A tin of condensed milk, Albert.'

As she was paying for it she said, 'Do you want to come for some dinner today, Edna?'

Over the past week, Edna had brought a sandwich and a flask of tea to the shop. It saved her making a mad rush home at dinnertime.

'That would be lovely, Mrs Pirie. I usually get off from twelve till one o'clock.'

'Well, I'll see you then, Edna.'

At twelve o'clock, Edna went to the close next to the shop. Mrs Pirie lived on the second landing and she was standing at her door, waiting for her guest.

'Come in, I've made some soup.' She had laid the table with a lovely embroidered cloth and there was a wonderful smell of cooking.

Edna was quite touched by all the preparation the woman had gone to and she said so.

'Just call me Dolly' she said as she sliced a loaf of bread and put it on a floral plate.

The room was small and although it was quite mild outside, there was a small fire burning in the grate, Apart from the table there was a sideboard that looked really old and two red fireside chairs. Another wooden table in the corner held a large wireless. Dolly had switched it on but the volume was turned down low.

A wedding photo was on the sideboard. A tall, thin man with a bushy moustache and dressed in a military uniform stood to attention beside a very pretty girl in a white dress.

Dolly said, 'That's my wedding photo. Ronnie and I were married in 1914, just after the start of the war. He went away to France and was killed at Loos in 1915. We only spent a fortnight together before he died.'

Edna was shocked. 'That's terrible, Dolly.'

'Aye well, that's what wars do to people. They take your men away and they never come back and there's nothing anyone can do about it.'

Dolly filled two plates with soup. 'Come and sit down, Edna.

You said you were a widow, Edna. Was your man killed in the war?'

Edna shook her head. 'He was in the army during the war and afterwards he decided to become a regular soldier. He said the pay was good and now that the war was over, the army would be a great job in peacetime. But then his battalion was sent to Palestine and he was killed in a bomb blast at a hotel in Jaffa. There were a large number of casualties and quite a number of deaths. His officer said he was in the wrong place at the wrong time. At the time I honestly thought what a stupid statement to make but now I can see what he meant.'

'But you've got your little boy. Does he look like his dad?'

Edna smiled. 'No he looks like my mother except he hasn't got curly hair. William never knew about Billy. He was in Palestine when I realised I was expecting and he was dead by the time Billy was born.'

Dolly looked visibly shaken. 'That's terrible. What did I say about wars.' She sounded angry.

Edna said, 'You must come and visit me sometime Dolly. I live at 41 Paradise Road.'

Dolly said she would. 'But you've got another few days to work so I'll see you then. I'm not looking forward to Nancy coming back and I don't think Albert is either. She's a sharp-tongued young madam and she throws your change down on the counter and then turns her back on you. It's like she doesn't value anyone's custom.' She turned to Edna and took her hand in her own frail looking, blue-veined one. 'I'm sure Albert would like to keep you on. You only have to ask him. All the customers like you. So does Albert . . . and Eddie,' she said with a twinkle in her eye.

Edna laughed. 'I've hardly spoken to him, he's so quiet.'

It was Dolly's turn to chuckle. 'It's the quiet ones you've got to look out for.'

Edna normally worked until dinnertime on Saturday and was surprised when Dolly and a few other customers came into the shop. Albert gave a little speech about what a great asset she had been to the shop and he presented her with a box of Milk Tray chocolates and a card.

133

Dolly started to applaud and said 'Hear, Hear' while Snappy Sal asked why Edna was getting a card and sweeties when she was also getting a wage.

Edna had to wipe tears away from her eyes. It was a lovely moment and it was gratifying to know she had been valued as a worker.

'I just want to say thank you to everyone. It's been a joy to work with you and to have met all your lovely customers,' she said, meaning every word she said. Dolly began to clap again.

Everyone laughed. Edna went up to Dolly. 'I'll stay in touch and come and see you if that's all right, and you must come and see me, Billy and Mum.'

Dolly looked as if she was going to cry. 'Of course you can come to see me and I'll visit you sometime. And I'll give you all the latest about the dragon queen, Nancy.'

Edna was getting her handbag from the tiny office when Eddie popped his head around the door.

'I was wondering if you would like to go to the pictures some night, Edna.' His face was bright red as he said it.

Without thinking, Edna turned her head to look behind her. There was no one there but she knew *He* would be watching and warning her away from any other man. She couldn't risk anything happening to Billy. She couldn't understand why it was all happening again. It had been three years since she had had any contact with him, so why now?

She put on a sympathetic face. 'Oh, Eddie, that would be great but I've got Billy to look after and I don't like asking my mother to look after him all day and then again at night.' Eddie said he understood and went back to the shop.

Dolly gave her a look as she left but Edna merely shook her head sadly.

# 21

The preparations for Saturday's party were in turmoil. It had been a hard week for Molly and the tension in the house was terrible. Lena looked distraught and ill. Her face was white and etched with pain every time she moved her arm but she wouldn't cancel the dinner, much to Joe's disgust and Kenneth's concern.

'You would be better off going to bed Lena,' Kenneth said, 'and getting some rest.'

'I'll be better by tonight.'

Molly had come in early because she knew everything was running late. She had had a quick sandwich with Marigold at midday then she had driven to Cliff Top House.

Lena had ordered in the food for the meal tonight instead of making it herself, She asked Kenneth if he would go to Goodfellow and Steven's baker shop where Lena had ordered meringues for the pudding and they needed picking up at the Broughty Ferry shop.

'I can't go, Lena,' said Kenneth. 'You know I have an appointment with a customer this afternoon in the shop.'

Lena was annoyed. 'Can't you cancel it?'

Kenneth was firm. 'No, I can't. You know this is an important sale and I have to finalise it this afternoon or else we might lose it.'

Molly was helping to lay the table with the lovely crystal glasses and silver cutlery when Lena turned to her. 'Molly, can you and Mike go over to Dundee on the ferry and pick up this order?'

Molly was horrified but she was torn between pleasing her boss and mortified at being in Mike's company for a couple of hours.

Joe said, 'I can't spare Mike. He'll be busy in the warehouse. We have a delivery to make on Monday and it needs sorting out today.'

Molly was relieved but not for long.

'Well what about Christie? He can take the van. Molly can go with him.'

It was settled. Molly and Christie would take the van and Kenneth would take the boat over to the Earl Gray dock and leave it there. After the shop closed he would then come back over the river.

Joe didn't look happy with this arrangement. Molly had to smile in spite of all the tension. Joe was like a spoilt wee boy when it came to the boat. He looked on it as his own personal possession.

Kenneth went away muttering and he didn't look pleased either. He was the first to admit he wasn't a sailor and he didn't like being on the water, which was why he normally took the train to work.

He didn't have to feel the motion of the waves. He didn't want to admit it but he always felt a bit seasick.

Molly was starting to get a headache and the day had hardly begun. She was hoping this job wouldn't last much longer. Her diary was beginning to fill up and there were other jobs she could be doing. It was Edna's last day at the grocer's shop and Molly would have to go into the office tomorrow and sort out the bookings.

Yes, she could have done without this party tonight.

Christie drew up with the van and she got in. Lena had given her the list of food and she said it would all be packed. They just had to pick it up and bring it back.

The van set off along the narrow road, dodging the potholes and they were soon on the main road and on their way to the 'Fifie.'

'How are you liking this job, Molly?' asked Christie.

Molly felt like telling him the truth but she wasn't sure about him. For all she knew he would maybe carry tales back to the Lamonts.

'I like it very much,' she replied, hoping she sounded genuine. 'What about you Christie, do you enjoy living over here? Don't you miss Canada?'

'Yes, I do, as a matter of fact, but I'm hoping I won't be here much longer.'

'You said you lived with your father. Will he be glad when you go back home?'

'I suppose he will. Although we share the house, we live separate lives. He does his job and I do mine.'

Molly noticed he didn't mention his mother. 'Does your mother live with you both?'

Christie was silent for a moment or two and Molly wondered if he had heard her. Then he said. 'My mother is dead. That was the main reason for coming over here. My parents were divorced but she wanted to stay in Scotland while Dad wanted to emigrate to Canada. All this was years ago when I was a small child. So I went with Dad. Last year, she was very ill and I wanted to see her again but sadly she died a few weeks after I arrived. After the funeral I decided to stay on for a while and get a job. And here I am.'

They reached the pier for the ferry and Christie drew in behind a small lorry, three cars and two motor bikes. They didn't have long to wait and once on board, Christie asked if Molly wanted to sit on the top deck.

'I like the wind in my face,' he said. 'Makes me think of Canada.'

'Do you live in a rural area?'

'Heavens no, we live in Toronto but when I'm at home I like to take my holidays near the great lakes. I sometimes hire a boat and go fishing or just enjoy being on the water.'

'You should have taken the boat across and let Kenneth have the van.'

Christie laughed. 'What, and spoil Joe and Mike's day? That boat is their hobby and they are always messing about with it, taking it across the river and bringing it back. They don't like anyone else using it. Did you notice Joe's face when Lena suggested Kenneth should take it to work?'

They both laughed and found a spot beside the rails. The breeze felt warm on Molly's face. Her headache hadn't gone away but she hoped she would feel better soon. If not she would take a couple of aspirins.

'How are your parents getting on in Australia?'

Molly said they were now at Nell and Terry's house and eagerly awaiting the birth of their first grandchild. 'I had a letter last week with all their news and they are having a great time. They can't get over how hot it is and the constant sunshine is a pleasure.'

Molly was surprised how easy it was to talk to him. She hadn't liked him to start with but he was good company. She still didn't trust him because he had lied about being in the house that day but she put all this out of her mind and decided to enjoy the trip.

She watched as the green braes of Fife slowly receded in the distance and viewed the industrial landscape of the city with its smoking chimneys and bleak looking buildings.

She knew the job with the Lamonts wouldn't last much longer, for surely Lena's arm would get better soon. When that happened, most of the work would be in the town and she would have to think about renovating the rooms upstairs from the office. It would save all this time travelling on the ferry.

Christie was silent as he gazed at the view.

'I was wondering,' she said. 'Why don't the Lamonts live in Dundee? It would make sense for them to be near the shop and surely they could rent somewhere with sheds and a warehouse.'

Christie didn't say anything but as the 'Fifie' slowly docked at Craig Pier, he said. 'I've often wondered that myself. But I suppose they have the best of both worlds living where they do. They travel a lot to Edinburgh and Glasgow, as well as having customers on the continent.'

Christie manoeuvred the van out onto Union Street and set off for the baker's shop in Broughty Ferry.

Molly said, 'Lena doesn't look well. In fact, she looks positively ill and should go back to the hospital for a check up on her arm. It ought to be getting better by now instead of worse.' She turned to Christie. 'How did her accident happen? She said she fell.'

'Yes. She was in the town one day and she fell off the pavement onto the road and broke her arm.'

When they reached Gray Street, Christie parked the van next to the shop while Molly went inside.

The woman behind the counter knew about the order and one of the bakers brought out a box and placed it in the van, 'You'd better drive carefully or else you'll break the meringues,' he said.

'Well, now we know what's for pudding,' said Christie.

Next they had to visit the City Arcade. Since Lena had ordered everything over the phone, the butcher's and the fruit shop had everything packed up and the boxes were waiting for them.

The journey home went without incident but Molly could hardly believe that it had required the two of them to pick up this order. Maybe, she thought, Lena wanted to go back to bed and sending them both meant she would be rid of everyone for a few hours.

Molly could have done with some time off herself as her headache wasn't getting any better. She hated taking any kind of pills when she was working but she knew the headache wouldn't go away without some aspirins.

'Could you stop at my house on the way back, Christie? I want to pick up some aspirin.'

He nodded. 'No problem. I've got to go to one of the other shops in the arcade but I won't be a minute.'

When they reached the house, Marigold was in the garden. She stared at Christie and Molly introduced him.

'Now what's someone from Canada doing over in our neck of the woods?'

Christie grinned. 'Just working like you, ma'am.'

'Well I hope everyone is making you welcome. We like our Commonwealth cousins to see our glorious country.'

Molly hurried out of the house before Marigold could ask him any more questions. As it was, she seemed fascinated by him.

'I'll be late home tonight, Marigold, so I'll see you in the morning.

'Christie gave Marigold a salute and she waved her hands as if she was trying to dry them in the sunshine. 'Who is that fine neighbour you have?'

Molly said she was a big help to her since her parents went abroad and she said. 'She also looks after our cat Sabby who doesn't like me.

Christie looked outraged. 'Who could possibly not like you?

Unsure if he was serious or joking, she didn't answer.

When they reached the house, Lena was lying down but she came downstairs when she heard their voices.

'Did you get everything?' she said.

'We got three boxes, is that right?' asked Molly.

Lena opened them and peered inside. 'Yes it all looks fine.' She turned to Molly. 'If you want to go home for a few hours you can, or else you can help Christie with the paintings and furniture which will be on show tonight.'

'If it's all right with you I'll stay and help Christie.'

Molly was annoyed because if she had known about this chance to go home she could have stayed at the house and let Christie bring the van back himself. Perhaps Lena should have listened to Joe and Kenneth and cancelled the event tonight. After all it was only another three couples and Nelly Marten.

When she joined Christie in the sheds, he said, 'The first thing I'm doing is putting on the kettle for coffee.'

Molly filled a glass of water at the sink and swallowed two of the pills, hoping the throbbing in her head would soon subside because it was going to be a long day.

After an hour or so, Joe and Mike arrived back. She saw them walking up the steps from the jetty and decided to go into the house and sit in the office. It was one thing keeping Christie company but she didn't relish the thought of being with Mike.

The office was quiet and cool now that the sun had swung behind the tall trees to the left of the garden. She checked the invoices and the lists of tonight's items. There was a fine collection of antique furniture and a dozen paintings. No doubt the guests would be spoiled for choice.

She knew Betty and Ronald were coming, that intrepid American couple who were furnishing their home in Edinburgh with fine things. She didn't know the other names on the list but no doubt they were also collectors or antique dealers.

She needed to use the bathroom and hoped Lena wouldn't be disturbed if she went upstairs. Walking very quietly up the thickly carpeted stairs, she reached the bathroom.

She was on the point of going back down when she thought she heard a voice coming from Kenneth's room.

The door was slightly open and she gently gave it a push. Silence. She must have imagined it, she thought. Then the voice came again. It was a programme on the wireless and Molly felt so stupid. Kenneth must have left it on when he went out.

As she hurried away from the open door, she noticed a painting on the wall. It was the one bought by Nelly at the last party.

Molly was confused. Why would an expensive painting bought by Nelly be hanging on Kenneth's wall?

Suddenly conscious that she was standing in Kenneth's private room, she hurried down the stairs. What business was it of hers to wonder about her employer's private lives? But it was strange, she thought.

Maybe Nelly was looking for a house and Kenneth was looking after it for her. But it was none of her business. Then something made her stop. Surely Kenneth had taken the boat this morning as Joe and Mike were to be busy in the sheds? But she had just seen the two men arrive on the jetty with the boat.

What a strange upside-down day it was turning out to be.

Sounds from the kitchen brought her back from these thoughts. Lena was busy opening the boxes and there were lettuces,

tomatoes, onions and potatoes on the table. Sitting on the draining board was a large basket of strawberries.

'How are you feeling now, Lena?' Molly was just being polite
because the woman looked really ill. In spite of the warm day, she
was wearing a long-sleeved jumper and tweed skirt. 'What do you
want me to do?'

Lena looked listlessly at the food, as if she couldn't make up her
mind, which was a big contrast to the Lena who had come into
the agency a few weeks before.

'Can you wash the lettuces, Molly? I'm just having a simple
meal tonight. Salad and cold meat followed by meringues and
strawberries.'

'I wanted to do another Coronation chicken dish like the one
I served last month. That was the meal served at the Coronation
banquet, Did you know that, Molly?'

'Yes, I read it in the paper,' said Molly.

'I did cut it out but I've lost it. It's probably been thrown out'.

Lena came over to the sink. 'Can I tell you something in confidence?'

Molly stopped washing the tomatoes and looked at her.

'When I had my accident and broke my arm, I didn't fall off the
pavement. I was pushed.'

Molly didn't know what to expect with this confidential chat
but was shocked by this revelation.

'Did you see who pushed you?'

'No, I just felt this nudge and the next thing I was lying on the
road. Of course there was all the fuss of people picking me up so
the person could easily have slipped away unnoticed.'

'Does your brother and husband know about this?'

'No they don't and I don't want to worry them.'

'Why didn't you go to the police, Lena?'

Lena shrugged her shoulders. 'Would they have believed me? I
don't think so.'

Molly could see that it would have been a difficult thing to
prove and what if Lena was wrong? It may have been someone
hurrying past and accidentally knocking into her.

She voiced this thought but Lena said no, she was definitely pushed.

Molly didn't know what to say. Then the door opened and Kenneth came into the kitchen. He looked tired and his face also looked pale and gaunt.

He filled the kettle and placed it on the cooker. 'If I don't get a cup of coffee I'll collapse.'

Lena asked, 'Have you had a bad day?'

'A bad day doesn't describe it. I was to meet Peter Richards from Fine Antiques. He was interested in buying a couple of tapestries and that table and six chairs but he never showed up.'

'Did Mike pick you up at the station?'

'Yes he did. He was waiting for me when the train came in.' He saw Molly's face and he explained. 'I know I was to take the boat over but after you both left Joe suddenly remembered he needed it so he took me over and I got the train back.' He sat at the table with his coffee. 'What a day.'

Molly tried not to smile. I'll second that, she thought.

Her headache was coming back so she decided to concentrate on washing the salad and leave all the confusion of the day behind. After all she was getting paid to work solely in the office and the household problems had nothing to do with her.

Before she turned back to the sink, Kenneth gave her a look, which made her blush. She hoped Lena hadn't noticed because she felt working here was becoming difficult.

Hopefully Lena would get her plaster off soon and Molly would be on to pastures new.

By six thirty, everything was ready. The table in the dining room was set and the food ready in the kitchen.

But as always, the food took second place to the grandeur of the room with its beautiful furniture and paintings. Christie had said it was contrived because it gave the visitors a taste of how rooms should look and he suspected that Ronald and Betty were planning a similar dining room in their Edinburgh house.

Betty and Ronald arrived first. Lena looked a lot better when she went to the door to meet them. The weary expression on her face was gone and she seemed carefree and happy.

Molly couldn't get over the transformation. Christie noticed it as well and said she was putting on an act for her customers.

The other four people arrived almost together as the two cars pulled up in the courtyard.

The first couple looked hesitant and shy but Lena soon put them at ease but the last two were totally different. The man was small and fat, almost to the point of obesity and his white shirt was strained across his stomach. His companion was tall, slim and had lots of black curly hair falling onto her shoulders. Her dress was skimpy with an off the shoulder neckline. The skirt barely reached her sun-tanned knees. She looked like a film starlet. Molly heard an intake of breath behind her and when she turned, she saw Mike gazing at this girl in awe.

Then Nelly arrived, last as usual, it looked like she wanted to make an entrance. When she saw the film starlet look-alike she stopped dead in her tracks and her eyes narrowed. Unfortunately, she didn't seem to have much dress sense because she was wearing a brown frock which did little for her complexion. She also wore the ruby necklace.

Kenneth and Joe handed round the drinks and Molly went into the sheds with the men. Her table was all ready with the price list and the blank invoices. Molly wondered if Nelly would buy another painting tonight and if so, would it also hang on Kenneth's bedroom wall.

Afterwards they all came out to look at the stock. The fat man whose name was Al was talking in a loud voice. 'As I was saying to Gloria, you can't have a successful business unless you buy the best.' He looked at Joe, 'But the best has to be reasonably priced.'

Molly didn't hear what Joe said but Gloria laughed. A laugh, which didn't match her looks as it was harsh and coarse. Betty and Ronald were too busy looking around the furniture and paintings to pay them much heed but the other couple, Don and Davina, seemed quite intimidated by Al and Gloria.

However, when they saw the stock, they moved around it and seemed quite transfixed by the beauty and the quality of the pieces.

Nelly came in with Kenneth and Lena exchanged an amused glance with him. Nelly immediately spotted the paintings and marched over. 'I must have this one, Kenneth.'

Kenneth said, 'As usual, Nelly, you have a good eye for a painting, This is another one by the Scottish Colourists.'

After an hour of browsing, Molly totalled up the sales and was again surprised by the amounts spent. Betty and Ronald had bought some bedroom furniture, a painting and a lovely table for their hall.

Strangely enough, Al and Gloria didn't buy a thing. He had kept muttering on about getting a discount but neither Joe nor Kenneth took him on. The surprise of the evening was Don and Davina. They bought a large amount which they quietly paid for with cash. Al noticed this and he warned them, 'Better keep that wad of cash out of sight, Don, or you might meet up with a thief.'

Don ignored this and went over to Lena. 'Thank you for a lovely evening but we have to go now. You said the things will be delivered next week?'

Lena said they would and thanked them for their custom. 'But you must stay for coffee and drinks.'

Don said no, they had to be on their way.

Al said, 'Well, we're waiting on more drinks,' while Gloria nodded enthusiastically.

He didn't notice the look Lena gave him. She would know he hadn't bought a thing.

Kenneth came over to the desk. 'Don't make an invoice up for Nelly, I haven't got the price for that painting yet.'

Molly didn't look at him and pretended to sort out the remaining invoices.

Nelly was trying to start a conversation with Gloria but Al kept butting in.

'I'm a self-made business man and my shops in Dundee and Glasgow all have wonderful turnovers. I sell a lot of cheap furniture to families who live in the single-end rooms in the tenements of Hawkhill and the Gorbals and places like that, but I also like to cater for the better off customers who have the cash to buy quality.'

Nelly looked at Gloria. She had a wicked glint in her eye. 'Do you work in the business along with your husband, Gloria?'

'My husband . . .? Oh yes, I do,' she said while Al glared at her.

'Yes, She's my partner in crime you might say.' He laughed out loud at his own joke. 'She keeps me right when a customer comes in. She's able to tell me if it's Utility stuff or old antiques they're looking for. If it's the Utility stuff I normally run a twenty-week hire purchase scheme. A wee deposit and six bob a week. But if they've got a bit of cash going begging then I show them my prestige stuff.'

'What a great business man you are, Al,' said Nelly. Lena gave her a sharp look.

Molly's headache had come back and she realised she had only brought a couple of extra aspirin with her, which she had taken before the dinner started. She wished this evening was over so she could be on her way home and get to bed.

Al stood up, followed by Gloria who almost toppled over on her high heels.

'Well folks, we'd better be off. We need our beauty sleep and all that.' He threw a wink at Nelly who beamed visibly.

'Of course you do,' she said. Her voice all sweetness and light.

Lena and Joe saw them to their car and watched as it drove off. Lena looked terrible and obviously needed her bed as well. Back in the lounge, Betty and Ronald, and Don and Davina, who had been persuaded to stay for a coffee, finished their drinks and looked ready to go as well.

Nelly stood up. 'Before you go, dear folks, we have an announcement to make.' She looked coyly at Kenneth. 'Kenneth and I want to announce our engagement.'

For a moment there was silence. The sort of silence that usually presages a storm. Lena's face went quite pale and she dropped her drink. Molly watched as the crimson sherry spread all over the beautiful Persian carpet but it was Kenneth's face she also noticed. He looked angry and not at all like a betrothed fiancé. Joe seemed to be quite amused by this statement and it suddenly struck Molly that he didn't particularly like Nelly. But then Molly didn't like her either.

Then Ronald spoke and shook Kenneth's hand. 'Congratulations, Kenneth.' He went over and said the same to Nelly. 'Have you set the wedding date yet?'

Nelly looked coy again. She was positively simpering. 'No, not yet, Ronald, but it'll be soon. We'll let you and Betty know.' She turned to look at the other couple. 'And of course, Don and Davina, you'll both be told as well.'

Molly sat transfixed in her chair. Kenneth gave her an agonised glance but Nelly had moved over and sat down next to him. She was showing off a gorgeous diamond ring and Molly could see from where she sat that it hadn't come out of Al's store for a wee deposit and six bob a week.

Then it was all over. The two couples drove off after making arrangements for the delivery of their goods and Molly went to put on her coat.

It was a lovely evening. The river shone like a silver ribbon under the moonlight and as she made her way to her car, she suddenly felt so weary. She struggled to open the door and she felt she could hardly keep her eyes open.

It was a horrendous journey. Molly's eyes kept closing and she had to give herself a shake to keep awake. She had all the windows down but there was hardly any air. There must have been a shower earlier when they were all inside because the road was wet and there was the smell of damp vegetation.

The drive towards the road was creepy as usual and the trees seemed to lean down and touch the car, as if trying to grab it in their branches. Molly shook her head. What a vivid imagination she was getting. It must be all the drama of the night. She remembered Kenneth's look. She was sure it had been a shock to him and that anguished glance he had thrown at her . . . What was that all about?

She drove for a mile and her mind started drifting. Suddenly a grassy back loomed up and she wrenched the wheel back onto the road. I must have dozed off, she thought and, to keep herself awake, she decided to sing 'I Believe' . . .'

Frankie Laine had nothing to worry about judging by the way she murdered the song but the singing did the trick. She was relieved when her house came into view.

Marigold's light was still on but Molly decided she was too tired to see her tonight. She would have put Sabby inside the house so she would go and see her in the morning.

Sabby was sleeping in her basket in the kitchen but ignored Molly when she poured a glass of water. Her headache was now a dull throbbing at her temples but she decided not to take any more aspirin. They were making her feel so tired and she didn't want to go over the stated dose.

Instead of hanging her clothes up in the wardrobe as usual, she let them fall to the floor and tumbled into bed.

*Molly was drowning in a cold emerald green sea. She felt the strong currents tug at her feet and legs and her mouth was filled with the sharp tang of salt water. She tried to swim to the shore. She could see it through the waves that lashed her face. It was a dim black thumbprint on the horizon. Everything was dark and there were no stars. Just an image of land in the distance. There was a light shining, like an isolated house on a lonely island. A large wave caught her and pulled her down but she struggled to reach the surface again. A moon appeared from behind a threatening bank of clouds and the land seemed to be nearer. She was shocked to see Christie standing on the shingle beach. She called out to him, her voice drifting over the water. He saw her but didn't move. She shouted out again and again until she was hoarse. The waves pulled her down and the last thing she saw was Christie walking away. Her ears popped and in the distance someone closed a door.*

Suddenly she was awake. She felt awful and was soaked with sweat. The nightmare was still vivid in her mind and she shivered at the thought of it. She recalled the tang of salt water in her mouth and she was parched with thirst. She still felt groggy but needed some water.

Padding down to the kitchen, she drank the cold water like a dehydrated woman and wondered if Sabby might like some milk. The milk was kept in a little food safe in the back garden, in a spot away from any sunlight.

She opened the door and almost tripped over Sabby who came running in from outside.

Molly was so surprised until she realised that the cat must have got outside somehow. But all the windows were closed. Sabby made a loud noise and stalked off to her basket.

Then the truth hit her. Someone must have been in the house and the cat must have gone outside. The back door wasn't locked so had Marigold come in? No, she wouldn't have allowed Sabby to be outside.

Molly quickly locked the door and went into the lounge. Everything seemed to be normal although there was a faint smell. Molly couldn't quite place it but maybe Marigold had been in the house earlier.

She was on the point of putting out the light when something caught her eye. She moved over to the writing bureau and there was a corner of a letter hanging out from one of the drawers. Molly was sure it hadn't been like that when she came in for the aspirins because that was where the bottle was kept.

She tried to think if she had opened that drawer but was sure she hadn't. She had lifted the flap and taken four aspirins out of the bottle then put it back. She gingerly pulled the flap down. The bottle was gone. Nothing of importance was kept in here except perhaps some bills and letters which were lying in a pile on the surface but when she moved them, the aspirins were underneath.

Now very alarmed, she ran around the house checking the windows and doors. The front door was locked and she had just secured the back door but all the windows were closed.

Moving to the back door, she reopened it and gazed outside. It was starting to become light and dawn was a golden streak in the east. The air felt fresh and there had been more rain during the night.

There was a stone step at the door but her father had made two little flowerbeds on each side of this step. To her horror, she saw a footprint on the wet earth. Maybe it's Marigold's, she thought. But she knew in her heart it wasn't. Someone had been in the house. What Molly couldn't understand, was why? Her parents had nothing much to steal. Then she remembered Christie.

He had waited for her yesterday afternoon and would have seen the back door. And he had been in her nightmare.

Why would a stranger, this Canadian, want to rummage through her house?

She was almost asleep on her feet so she made her way back to bed, but not before she pulled the small bolt at the foot of the kitchen door.

She would see Marigold later and maybe her neighbour would stay with her at night, in case the intruder came back.

# 22

Someone was knocking on the door and Molly could hear a voice calling. It was all part of her dream she thought. Then the knocking became more insistent and she woke with start and jumped out of bed.

Her head felt like a lump of cotton wool and she couldn't remember what day of the week it was. She heard the voice as Marigold tried to unlock the door. Molly then remembered that earlier she had pushed the bolt at the bottom of the door Marigold came into the kitchen with a bottle of milk in her hand and a parcel in the other.

'I've come to feed Sabby,' she said

'What time is it?'

'It's half past eight. I wouldn't have bothered you but I heard her crying at the window. Then I couldn't get the door to open and I thought something was wrong.'

With the sun shining, Molly felt stupid about her fears the night before. She still felt woozy and slightly sick and hoped she wasn't coming down with something. Being ill was the last thing she needed.

'Come into the kitchen, Marigold, and I'll make some tea and toast.'

Marigold fussed around Sabby who weaved in and out through her legs, making purring sounds while she filled her saucer with the milk.

Then Molly remembered she had been going to give her milk last night when she saw the footprint.

'Marigold, you didn't step on that patch of ground by the back door, did you?'

Marigold looked surprised. 'I don't think so, Molly. Is there something wrong?'

Molly shook her head. 'No, it's just that I saw someone's footprint there and I was worried.'

Marigold went to the door and looked out. It was clear someone had stood on the patch but it could have happened at any time.

'Maybe it was the postman. Oh I almost forgot, the postman must have left this packet yesterday. I expect it was too thick to go through the letterbox and he left it at the front door. I saw it at teatime and took it home but I thought you might be tired last night so I didn't come over.'

Molly looked at the small brown parcel. It had a foreign stamp on it but the postmark was so blurred that it was difficult to see when or where it had been posted.

She opened it quickly. A small but quite thick diary lay in the folds of paper.

'Oh it's a five-year diary,' said Marigold. 'It must be from your parents as a present from Australia. Look it has a wee lock and key to keep all your secrets intact.'

'There's nothing with it to say it's from them,' said Molly, 'but it must be because of the stamp. Can you see Australia on the stamp?'

Marigold took the paper and scrutinised it. 'The postmark is covering it and it's difficult to make out where it was posted.'

Then Molly thought. 'It'll be from Nell. She was always writing up her diary and telling me I should do the same. I bet she's sent it.'

Marigold was looking at it in dismay. 'The lock is broken and the key doesn't work. It must have got damaged in the post.'

'Well, it doesn't matter. I don't have any secrets to lock away.'

'Oh I almost forgot,' said Marigold. 'And that is the reason I'm over so early on a Sunday morning. There was a policeman here to see you yesterday.'

Molly suddenly felt faint. 'A policeman? What did he want?'

'He didn't say but I told him you normally go over to the office on a Sunday and he would be able to catch you there. I said around twelve o'clock.' She stopped when she saw Molly's white face. 'I hope I did the right thing.'

Molly quickly recovered from the shock and said. 'Yes you did, Marigold. I've got to go over to Dundee so I better be getting dressed.'

Marigold sat with her cup of tea as Molly rushed upstairs to get ready. Going to the office was the last thing she wanted to do today. She would have loved to stay in bed and have a long sleep.

Marigold was folding up the brown paper when she came downstairs.

Molly gathered her handbag and the diary and made sure everything was switched off. 'I hope there isn't another incident like last Saturday,' she said.

'What was that?'

'Oh, a woman had her handbag stolen as she was getting off the 'Fifie'. She nearly fell into the water. Poor woman, she had all her housekeeping money in the bag.' Molly didn't mention the old woman's strange theory that she had been the intended victim.

Marigold said, 'I read about that in the paper but some young girl found the bag at the Victoria Arch and handed it to a policeman. The money was seemingly still in her purse.'

Molly was puzzled. 'Why would anyone steal a bag then not steal the money?'

Marigold shrugged. 'It's a funny world.'

'Well I'd better be off as I've lots to do today. Did the policeman say anymore about what he wants?'

Marigold said no he hadn't, but she added, 'Maybe it's because you were a witness to the robbery. He maybe thinks you saw the thief and can give a description.'

Molly was relieved. 'Of course, that's what it's all about. Well he's going to be disappointed because I didn't see the thief. I only heard all the commotion.'

Molly waited at the pier for the ferry and she still felt ill. She was aching all over and the headache was still there. She hoped it wasn't a summer cold or even worse, the 'flu.

She sat on the top deck and let the river breezes sweep over her. Her stomach was churning and she thought she might be sick but thankfully the water was calm.

She thought about the strange events of yesterday; Kenneth's engagement and the intruder, if that's what it was. Sitting in the warm sun made her doubt her feelings about last night.

By the time Molly walked to the Wellgate, she decided to go and see Edna first. It was such a lovely day that she suspected the family would make the most of it and take Billy out. When she reached Paradise Road she was suddenly stopped in her tracks by the smell.

Edna was on her knees scrubbing the stairs. She looked surprised to see Molly but said, 'I won't be five minutes. Just go up to the house. Mum and Billy are in and she'll make you a cup of tea.'

'Edna, what is that smell?'

Edna was confused. 'Smell, what smell?'

'The smell from your bucket'

'It's just soap, water and Dettol disinfectant'

Dettol. Molly recognised it now. That had been the smell in the lounge last night but she hadn't been able to identify it.

Edna gave her a queer look but Molly said she would see her in the house. True to her word, Edna appeared five minutes later, her face all red and sweaty. She pulled off her overall and took the scarf from her hair.

'That's better,' she said. 'I should have done our turn of the stairs last night but I was too tired. I'm hoping the stairs will be dry before the upstairs neighbours go to church.'

Irene was bustling about making sandwiches and filling a large message bag with a flask, cups and a small bottle of lemonade. Billy was playing with his cars.

'We're taking Billy to the beach at Broughty Ferry today. The forecast says it's going to be a glorious day and we want to make the most of it.' said Edna.

'I'll not keep you more than fifteen minutes Edna,' said Molly 'I want to make up the timesheets today and Mary will invoice the grocer's shop with the bill. How did you get on?'

'Oh, I loved it. The people were great and made me feel welcome, and in a way I'm sorry the job is finished but Nancy, the clerk, is coming back tomorrow.'

Molly said. 'I was in the office on Friday and there are some more new jobs that have come in. I'll leave the details with Mary and you can pick them up tomorrow morning. Now I'll not keep you back from the beach.' She gave Billy a smile. 'You'll be wanting to build sandcastles, won't you Billy?'

He gave her a shy look and nodded.

'I'll walk down the stairs with you,' said Edna.

When they were outside the door, she said. 'Why were you asking about the smell, Molly?'

Molly hesitated, She didn't want to commit herself to admitting someone had been in the house and the Dettol may have been used by Marigold. But Edna was waiting for an explanation.

'I had a terrible day at Cliff Top House yesterday. Everything seemed to be wrong, I was sleepy when I left and almost had an accident with the car. Then, when I got home, I fell asleep but was wakened by a sound. Sabby, that's our cat, was in the house when I went to bed but, when I woke up, she was outside and there was a faint smell in the lounge. I couldn't put my finger on it until now, but it was like the smell of Dettol.'

Edna looked astonished. 'Dettol?'

Molly was embarrassed. 'Well I think it was but now I'm not so sure. Then there was the surprise engagement of Kenneth to Nelly Marten. I've mentioned her to you. I can't get over the feeling that it was all news to him, and his sister Lena certainly wasn't happy about it.' Molly realised she was talking too much but she had to get it all straight in her head and maybe Edna could give her some help, even if it meant rubbishing all she had said. Then she remembered the footprint and mentioned that.

Edna looked worried. 'I think something's not right Molly. It's probably a domestic situation but you're right in the middle of it. How long do you think the job will last?'

That is the question, Molly thought. 'I hope it'll be a week or two at the most. Lena's arm must be getting better and hopefully the plaster will be coming off soon. In a way I'll be glad to finish but it pays well and it's keeping the agency afloat because I get my money every week.'

Molly looked back at the close. Two elderly women were coming down the stairs. They looked at Edna and one said. 'I see the stairs have been washed. We always do our turn on a Friday, Edna.' With that they walked away down towards Dudhope Road.

Edna smiled at them but after they passed, she said, 'But you don't hold down a job and have a five-year-old boy, Missus Bell.'

Molly noticed that she looked drawn and worried. 'Here I am talking about myself. What about you, Edna, are you all right?'

Edna said she was fine but added, 'Sometimes it all gets a bit much, Molly. Mum tries her best and I'm grateful for her help with Billy, but she shouldn't be lumbered with a young child all day. Still we're going to have a good day out at the beach but I expect there will be a long queue for the buses.'

Molly left her to finish her Sunday plans and hurried to the Wellgate. The office was dim and cool and she got that feeling of pride when she entered the building. This is all mine, she thought.

Mary had left a detailed account of the jobs waiting to be filled. Some of the smaller ones had been allocated to Jean and Betty but there was one that would suit Edna; two weeks at an office in the Eagle Jute Mill. The address was Dens Road. The wage clerk was off ill.

Molly put on the kettle. She still felt slightly woozy and sick but there was work to be done so she quickly wrote out the details of jobs that were now complete for Mary to make up the invoices tomorrow and get them posted.

Molly's mum had a saying, 'Think of the devil and he will appear.' And she was thinking of Mary when the girl appeared at the door, with a friend.

'I thought I saw you, Molly,' she said. 'We're off to the beach at the Ferry. This is Margaret, my friend.'

Molly had a quick word with Mary about the work the next day and as they were about to leave, Mary said, 'Last Saturday, when Rita and I went to the swimming baths, we found a handbag, which turned out to be stolen. I saw that chap, the one I met at the dancing. He was on a boat with an older man. Rita left me and I think she was on that boat. Something happened because she hasn't been out all week and she'll not talk to me about it. She looks scared.'

Molly felt herself go cold. It must have been Mike and Joe. She shuddered at the thought of a young girl being with Mike.

'They live in the house I'm working at so I'll tackle them tomorrow and find out what's been going on. Now, away you go and enjoy yourself.' Molly went to the door and watched as they walked down the street.

Well that was clever, she thought, offering to tackle the gruesome pair, but if Rita had been harmed, they shouldn't get away with it.

Life was becoming more complicated by the minute. And she hadn't seen the policeman yet.

Charlie made his way to the Wellgate a good half an hour before his appointment with Molly McQueen. He wanted to see the agency for himself and see if any visitors went in or out.

He was standing across the road, smoking a cigarette when two young girls went in. It looked as if one of them knew the owner as she was really chatty while her friend stood in the background. Then they were gone.

The owner had come to the door with them and he was surprised to see a young woman. He had somehow thought she would be older. She was a very attractive girl.

He threw the cigarette down on the road and ground it out with the heel of his shoe before walking over to the shop. He noticed it had been newly painted and looked quite smart and fresh. He knocked on the door.

Molly, who was doing her invoices, looked up. Charlie held up his warrant card and she opened the door. The interior of the office was as fresh and as smart as the exterior and although there wasn't a lot of furniture, it still looked business-like.

Molly sat down behind the desk while he took the other seat across from her. He would have preferred the interview to be held without a desk separating them but there was no way he could request this.

As it was, Molly was nervous. Not that this meant anything because Charlie knew that even the most innocent of people were usually nervous when faced by the police. In fact, some of them looked downright guilty even if they hadn't committed any offence.

'I just want to ask you some questions, Miss McQueen,' he said, hoping his voice sounded casual. Molly said she didn't understand why he should come to see her.

Charlie took the small photo of Harry Hawkins from his pocket and placed it on the desk.

'This man was a steward on *The Golden Queen* last year. A ship I believe you were on when you returned from Australia. Have a look at it and tell me if you remember him.'

He was looking at her as she took the photo and scrutinised it quite intently. She frowned in concentration 'Yes, I do remember him being on the ship.'

'Have you had any contact with him since then?'

'Contact? Of course not. I hardly spoke to him on the ship and I've not seen him since. Why are you asking all these questions, Detective Sergeant Johns?'

'This man drowned a few weeks ago in the harbour and I have reason to suspect it wasn't an accident.'

Molly looked at the photo again 'Oh, I'm really sorry about that. He was so kind to me on my journey home.'

Charlie looked at her sharply. 'So you became friends?'

'No, no, He would come to the cabin to tell me when the meals were being served and because I didn't go to the restaurant during the day, he very kindly offered to bring me some food to the cabin.'

Charlie didn't say anything but looked at her.

Molly knew she would have to tell the entire story; something she had decided to lock away but now this policeman was sitting there and watching her.

'I left Dundee with my sister Nell in 1949 for a new life in Australia. On the trip out we met up with Tom who also came from Dundee. When we settled in Sydney, Tom and I became good friends and we talked about getting married. Then Nell got a job in Queensland and I went to visit her. She had met a man called Terry and they were getting married. I was a bridesmaid at the wedding and we all had a wonderful day.

'Tom couldn't come because of his job. He was an electrician in a small company and they had a big contract to finish. After a great holiday with my sister and her husband I set off for Sydney but when I arrived I was met with the news that Tom had been killed in a car crash. The man who was driving the car didn't have a scratch on him. Tom used to tell me about this colleague and his driving. He said he was one of the worst drivers he had ever met. I begged him not to travel with him, but as it was the company's van, Tom had no choice.

'I went slightly berserk with grief, especially as the culprit had escaped with no injuries and he didn't even go to court. He claimed a small child had run out in front of him and he had to swerve to avoid him. It was all put down to an unfortunate accident. Then I heard later that he caused another two crashes but thankfully no one was injured badly. He got the sack after that but it was too late for Tom.

'I stayed on for a short time then decided to come back home. On the ship, I wasn't the best of company so I kept to my cabin except for my evening meal and a walk around the deck late at night. This man, Harry, was very kind and seemed to be worried about me but that is all. I never saw him again and I didn't know he had left *The Golden Queen*, let alone was in Dundee, and that's the truth.'

She suddenly got up and walked to the filing cabinet. 'Why was he in Dundee? The big liners don't come here. Did he have family here?'

Charlie sighed. 'No, Miss McQueen, he didn't. As far as Harry was concerned he was a stranger in a strange city yet he met someone who knocked him out and pushed him into the river.'

Molly shivered. 'That's horrible. He was a really nice man and didn't deserve to die like that.'

Charlie stood up. 'I think that's all, Miss McQueen. I was hoping you could give me some information on him and I'm sorry for your loss. It must have been a hard time for you.'

'Oh, it still is, believe me, but I'm hoping this venture with my agency will keep me busy and take my mind off my loss.'

'Are you back living with your parents?'

'Yes I am. They've gone to Australia to be with my sister Nell when she has her baby in a few weeks time. My father retired recently and this is a holiday for them, as well as being there for the birth of their first grandchild.'

'Do you know anything about the people who bought your parents' house in Strathmartine Road?'

'No I don't. My mother wrote to me in Australia and said they were selling up and moving across the water to Newport. It was all done by the time I came home.'

She sat down again. 'I've got lots to do. Is that all you want to ask me?'

'Yes it is, and thank you for seeing me.' He went to the door and Molly saw him out.

When he reached the pavement, he heard her lock the door and he smiled to himself.

He was no further forward and he suspected that this case might never be solved. It would be treated as an accident, just like Miss McQueen's friend Tom. No doubt the driver was going too fast and driving recklessly but he had escaped Scot-free. But that's life, he thought as he made his way home to his flat in Dens Road. Not all the baddies face justice.

Tam was having mince and mashed tatties for his dinner and Ina Kidd said there was pudding. 'I've made custard with a dollop of jam,' she said.

Tam still hadn't been out since his assault and Rover sat in his basket and looked at him with a baleful eye. Tam tried to ignore him but Rover kept making little yelps as if to get his attention.

'I know I haven't been out with you, Rover, but Jock takes you out.'

Rover got up and wagged his tale. He came over to the table and sat looking up at his master.

Mrs Kidd came in with the plate of custard and jam and a bottle of milk. She was followed by Jock.

'I was just thinking, Tam,' said Jock. 'What about going out with me and Rover for a walk? It's a great day.'

Tam felt his throat constrict with fear and he gazed at the plate of yellow custard and red strawberry jam. He wasn't sure if he could manage to eat it.

Jock was still talking. 'It's not like you're going to be out on your own. I'll be there and nobody will tackle me willingly.'

That was true because Jock manhandled a crane every day at the docks and he was a big, muscular man.

Tam started to say he couldn't but he caught sight of Rover gazing up at him with his brown pleading eyes.

'All right, Jock.' He looked at Mrs Kidd. 'I think I'll leave my pudding and have it at teatime, if that's all right.'

He got up and put on his jacket. Jock beamed. 'That's the spirit, Tam. Never say die.'

Rover was ecstatic and danced around the two men as Jock tried to put on his lead. 'Now, lad, calm down or we'll never get away.'

The heat hit Tam as soon as he stepped out onto the pavement. The street was busy with families all heading off somewhere for the day and there was a festive spirit in the air.

Tam suddenly felt enjoyment as they strolled towards the docks.

The Shore Terrace bus stances were busy, especially the one for Broughty Ferry. The queues stretched right beyond the City Arcade and almost reached Crighton Street. The children were becoming fractious in the heat, wondering when they were going to see the sand and sea but there had been extra buses laid on and the queue slowly made its way towards the front. However, more people kept joining and it never seemed to get any shorter.

The two men made their way to the Victoria Arch and meandered towards the various wharves and bridges that connected the various small docks It was quite busy here as well as people took the chance to walk in the warm sunshine. Jock let Rover off the lead and he briskly made for the edges of the road where there were a hundred smells to be investigated.

Jock said. 'Is that where the man drowned?'

Tam said no, it was nearer the cargo ships that were docked at the wharf but he didn't want to go there, he said. So the two men turned and walked back. They were almost at the entrance to the Victoria Arch, or the Pigeon's Palace as it was also called, when Jock called Rover to come and get his lead back on.

There was a huge crowd of people all strolling or walking at the entrance and they mingled with the crowds standing at the bus stances. Suddenly Rover took off. He was barking loudly as he ran towards the road. Some of the people scattered out of the way and Jock, taken by surprise, said, 'What on earth is he up to?'

Tam darted forward and called his name. Rover stopped and came back to the two men.

He was still growling quietly and he was shaking.

Jock put on his lead. 'He's never done that before, Tam. What got into him?'

Tam was suddenly very afraid. 'He saw who attacked us, Jock.'

Jock looked sceptical. 'How can you know that?'

'When he was a puppy, the man in the shop where I bought him hadn't been very good to his animals and Rover always growled every time we passed the shop. Just like now. After the shop was sold to someone else, the growling stopped. You can take my word for it . . . he saw our attacker just now.'

Jock looked towards Shore Terrace but there were hundreds of people there. The person responsible for the attack on Tam and Rover could be any one of them. He scanned the crowd but no one looked suspicious. He said this to Tam.

'Oh no, the person is long gone. Otherwise Rover would have bitten him and we would know who he was.'

As that person hurried away, they were in shock and a deep anger welled up inside. They made up their mind to sort out that yapping dog and the old man once and for all.

# 23

Edna was washing her hair which was full of sand. They'd had a great time at the beach, Billy especially. Edna and her mum had relaxed on deckchairs which they had been lucky to hire, while Billy had spent the entire afternoon building his sandcastle. Although Edna looked calm, she was still nervous and apprehensive. There hadn't been any more contact since Arbroath but she sensed he was still watching her.

The entire beach was a mass of humanity as people were all intent on enjoying the warm sunny day. Children ran in and out of the sea. In spite of the weather, the water was cold, so not many swimmers lingered for long in the waves.

When she bent down to help him finish off his masterpiece, Billy had scooped a bucketful of sand which he had tipped accidentally over his mum's head. Edna had tried combing it out but she could still feel the tiny gritty bits in her hair.

Billy was now in bed and Edna was getting ready for her new assignment in the morning. Molly had left the job sheet in the letter box and she had read it when she returned from the beach.

She had laid out her suit and white cotton blouse and the new pair of nylons she had bought in D. M. Browns. She had never been in a jute mill before so this new job promised to be a challenge. Seemingly the wages clerk was off ill so Edna would be in charge of overseeing the pay packets of hundreds of mill workers for next Friday's shift.

It was still as hot the following morning and she debated about wearing a dress instead of the suit but she wanted to give a professional image on her first morning. The hours were seven thirty till five thirty so Billy was still asleep when she left the house and walked quickly along Victoria Road to the jute mill.

The mill road was as busy as the beach had been yesterday, as hundreds of mill workers converged through the gates. Edna wasn't sure where she had to report but she found the lodge and asked the man in charge of the timekeeping machine where the office was. He pointed to a long corridor which had windows along one side and said the office was situated half way along.

Edna wasn't usually so unsure of herself but she felt her stomach churning as she knocked on the door. It was opened by a tall woman with grey hair and a grey dress.

'Yes, can I help you?' she said politely.

Edna held out the job sheet, which Molly had typed out. 'I'm the agency worker who's covering for your wages clerk. The one who's ill.'

The grey-haired woman looked surprised. 'Our clerk?'

'Yes,' said Edna. She a little worried by this cool reception. 'I work for McQueen's Agency and this firm requested a temporary clerk to make up the wages. It was to be a two or three-week job.'

The woman said, 'You'd better come in.' She ushered Edna into a large office. There were quite a few people already working at the desks. 'Please take a seat while I get Mr Davidson.'

Edna felt self-conscious as she sat down but no one paid her much attention. This didn't feel right, she thought, and hoped Mary hadn't taken down the wrong address.

After ten minutes, the woman returned with a small, stout man in tow. He was bald with a round, pink face, and was wearing a pin-striped suit with a waistcoat which had a watch and chain across the front of it. He looked important.

The grey-haired woman was still holding the job sheet. 'This is Mrs McGill,' she said, then left and went to sit at one of the desks.

Mr Davidson introduced himself and said, 'We're at a loss about this appointment, Mrs McGill. We never contacted your

165

agency about a job and Miss Evans,' he indicated the grey-haired woman, 'Well, she's our wages clerk.'

Edna was speechless. Mary must have made a mistake and now she would have to go and sort out this mess.

She said, 'I'm very sorry, Mr Davidson. There must have been a mistake at the office. It must be some other jute mill that's needing some office help.' She stood up to go. The quicker she was out of this terrible situation the better.

Mr Davidson walked with her to the door, full of apologies. Edna found herself standing outside on the sunlit pavement, totally flummoxed.

She walked to the Wellgate and into the office. Mary was busy typing and looked surprised when she saw Edna.

Edna could hardly contain her annoyance but she didn't want to accuse Mary of making a mistake until she had heard what the girl had to say.

'Mary, you did say this job was at the Eagle jute mill today, didn't you?'

Mary said it was. 'Have they changed the work times, Edna? They did say to start this morning.'

Edna slumped down on the vacant chair. 'Well, I turned up for work at seven thirty this morning to find that they have no record of being in touch with this agency, or any other agency for that matter. The wages clerk is a grey-haired and very efficient woman and she doesn't look the least bit ill.'

Mary remained silent during this speech then she got out the diary and showed it to Edna. It stated quite clearly: 'Wages clerk for two or three weeks at Eagle jute mill, Dens Road.'

'Do you think you could have taken down the wrong name, Mary? Maybe it was another mill with a similar name.'

Thankfully, Mary didn't look offended. 'No, Edna, I wrote it down right away as the person on the phone was saying it. They said you couldn't get lost because it was at the end of Victoria Road and was well signposted. I remember the man being quite clear in his instructions.'

Edna tried to recall if she had seen any men in the office but she couldn't remember.

'Well that's one job that doesn't need done. Have you anything else on the books?'

Mary looked embarrassed. 'We did have but Jean and Betty are away doing them. I'll have to phone Molly but she'll be at her work at Cliff Top House. I won't be able to get her until she gets home tonight. I'm really sorry.'

Edna felt for the girl. 'It's not your fault, Mary. Maybe the original mill office will call back wondering why I haven't turned up. If that happens, can you let me know?'

Mary said she would and Edna left to go back home. Her mother was surprised to see her. 'What's happened?' she asked.

Edna said there had been a mix up with jobs and Mary was going to try and get hold of Molly tonight. Billy wasn't in the kitchen. Edna asked, 'Where's Billy, is he still in bed?'

Irene said he was downstairs playing with his friend and the Meccano set.

'Can you not go back to the office this afternoon and see if anything else comes in?' suggested Irene.

Edna said she would do that. She felt very unsettled about this whole chapter and hoped it wasn't going to be the start of a lot of job mix-ups because she really needed the regular wage coming. Still Molly would sort it out when she got to hear of it.

Edna tried to get on with some housework but her heart wasn't in it. Irene was putting on her coat to go to the shops but Edna said she would do the shopping.

'It'll take me out of the house,' she said.

She walked to Willie Low's grocery shop on Victoria Road and got some bread, cheese, eggs and milk. As she passed the Wellgate steps she decided to go and see Mary, to see if the mistake had been sorted out. Not that she held any hope because it was barely ten o'clock and she knew Mary couldn't get in contact with Molly till the evening.

When she went into the office, Mary said. 'Oh, I was coming round to see you at dinner time, Edna. I've had the manager of that job this morning at the Eagle jute mill on the phone and he apologises for getting the name wrong. He meant to say the Bowbridge Works, on Main Street. Can you start there tomorrow morning at seven thirty?'

Edna was puzzled. 'Why did he say the Eagle jute mill?'

'He explained that. He said he was the manager there up till two months ago when he moved to the Bowbridge Works, and he must have had a slip of the tongue.'

Mary seemed pleased that it had all been sorted out and Edna was relieved as well. Now that she had a definite job tomorrow, she could enjoy the rest of the day off.

She would take Billy to Dudhope Park later and let him play on the swings to give her mum a rest.

Billy was excited at the thought of the outing. The swing park was busy with children playing but Billy managed to get a swing and Edna pushed him.

'Push me higher, Mum,' he said. 'I want to go right over the bar.'

Edna laughed. He didn't know what that meant and was just copying the other children who were shouting while trying to swing higher and higher into the air.

'That's high enough Billy,' she called but his little legs thrust forward and backwards and this was taking him higher.

Edna became alarmed and frightened he would fall off and she tried to grab the wooden seat to slow it down. She couldn't quite catch it but a man stepped in beside her and grabbed the swing, almost bringing it to a halt.

Billy wasn't pleased. 'I wanted to keep swinging.'

Edna turned to thank the man and was surprised to see John Knox.

'Hello again,' he said. 'How are you keeping?'

Edna was flustered. 'John. How nice to see you.'

Billy was swinging idly with his feet still on the ground.

Edna said it was time to go home and Billy ran to her side.

'It was nice seeing you again, John. I heard Mary did a great job with your book.' John said, yes she had.

'Well, I'd better get this wee lad home for his tea.'

John looked at her and said he'd better be getting back home also, then he turned and walked away. Edna gazed after him but he didn't turn round.

Billy was running towards the merry-go-round. 'I want to go on that,' he said.

'I don't want you to be sick.' Edna had vivid memories of days gone by when she had always been sick riding this circular swing.

Her mind was in turmoil. Why hadn't she been more welcoming to John? Why hadn't she suggested having a walk along some of the paths with him and Billy?

Well, it was too late for regrets now. She probably wouldn't see him again. Billy was having great fun sitting beside the large group of children who were going round in circles. Their screams and childish voices floated over to where she was standing.

Suddenly she felt cold and sensed someone was staring at her. She turned around but there were only the other mothers and one or two fathers either pushing swings or sitting on the benches.

She looked to see if John was watching her but she saw his figure marching up the path as he made his way home. She almost shouted out to him then felt stupid.

No one was watching her. She was just feeling jittery after the strange morning she had experienced.

She looked over to the merry-go-round. It had stopped and Billy was nowhere to be seen. She ran over and asked one of the mothers if she had seen him but the woman hadn't noticed.

'I've got three kids here and I was busy looking after them,' she said.

Edna rushed around the playground but there was no sign of Billy. She felt sick with apprehension and worry. Billy would never go off without her. She called out his name but he wasn't answering.

Edna didn't want to leave the playground but it was clear that he wasn't here so she hurried up the path that climbed up to the grassy stretch in front of the Royal Infirmary.

The grass was covered with checked blankets and coats as people settled back in the sun and although there were loads of children, there was no sign of Billy.

By now Edna was crying. She couldn't think where he was and thought of running for John and getting him to help but that meant leaving the park. Some people were giving her strange looks but she didn't care. They were sitting with their families tucked in beside them, but her son was missing.

She ran back down to the playground where she found Billy sitting on one of the swings

'Billy where have you been? I've been looking all over for you.' She grabbed him from the swing and hugged him.

'The man said he would show me the big gun, Mummy.'

Edna went cold. 'What man, Billy?'

Billy looked around him. 'He's not here now but he said I could go and see the big gun.'

'You didn't go with him? You know what Granny and I have said about going off without us, don't you?'

Billy looked virtuous. 'No I didn't. I said my mum wouldn't like it and he left.'

'But where did you disappear to, Billy? I couldn't find you.'

'I went and hid in the bushes till he went away and when I came out you were running up that path.'

Edna took his hand. 'I was looking for you.' She knelt down beside him. 'Promise me you won't ever go off with anyone.'

Billy said he wouldn't and they made their way home.

Back in the house, Edna told her mother what had happened. Irene was shocked. 'Do you think it was John who talked to him?'

'No. I was watching John as he went up the path so it couldn't have been him.' Edna didn't say, but she knew who the man was and was very afraid.

'I promised Billy that we would have ice cream for our tea so I'll run out to the ice cream shop on Victoria Road and get some.' She took a small bowl with her for the Italian man behind the counter to put three scoops into. 'Mind and get some raspberry sauce over the ice cream, Edna,' said her mum.

Edna still couldn't get over the feeling that she was being watched and she knew he was back.

The next morning, Edna warned her mum to keep Billy in her sight all day. 'I don't want a repeat of yesterday.'

Irene said she would keep her usual eagle eye on the boy. 'In fact, I'll get Brian from downstairs to come up here and play so I can keep my eye on him.'

With that promise in mind, Edna hurried to the Bowbridge Works. She caught the tramcar at the stop outside the Victoria Cinema. Her destination was Moncur Crescent and the bottom of Mains Road. It was only a short walk to the main door.

There were two men in the lodge. One man was small while his companion was tall. The tall man looked like a retired policeman and it was to him that Edna showed her job sheet.

'I've come from McQueen's Agency as a temporary worker in the office,' she told him.

'Right, lass, if you just wait here, I'll go and get the office manager.'

The other man was brewing a pot of tea. 'Do you want a cup?' he asked.

Edna said no, she had not long had her breakfast.

'Neither have I,' he said with a crooked grin, 'But I've always got time for another cuppie.'

Edna waited for about fifteen minutes and was wondering where the man had got to when he appeared with another man in tow. This man was tall and thin with a shock of grey hair and a kind face.

He had the job sheet in his hand. Edna had a terrible thought.

'You say you've come to work in the office and that we contacted McQueen's Agency?'

'Yes,' she said, her voice dry and croaky.

'I'm afraid we have no record of this and I'm very sorry but maybe you've got the wrong address.'

Edna was aware that the three men were watching her intently.

'I can't understand it,' she said. 'This was the address the manager gave to the receptionist yesterday morning.'

The manager looked at a loss for words. 'I don't know what to say, Mrs McGill.'

Edna took the job sheet. 'I'll go and check with the office to see if they've given me the wrong place.'

The manager looked relieved, the small man stirred more sugar into his tea and the other man, the one who looked like a retired policeman gave her a strange look.

Edna escaped out on to the street and promptly burst into tears. She tried to dry them with her handkerchief but she was too distressed. She didn't realise the tall man was standing at her side

'Come back inside and have a cup of tea and tell me what this is all about.'

The small man, whose name was Ron, hurried to make another pot of tea.

Edna told them all about the mistake yesterday and now this one today. The tall man, whose name was Alex, looked angry. 'It looks like somebody's playing a nasty trick on you, lass. Have you any idea who could be doing this rotten thing?'

Edna said no but she knew all right. But there was no way she could explain to these two strangers, although they were both being kind and helpful.

She would have to see Molly and hand in her resignation. She couldn't take any more of this and Molly wouldn't want all this trouble. That was now two jobs that the office staff knew about and the name of McQueen's Agency would become associated with blunders.

Edna knew that Molly was running the agency on a shoestring at the moment. and it was surprising how quickly word got around about blunders and sloppy working practices. No, she would offer to leave and take this horrible problem with her.

She made her way down the Hilltown, barely registering the people who were going to the shops or to work.

Molly had given her a key for the office so she decided to go there as she didn't want to alarm her mother with this latest development.

The office was cool and quiet. Edna made her way upstairs and washed her face in cold water and then gazed at her reflection in the mirror. Her face looked gaunt and drawn and she was annoyed that she didn't have her make-up bag with her. Maybe a little touch of lipstick would have helped.

She thought about the two threats to Billy and the voice warning her to stay away from John. Well, she had done that but it hadn't stopped the torment.

She then went downstairs to wait on the office opening and after Molly accepted her resignation then she would have to face this threat on her own and deal with it.

These two job offers hadn't been blunders, she now realised that. Someone had gone out of their way to send her on two hoax calls.

She suddenly felt sick with worry.

Back at the Bowbridge Works, the manager and Alex, the man from the porter's lodge were deep in conversation.

'I don't understand why that agency sent someone to work here,' said Mr Marr, the manager.

Alex, who was indeed a retired policemen, had an angry gleam in his eye.

'Oh I think whoever sent her knew what they were doing and it's a dirty nasty trick to play on a young woman. There's a lot of malicious and criminal people out there.'

Mr Marr walked away. He was still shaking his head at the morning's events while Alex made his way back to the cosy porter's lodge and Ron who gave him a quizzical look as he entered.

'Did the young lass find out who made the mistake?'

Alex shook his head 'I wonder if she knows herself but I hope she gets some help with this as it's some malicious and nasty beggar who needs to be sorted out.'

# 24

Molly took the frantic phone call from Mary on Tuesday night when she arrived home from Cliff Top House. She was crying and Molly, who was immediately filled with misgivings, had to tell her to calm down.

'Just slow down, Mary, and tell me what's the matter.'

'It was the two jobs that Edna went to. They were both hoax calls and Edna is in a terrible state.'

'Tell me what happened, Mary.'

Mary related the phone calls with the jobs. The first one was for a wages clerk in the Eagle jute mill, which was a hoax. Then the same man called back to apologise for his mistake and he said the job was in Bowbridge Works, but that also turned out to be a hoax. Mary stopped to catch her breath. 'You'll be thinking I took down all the wrong details but I didn't. I swear it.'

By now Molly was worried. What on earth was going on?

But Mary wasn't finished. 'Then I got another phone message which I'm sure is from the same man. He wants a clerk at his office on Friday morning. He said he would phone back with the details. What shall I do?'

Molly, who had a busy day ahead of her tomorrow, had to give this some thought.

'Should I give the job to Edna?'

Molly's voice was sharp. 'No, Mary, don't mention it to her. Tell her I said to take the rest of the week off and I'll come through to the office first thing on Friday morning. If this man calls back, tell him we'll take the job but don't say who will be going.'

Mary seemed calmer after this conversation. It was a relief to leave it with Molly.

When Edna came in the following day, Mary told her what Molly had said and although Edna didn't seem very sure of having time off, she had to admit she was exhausted after all the drama.

Molly hadn't managed to catch Joe and Mike on their own to question them about Rita being on the boat but she was just biding her time. When she turned up at the house the next morning it looked as if that time had arrived.

Lena and Kenneth were planning to go to the shop for the day. Lena still looked dreadful but said it was just a summer cold and she would be fine in another few days. Joe and Mike were in the sheds and there was no sign of Christie. She heard Joe call out.

'Mike, we've to go over to the docks to see if that cargo of furniture and paintings have arrived.'

Molly saw Joe sitting at the desk. She asked him, 'Are you going over in the boat?' Joe looked at her but didn't reply.

Molly was determined. 'It's just that a young friend of my receptionist was seen on your boat a week past Saturday. Her name is Rita.'

Still Joe stayed silent.

'She had such a traumatic time that she hasn't left the house since then.'

Joe went to walk away. By now, Molly was furious. 'Don't you dare walk away from me because I'm going to suggest that she gets the police on to the pair of you. For heaven's sake, she's only sixteen. What gives the pair of you the right to scare a young girl like that?'

Joe stopped and turned to look at her. His expression was more sympathetic. 'Yes, she came on board because she fancied Mike. She had been swimming and Mike said she could swim back from the middle of the river. He likes to make these jokes. Thinks it makes him big and manly like his idol, Marlon Brando. He didn't mean it but she got a fright. I knew she was on board but when she burst into the cabin in tears, I made Mike turn the boat around and we took her back to where Mike had picked her up. That's all that happened, I swear to you.'

'Thank you,' said Molly, 'But you know something, Joe, if you hadn't been on board I'm sure Mike would have had great pleasure with his threat. Even if he was just fooling around. Rita suspects that as well and that's why she's so scared.'

'Well give her another word of warning from me. Tell her to keep away from him. He was in the army during the war and he got used to killing people and shall I tell you something? He liked it. He likes this image of scaring silly young girls but that's the least of his problems.' With this statement, he went out of the shed and down to the boat.

Molly returned to the house. She would be glad when this job was over. It was a good paying position but there was an atmosphere here and Molly suspected Mike was the cause. Was that why Lena looked so haunted and ill?

She heard the boat's engine start up and saw it chug away over the choppy water.

There was a strong wind today and the river looked rough.

She wondered where Christie was and as she went into the house, she passed him coming out. He seemed cheery enough and didn't look suspicious but Molly wondered why he was there in the first place. He was certainly a lot more likeable and attractive than Mike, but he was always in the house when everyone was out. He was another shady character. He said he was Canadian but anyone could say that and who would question it?

After he had gone, Molly went upstairs on the pretext of going to the bathroom. Kenneth's door was closed but she went and stood outside it. She felt terrible spying on her employers like this but she had to know if the second painting was here or had Nelly taken it away.

She turned the door handle and the door opened silently. The two paintings hung side by side on the wall. Molly had her answer. She closed the door and went back to the office.

Of course, if he was going to marry Nelly then perhaps they would stay in this house and that was why she was buying expensive paintings. Maybe the paintings were his engagement present. After all her engagement ring was a beauty; a large solitaire diamond. A ring like that never came out of a Christmas cracker.

What Molly didn't know was that Nelly's ring had been her engagement present from her first husband.

Normally, Molly loved the house when it was quiet like this but today the stillness felt unsettling. Still, she would soon be going home. Lena had said to leave early if she managed to finish all the work so she began to tackle the pile of invoices and all the week's filing. By three o'clock, she was finished and put on her coat.

She decided she wouldn't go home but instead go over to the office and see Mary, to sort out the other unsettling incident.

Mary was on the phone when she arrived, looking slightly panic-stricken. She held up her hand as if to tell Molly to stay silent.

'Yes Mr Archibald, we will send one of our secretaries to see you tomorrow. What is the address, please?'

She scribbled something down on the message pad. When she put the phone down, she said, 'That was the same man. He said he had heard good reports about a Mrs McGill and was it possible to send her.'

Molly looked at the message pad and saw the address was in Union Street. 'Don't mention a word about this to Edna. I'll go tomorrow and see who this joker is.'

Mary's face was a picture. 'Oh you will be careful, won't you? He might be a murderer or he might have escaped from some asylum.'

Molly laughed. 'You read too many detective books, Mary.'

But Mary still didn't look happy.

'By the way, Mary, I tackled the men who were in the boat with your friend. Their names are Joe and Mike. Joe said Rita was on board but Mike, the one you've met at the dancing, was the one who threatened her. Luckily for her, Joe got him to turn the boat around and she landed safely, but if you get the chance to talk to her, tell her he's dangerous and to stay away from him.'

Mary said she still hadn't seen Rita but when she did, she would let her know.

Molly couldn't sleep that night. Her mind was going round in circles. She was worried about the future of the agency and the welfare of Edna. She would have to go and see her and try to get to the bottom of all this mystery.

If these hoax phone calls kept coming in then there was no way she could send Edna out and if no other work came in then what? She didn't want to think about that.

She was also hoping to finish at Cliff Top House. Ever since Nelly had announced the engagement, the atmosphere had been difficult. Lena looked terrible, Kenneth hardly spoke or smiled these days and as for Joe and Mike . . . they remained their usual surly selves. Then there was Christie; another mystery man.

Molly must have fallen asleep around five o'clock and when the alarm went off, she didn't want to get up. Then she remembered her assignment for the day; the meeting with the possible hoaxer. Although she had scoffed at Mary's suggestion that he could be dangerous, Molly still felt uneasy.

The ferry trip across the river didn't help. It was a cold day with heavy rain and a sharp wind. More like autumn than summer.

She had one amusing thought as the ferry battled its way across the stormy river. Her hand closed around the small box of pepper she had put in her coat pocket. She suddenly wanted to burst out laughing at the melodrama of this precaution.

Heavens, she thought, it's as if I'm in an old spy picture like *The Third Man*. The only thing missing was the haunting zither music.

Molly reached Union Street a good ten minutes before the appointment. The address was a shabby looking close with a couple of grubby brass plates at the entrance. The writing on both was so faded it was difficult to make out the writing.

She stood across the road at Henderson's jewellery shop and viewed the windows above the close, trying to look as if she was looking at the jewellery. Every so often she looked at her watch as if she was waiting for someone.

The windows across the road were as neglected as the entrance. Net curtains that had once been white now had a yellow tinge and the windows looked as if they could do with a good wash.

Suddenly one of the curtains moved and the shape of a man filled the window frame. Molly couldn't get a clear look at him because he stood behind the curtain. It was just an indistinct image she had. She looked at her watch again and it said nine o'clock. It was time to go.

She crossed the road and climbed the stairs, which hadn't seen a brush in a long time and were decorated with balls of fluff and discarded litter.

She reached the door and knocked. There was no answer. She knocked louder and called out, 'McQueen's Agency.'

All was quiet but she felt something wasn't right. She tried the door handle and the door opened. She called out again, 'I'm from McQueen's Agency.' Her hand held on firmly to the pepper pot.

She had taken a dozen steps inside when the door suddenly slammed shut and she heard the sound of feet pounding down the stairs. Running over to the window, she caught a glimpse of a man sprinting down the street. He didn't look back so she didn't see his face.

Molly realised she was in a strange room with a possibly locked door, but when she tried the handle, it opened. She looked around the room but it was unfurnished. It must have been an office at one time because a few wastebaskets lay in the corner and there was a scratched, grey filing cabinet in the other corner.

Hurrying out, she ran down the stairs into the wet street. The man was long gone so Molly headed for the office. She would have to see Edna this morning to try and get some sort of explanation. This man was obviously following her and she needed help.

Molly suddenly remembered the policeman who had questioned her last week and she wondered if he could help Edna.

Should she suggest it? She wasn't sure if Edna would want the police poking into her affairs.

Charlie had come to the end of his enquiries and there was nowhere else he could go to get to the truth about Harry's death. He knew Tam was adamant that Harry had been murdered but there was no proof and Charlie would have to tell him that.

Tam was listening to the wireless when Mrs Kidd arrived with his tea. She was wearing her beige waterproof coat with the hood.

'What a day it is with all this wind and rain. I got soaked at the shops.'

Tam said. 'You're not to go out in bad weather just for my messages.'

Mrs Kidd laughed. 'Oh, I've got to get Jock's tea as well so it's no a problem. I've got three bridies out of Wallace's in Castle Street so I'll heat them up. Do you want me to open a wee tin of beans with your bridie, Tam?'

Tam said no, the bridie would be fine on its own. He moved to the cupboard to get a tin of dog food out for Rover and filled his dish up.

As Mrs Kidd brought out the bridie from the oven she said. 'You'll have to save up and get one of the televisions that are on sale. Folk are saying it was great watching the Queen's coronation on it. It would be great company for you, Tam, especially as you live on your own.'

Tam said he would think about it but at that moment, television was the last thing on his mind. He was trying to visualise the scene from the other day when Rover had gone wild. He could remember a lot of people but no one in particular stood out. Still, that was the worst thing about criminals. They looked normal like everyone else and didn't look like Hitler or Mussolini, or like a deranged killer.

Tam had never locked his door before being attacked. He had nothing to steal and his neighbours all looked out for one another but since that first attack he had locked the door every night. On this night of inhospitable weather, he turned the big key in the lock before going to bed and also pushed the big bolt in place. A bolt he had got from Jock who had fixed it in place.

The figure moved quickly towards the house, glad that the bad weather had kept most people indoors. Thankfully it was quite dark as they moved to Tam's close and climbed the stairs. Some of the houses still had lights in their windows so the figure waited in the tiny outside toilet, which lay on the curve of the stair.

Their watch said eleven thirty. Common sense told them to leave well alone and not go near this old man again but it was now a personal thing. That dog had given the individual a nasty bite and now it was time for revenge. Gaining entry would be easy. No one in these tenements ever locked their doors.

It was stormy outside and Tam didn't sleep well because of the rain beating down on the window. About eleven o'clock the wind died down and the rain stopped. He got up and looked out. The sky had cleared and a moon appeared between dark scudding clouds.

He went back to bed and must have fallen asleep at once. He was woken by the sound of someone trying the door.

'Is that you, Jock?' he called out. Someone pushed hard against the door and Rover started to bark loudly. He ran to the door and began to scratch at the base of the door as if trying to get out.

Tam was frightened but he called out again, 'Who's there?'

Meanwhile Rover's barks became even louder and Tam tried to stop him. 'Be quiet, Rover.'

Rover moved back to his basket but continued to growl loudly. Tam got up and moved to the window. He opened it and leant out. A dark cloud had covered the moon but he caught a glimpse of a figure running down the road towards Dock Street.

Molly arrived at the office and Mary looked relieved. 'Did anyone turn up?' she asked. Molly nodded. 'I have to go and see Edna but I'll not be long.'

But she was just picking up her handbag when Edna arrived. She looked surprised when she saw Molly.

'I thought I would come in and see if there was anything for me,' she said hesitantly.

Molly asked Mary to make some tea and bring it down into the office. Mary did as she was told but she looked disappointed at being asked. Molly reckoned that this would be the quickest pot of tea on record.

Molly decided the best way was to tell Edna all about this morning. As she related the incident, Edna's face turned white.

'Mary recognised the man's voice so that's why I went. You're in danger, Edna, and I think you should go to the police. I know someone I could put you in touch with.'

'I think I should hand my notice in, Molly. You have enough work running this place.'

'Nonsense, Edna. I don't want you to leave but what's going on?'

Mary arrived back and looked at the two women with undisguised interest.

'I can't tell you at the moment,' said Edna, 'But I know the man and want to meet him face-to-face. I can't live like this. I don't want the police coming round.'

Molly had worked it out. 'What I'll do is this. I'll send Mary out on the jobs and you can stay working in the office, just until this is sorted out, or until I'm sure the job is genuine.'

Edna said that would be fine while Mary beamed at the thought of going out on assignments.

'Take today and tomorrow off, Edna, and we'll sort something out for next week.'

As she watched her walking up the Wellgate, Molly wondered about the other weeks. How long would this last?'

She was about to leave to go home when the phone rang. Mary answered it while Molly held her breath. Mary wrote down all the details and said that someone would be there on Monday morning.

When she put the phone down, she said. 'That was Albert's Stores asking if Edna could do another two weeks. The clerk is off work again.'

'Do you think it was that man's voice, Mary?'

Mary said no.

'Well I'm going to check it out to see if the grocer did ring and make sure that Edna will be safe with that job. At least there's all the staff and customers to watch over her there.'

Mary looked disappointed. She realised that Edna wouldn't be manning the phone if the job turned out to be genuine.

Molly noticed this and said. 'Never mind, Mary. In a few months time I'm thinking of hiring another school leaver and you can join the outside jobs. After all, you were very clever at recognising that the man's voice was the same as the hoax caller.'

This pleased Mary and she felt an important part of the business.

Molly caught the tramcar and was soon at Albert's Stores on Arbroath Road. There was just the one customer and she waited until the cheery looking man behind the counter served her.

She introduced herself and said she had got the call about a replacement for his sick clerk.

'That's right,' he said. 'I'd like Edna back if that's possible. She's a great worker and good with the customers and my assistant,' he pointed to a slim young man with red hair, working at the far end of the shop, 'especially Eddie,' he said with a wink. 'My clerk Nancy is a proper wee hypochondriac. Now she's got a cold and tells me she can't count properly because of her headaches. Quite honestly she can't count without a headache but that's just my opinion. In fact, I would sack her but she's my niece and my brother would kill me if his precious daughter was on the dole.' He laughed loudly and Eddie looked at him.

Molly came away feeling better about this turn of events. Edna would be able to work and surely the mysterious man wouldn't be able to accost her in this very public environment.

# 25

It was a Sunday and Marigold had invited Molly and Peggy for afternoon tea. It was a lovely sunny day and she set the table, which was situated by the large bay window overlooking the garden. She had spread the fine old embroidered cloth on the table and set out the best rose-patterned china tea set.

Marigold belonged to the old school that believed in the niceties and the good manners of a bygone age. She had made a sultana cake and scones with homemade jam, plus dainty tomato sandwiches.

Molly arrived first but Peggy was just a minute or two behind her. Peggy was used to these afternoon teas with all the gracious trimmings but Molly was taken aback, although secretly delighted by all the preparation her neighbour had gone to.

Molly smiled as she viewed the two ladies. They came from another age when manners and customs were more leisurely. Marigold never even went to the local shops without her hat and white gloves. Sabby was lying in a shady spot of the garden and she never gave Molly a glance when she passed.

Marigold saw this and muttered. 'That is one Prima Donna cat. 'I was telling Peggy that you work at Cliff Top House, Molly,' she said.

Peggy said she remembered it when it was called Tayport Farm and was owned by old Mr Abbot. 'People called Lamont have it now, Molly.'

Peggy said, 'Old Mr Abbot had a daughter who was a bit wild. She ran off and got married when she was seventeen and I recall she had a child but I can't remember if it was a boy or a girl. She came to visit her father on her own in about 1925 and she said the child was around ten years old if I remember it right. There was a rumour going around at the time that she had remarried and was going to live abroad but whether that was true I don't know. How old is this Joe Lamont, Molly?'

Molly hadn't given this much thought but she tried to put an age to him. 'I think he'll be almost forty, Kenneth will be about forty-five and Lena will be . . .' she hesitated.

On the very first meeting with her, Molly had estimated her to be ages with herself at twenty-seven but she had to admit that Lena now looked about forty.

'I've no idea how old Mike is, perhaps twenty-nine and Christie is about thirty I would say, but I could be wrong.'

Marigold smiled. 'Our colonial friend Christie,' she said, turning to Peggy. 'He comes from Canada.' She looked at Molly, 'Have you started to write in your new diary yet. The one you got from Australia?'

Molly was flustered. 'Oh the diary. I'd forgotten all about it. I've left it in Mary's drawer in the office.' She didn't mention all the hassle that had been taking place there, hence the reason for not remembering it. 'I must write and thank Nell for it.'

Peggy was wanting to hear about her parents' adventures in Australia. 'I think it's absolutely wonderful that they've gone to the other side of the world at their age. And how is your sister and her husband?'

Molly said their last letter had been full of their travels and now that they were with Nell and Terry. They had described the house and the area, how wonderful it was and, although it was winter over there, how the sunshine was better than a Scottish summer. Molly had to laugh when reading this letter as her parents were describing everything she had witnessed personally. It was almost as if they had forgotten she had been in Australia with Nell.

185

After the meeting Molly had lots of invoices to make up and was thinking about bringing forward her plan to recruit another receptionist. Mary was shaping up well. She had done a good job filling in for Edna at John Knox's house and her handling of the hoaxer had impressed Molly. She thought she would put an advert in the paper at the end of August or September.

She was sitting in the living room with her typewriter on a small table. She had totally forgotten all about the diary but made a mental note to bring it home next week. Thinking about the diary brought back the memories of that dreadful Saturday and the party when Nelly had announced her engagement to Kenneth.

Then there had been the break-in when nothing had been stolen. And that strange smell in the living room. The more she thought about it, the smell had been Dettol. It had been an antiseptic smell; like a hospital odour. And what, she wondered, was she to make of Detective Sergeant Johns and the dead steward? She remembered him clearly from the homeward-bound ship and how kind he had been. She was sorry he had come to such an awful end.

Still there was no use sitting thinking about things, as she had to finish her paperwork before the start of the new week. She was glad that the grocer's shop job had materialised again, and it would keep Edna safe for at least two weeks. Although Molly had not accepted Edna's resignation, she was realistic enough to realise that if the problems continued then she might have to let Edna go.

She had been sitting with her back to the window but after an hour of typing she got up to stretch her legs and wandered over to the window and got the shock of her life when she saw Kenneth sitting in the van outside. She stepped back into the shadow of the room.

It was clear that he was looking towards the house.

Did he have a message he wanted to pass on, she wondered? But surely he would have phoned? The Lamonts had the phone numbers of both the office and the house.

She moved nearer the window but he had disappeared. Perhaps he was on his way to the ferry and had stopped to pass on some message about next week's workload. It was going to be a heavy week work-wise. A large consignment of paintings and furniture had been bought from a large house sale in Perthshire, that had been a grand stately home until the First World War. Now it was up for sale along with its contents.

Kenneth and Joe and gone to the auction last week and everything was being stored in a warehouse in Dundee. The plan was to transport the items in their own van so maybe that's where he was going. Still it was strange he hadn't come to the door.

The sight of Molly appearing at the window had taken Kenneth aback. He had stopped on an impulse, debating whether to go and knock on the door and see her. But he didn't.

He felt he was being boxed in with his life and there was little he could do about it. Nelly was demanding they set a date for the wedding but he had told her he wasn't going to marry her, or anyone else for that matter. She had simply looked at him with astonishment.

Then there was the worry about Lena. He had told her she should go back to the hospital about her arm, but she said the doctor had told her it would take a few months to heal. But she seemed to be in constant pain. Then there was Joe's sore arm where he had stumbled on the beach. He said it was getting better but Kenneth had noticed a spasm of pain on his face while lifting something heavy.

He had arranged to collect this latest consignment from the warehouse and transport it to the house because most of the items already had prospective buyers. He knew he was lucky to have this lucrative business, but what did money amount to without happiness?

Yes, he should have marched up to Molly's door and told her how he felt about her. He smiled grimly. What would her reaction have been he wondered? After all, he was almost twice her age and a young woman like her must have a man in her life, although she had never mentioned anyone. But then again, would she have mentioned her private life? He thought not.

Lena was waiting for him at the warehouse. She had come over with Mike and Joe on the boat. He was the only one who didn't like the boat, much preferring to travel on the train or the 'Fifie'. Joe said the boat was safer than the rail bridge because that had fallen down once and could maybe fall again. Quite honestly, the way he felt today he wouldn't have minded if it had.

Joe said, 'We'll take some of the smaller bits of furniture and some of the paintings today and come back tomorrow for the rest. I've left Christie sorting out the sheds to make room for this lot.'

Kenneth took the key for the warehouse from his pocket and they made their way into the building. It wasn't a large warehouse, more of a converted shed, but the pieces of furniture were stacked against the wall, covered by protective covers.

Kenneth was concerned about Lena. She looked terrible and she should have stayed at home. Christie could have come and helped. They could have done with another man to help carry everything to the van.

After three hours' hard work, the van was full and Kenneth set off to catch the ferry. He wasn't looking forward to the return journey. The boat was full of families with noisy children running around, making for the shores of Newport to have picnics and enjoy the sunny weather.

He usually liked the sound of children's laughter but not today. His mood was too dark for any frivolity and it was all because of Nelly. On most trips across the river, he normally stayed inside the van but today, maybe because the sun was shining, he wandered up to the top deck. For a moment he couldn't believe his eyes. Molly was sitting by the rail. She looked beautiful in her yellow dress.

He went over to sit beside her. She turned with a look of surprise. 'Kenneth how nice to see you. I saw you outside the house, you should have come in.'

'I did stop with the intention of dropping in to see you but then

I thought you might be busy.' He hoped this explanation would satisfy her. 'I've been over to get some of the stuff from the sale last week. It's in the van. The rest is coming back by boat. I think Lena, Joe and Mike should live aboard that ship as they are never off it.'

Molly said, 'I didn't realise that Lena liked sailing.'

'Oh yes, she used to do a lot of sailing when she was young and although she can't use her arm just now that doesn't stop her being a passenger.' He looked at her. 'Have you been over on business as well?'

'Yes, I've been to the office, just for a quick visit to leave all the invoices with Mary, my receptionist.' Actually this wasn't the whole truth because she had gone over to pick up her diary, which was tucked into her roomy handbag. 'Kenneth, how long do you think you'll need me working for you?'

Kenneth was stricken. 'I've no idea. Until Lena's arm gets the all clear from the hospital, I suppose. I've told her to get it checked out soon. Why, do you want to finish?'

'Oh no, I just wondered,' she said. *Did* she want to finish, she asked herself? On one hand, she did but the money was good and it was keeping the agency afloat until it became better known with more customers.

Edna's job with the grocer's shop certainly helped as well. It was these longer spells with one employer that made the money.

'Why do they call this ferry the 'Fifie'?' he asked.

'It's just an affectionate name because it crosses the Tay to Fife. I suppose it could have been called *The Dundonian* by the people of Newport.'

'Your father worked with these 'Fifies', you said?'

'Yes, he worked in the ticket office at Craig Pier but as I told you, he retired this year. I've put his painting away until my parents get back from Australia.'

By now, the ferry had docked and Molly went to the lower deck where the van was parked.

'Let me give you a lift home,' said Kenneth.

Although she didn't live too far away from the pier, Molly was still grateful for the lift.

When they reached her house, he said, 'It's a lovely house, Molly.'

She laughed out loud. 'It isn't as grand as Cliff Top House.'

His face became sad and she was sorry she had been so flippant.

'Come in and have a cup of coffee or tea.'

For a moment she thought he was going to accept but then he said, 'I'd love to come in but I've got to get all this furniture back so that Christie can pack it away. I have to do another trip tomorrow, so it'll be a busy day for you too. And I'd better be back before the three intrepid sailors reach shore. Also, Ronald and Betty are coming to the house next Sunday. They want to have a look at the new stuff we've bought. There's a lot of good quality furniture and art and you know what they're like? It's only the best for their new house in Edinburgh. Still they are great customers and have bought quite a lot of our stock'

But he was back for over an hour before they arrived and had just placed the last of the paintings in the shed when he heard the sound of the boat chugging in to the jetty. I could have had that cup of coffee with Molly, he thought bitterly.

The figure walked up the Wellgate. Even though it was a Sunday, the street was busy with people walking into town. Passing the agency, the person glanced into the windows of shops as if killing time, then they walked back slowly, took the duplicate key from their pocket and slipped inside the agency. Everything was quiet. A quick look around downstairs produced nothing. A pile of invoices had been left on the desk beside the typewriter, and the diary only showed a list of jobs and customers.

The pile of invoices slipped from their hand. Shoving them back on the desk the figure resumed their search.

There was no sign of what they were looking for and it hadn't been in the house either, because the person had already searched there.

Upstairs, they were taken aback by the unfinished look of the two rooms with the little sink at the window and the small cooker. Otherwise, everything was neat and tidy.

The figure slipped out, locking the door behind them.

# 26

Edna was glad to still have her job. She really thought it had been touch and go last week after the terrible hoaxes played on her. Thankfully, Molly hadn't gone to the police but she knew everything would have to be sorted out soon.

She had no doubt that her tormentor would be in touch again. Little did she know that as she walked to work on the Monday morning, he was nearer than she realised.

The man was puzzled about her destination but was determined to find out where she was going as soon as possible. He couldn't understand why the other woman had turned up for the job. He had specifically asked for Mrs McGill and had gone to the bother of enquiring about renting the empty office in Union Street, just so he could meet her.

He had had a long wait until he was sure the other woman had left before going back and locking up. He planned to wait a week or so before making another move but now he wanted to see what Edna was up to. He smiled to himself when he thought of her going to the two non-existent jobs in the jute mills. These little acts gave him pleasure; made him feel powerful.

Edna reached the shop and was greeted cheerfully by Eddie who was working at the counter.

'Albert is in the back shop,' he said, 'But it's good to see you again, Edna. We've missed you.'

'I've missed you all as well,' she said. His face went red.

Dolly appeared. 'It's like I always say, Edna. There's a Lord in heaven looking after grocers' shops.'

Edna and Eddie laughed as she put her white overall on.

'What can I get you, Dolly?' asked Eddie.

'A tall, rich man with loads of money and good looks for a start, Eddie, but failing that I'll settle for a quarter pound of cheese.'

The man had stationed himself across the road. Standing in a convenient close entrance, he was able to view most of the activity in the shop. So this was the new job he thought, a grocer's assistant.

He waited for a half an hour then left. He would come back at closing time and follow Edna home.

Charlie decided to go and see Tam, who told him about the intruder at the door and Rover's behaviour at the Victoria Arch.

Charlie looked worried and asked if Tam had any relations he could go to until this was cleared up but Tam shook his head.

'No, there's just me left.'

'Well I have to be honest, I haven't managed to get any further forward with Harry's investigation.'

'I'll be careful,' said Tam. 'Rover is a great watchdog. He barks really loudly so whoever it was, he got frightened and ran away.'

Charlie asked if he got a good look when he opened the window but Tam said no. 'The weather was awful with wind and rain and it was just the figure of a man running down the road towards Dock Street.'

'Does Jock still take Rover out?'

'Sometimes I go along with him, just to get out the house and get some fresh air.'

'Be careful, Tam.'

When Charlie left he once again pondered this strange affair. Harry had been a stranger in the city, he hadn't been able to find anyone who knew him, yet someone had most definitely assisted in his death, either by pushing him in the water or not getting help if Harry had fallen accidentally.

Then that person had seen Tam looking at the scene. The newspaper had also reported that the last known person to see Harry alive was Tam, giving some details and printing Tam's name and address. Had that person read it and decided to silence the old man in case Harry had passed on any information about his intended meeting? Thankfully, Rover had saved him, not once but twice.

Nelly arrived dead on seven o'clock. Lena had a face like thunder and Joe wasn't in he best of humour either. Nelly seemed oblivious to the tension in the air and she settled her ample bottom on the sofa. She was dressed in the awful bronze coloured dress again, the one that stretched over her stomach in large puckers while the buttons on the bodice looked as if they would pop off at any time.

Thankfully, Ronald and Betty seemed not to notice the tension. They were so ecstatic at the quality of the furniture and pictures on sale.

Good manners made Kenneth pour out drinks but he wished Nelly hadn't come tonight. But she also said she wanted to view the items. His mind was still on the wonderful afternoon with Molly on the ferry last week.

Later, when Ronald and his wife had gone out to the sheds with Christie and Mike, Nelly suddenly said, 'Now Kenneth, we'll have to discuss our plans for the wedding. I thought we could get married in the Registry office or would you prefer a church wedding? I also thought we could have Lena and Joe as witnesses.'

Joe scowled at her while Lena looked as if she would throw her drink over Nelly's bronze frock.

To everyone's surprise, Kenneth stood up and said, 'Goodnight Nelly.'

'But we have to make our plans.'

Kenneth stood in the doorway and looked at her. 'There are no plans to make because there isn't going to be a wedding. Now, I'm going out to help Ronald and Betty choose their furniture.'

He turned and marched through the door. Leaving Joe and Lena with small smiles on their lips which they tried to hide.

Nelly's mouth was wide open. She was an astonished and unhappy woman.

Nelly was furious as she remembered Kenneth's cold voice saying there would be no wedding. She wandered around her house which overlooked the Magdalen Park bandstand.

Although it was almost midday, she was still wearing her nightdress and dressing gown which had been a present from her late husband, Hans.

Her marriage had been a loveless match, at least on her side but had been a reasonably happy one, and she wasn't daft enough to throw away any good quality clothes. Nelly didn't have Lena and Kenneth's good taste in clothes although heaven knows she tried hard enough.

She made some coffee in a pot but didn't drink it. She was so sure Kenneth would have been overjoyed at this marriage proposal. He knew she had been in love with him ever since she met him and she was an important customer to the firm. Surely he hadn't found someone else, had he?

Her eyes narrowed as she thought of Molly. Nelly had seen how he looked at her and although she was sure the girl didn't reciprocate his feelings, things could change rapidly.

The fury returned. So he wouldn't marry her, well she would see about that.

Now that she had made up her mind on her next course of action, she poured herself a cup of coffee.

Molly was in the middle of a hectic morning. Kenneth had brought back most of the house sale items and Christie and Mike had already been out on the road delivering some of them. As usual, Ronald and Betty were waiting for some pre-war items they had purchased on their last visit. This time it was an arts and crafts cabinet and sofa plus two oil paintings.

Lena was lying down, said Joe. She wasn't feeling well but hoped to be up and about later in the afternoon. Molly typed out all the invoices and catalogued the furniture and paintings that were as yet unsold. She was sending out letters and price lists to some of the shop's regular customers.

Mike was in a particularly bad mood and even Joe was staying out of his way. The weather was hot and humid. Molly wondered if a thunderstorm was imminent. Even with the office window open, there was hardly a breath of air.

She heard a noise at the door and when she turned around, Lena was standing there, moaning. Molly ran over and helped her to a chair. Lena was wearing a long woollen dressing gown and the edge of her plaster peeped out from the sleeve.

'You should be back in bed, Lena. You don't look well.'

Lena grabbed Molly's hand with her good arm. 'I think I'm going to die, Molly. Where's Kenneth?'

Molly ran out to the shed where Joe and Kenneth were arguing about where to place a large sideboard. They both looked up when she ran in.

'It's Lena . . . She's downstairs and she's ill. She's asking for you.' She didn't mention it was Kenneth she had asked for. After all, maybe Joe would be hurt to know his wife had asked for her brother before her husband.

The three of them went into the house but there was no sign of Lena.

'She must have gone back upstairs,' said Joe, as the two men went to look for her.

When they came back down, they gave Molly a queer look.

'Lena said she's been in bed all morning. She says she never came downstairs and that you imagined it.' In fact, Joe was lying when he mentioned this last bit as Lena had said that Molly was lying.

Joe left but Kenneth remained. Molly went to the desk and sat down. Why would Lena lie about coming down?

Kenneth said. 'I believe you, Molly. Lena's not herself at the moment and I'm making an appointment at the hospital to get a doctor to look at her arm. We have to make an allowance for her just now. I think she's suffering from an infection in her arm and the sooner we get it sorted out the better.'

196

'She told me she was dying.'

He laughed. 'Nonsense! She's just feeling a bit sorry for herself because she thinks the business can't run without her and of course it can.' He gave her a smile as he turned to go. 'Only don't tell her I said that. It'll hurt her feelings.'

Molly sat for ages after he left and tried to think things through. The Lena she had seen today was a shadow of the woman who had come into the agency a few weeks ago. Then she had been a vibrant, confident woman and now she was a ghostly waif-like figure. Molly looked outside where the heat was shimmering on the river. Voices floated from the sheds and the sound of the van driving into the courtyard, filtered through the open window.

She made up her mind. She would finish at the end of this week. Even if it meant losing the lucrative contract, she would go out to the temporary jobs that Betty and Jean were now doing. Some of the work was a few days at a time or maybe a week at the most.

The postman arrived and there was the usual pile of business mail plus a letter for Kenneth. Large, flowing handwriting took up all the space on the cream envelope; a woman's handwriting Molly thought. She dealt with the business mail and left the personal letter on the desk but Kenneth didn't come back in.

Christie wandered in for some of the invoices. Molly asked him to tell Kenneth that a letter had come for him.

'Oh, he's away with the van. He's taking some things over to the shop but he'll be back by early afternoon.'

'Well, will you tell him it's here. I'll probably be away by then.'

But she wasn't. Joe came in with some extra work at about four o'clock and it took an hour to deal with it all. She was on the verge of leaving when Kenneth arrived back. He looked weary as he threw himself down in the chair.

Molly asked, 'Can I make you a cup of coffee or get you some water?'

She handed him the letter and went into the kitchen. She was coming out with the cup in her hand when he passed her. He looked like he'd had a shock. He looked stunned. Then to Molly's horror, his face filled with fury and he marched back into the office.

She put the cup down on the small table beside him but he didn't seem to notice her. Then he went upstairs.

Picking up her bag from under the desk, Molly went quietly to the front door and let herself out. The voices were angry and loud. It was Lena and Kenneth. Molly stopped, wondering what was going on then she realised they were arguing. Kenneth's voice was filled with anger and fury.

'This is Lizzy and Ben we're talking about. What about them Lena? And the baby?'

Molly didn't hear Lena's reply.

When she got home, the weather darkened and rain poured down the windows in a torrent. Thunder and lightning crashed in the sky and it seemed as if the very heavens were having temper tantrums.

She lay down on her bed and fell fast asleep.

The man was trying to shelter in the doorway but the rain was coming down in large wet drops and he was soon soaked. His good shoes which he had just bought from Birrells in the Overgate were going to be ruined if he stayed here much longer.

He had been coming to check on Edna most mornings and then again at closing time. Up till now she seemed to be doing a job and nothing else, although he could tell that the red-haired guy was attracted to her. Still he was no threat. A young skinny lad like that.

Dolly went to the window. That man was there again. He came most days and seemed to look at the shop. He didn't always stay in the same close or doorway and today he was sheltering diagonally across from her window.

Suddenly, as if he became aware of someone's scrutiny, he looked directly at her. Keeping her composure, she pretended to sort out her curtains, twitching them back and forth as if shaking dust form them. Then she drew a pretend duster over the sills, keeping him in her sights.

He looked away and went back to glancing at the grocer's shop.

'That'll sort you out, my lad,' she said out loud. 'Thought you would scare me, did you? Well my old granny always said the Pirie family never fell aff the back o' a bus.'

But she was worried nonetheless and went back to the window with feather duster in her hand. He must have been watching someone in one of the shops across the road.

But when she looked out again, the doorway was empty.

# 27

The man was becoming desperate. He didn't have much time left and he had to deal with Edna before he went. This job in the shop seemed to be going on forever. It was now the start of a second week and he had no idea how long she was hired for.

He saw her come out of the shop with a bank bag in her hand and walk down the road towards the bank at the corner of Arbroath Road and Princes Street. He decided to make his move and went into the shop.

The skinny lad served him with some biscuits. A fat woman was being served by the cheery faced man and she was enjoying a good gossip.

'When's that sour-faced Nancy coming back?'

'Now, now, Mrs Baxter, she's my niece so no bad mouthing her, and she's due back next week. You'll only have another week of Edna so make the most of it.'

The man picked up his bag of biscuits and hurried out. He didn't recognise Dolly when she came in but she knew him.

'Eddie, see that man. He's been standing every day last week watching somebody and I think it's this shop. Do you think it's Edna he's watching?'

Eddie looked worried but wasn't sure if Dolly was fantasising. Living on her own, maybe she liked a wee bit of drama in her life. Still he was going to be vigilant.

Edna came back but neither Dolly nor Eddie said a word.

Perhaps the man had nothing to do with her and it would be a shame to worry her needlessly.

Mary was puzzled. Molly had brought some invoices into the office but she normally left them in alphabetical form. Ever since she had started here, that had been Molly's way. In fact, Mary had a quiet laugh at this little foible. But this morning it was different.

Jean had worked a week at Acorn Potato warehouse and Edna at Albert's shop. They should have been on the top of the pile but they were in the middle. Molly was at the Lamont's business and Betty at a firm called Williams the Ironmonger. The William's invoice was on top and Molly's one was at the back.

It was almost as if someone had rifled through them and had not put them back the way they were.

Then the phone rang and she forgot all about it. The caller, a woman, wanted a temporary secretary to work next Monday. Mary wrote the address down and said someone would be there at nine o'clock as arranged.

The woman came out of the call box and looked at the man. 'Is that all you wanted me to do?' she asked.

The man's voice was barely audible. He must have a bad cold the woman thought. Poor soul, and him such a big strong fellow.

'I'm really grateful,' he croaked. 'I've lost my voice and I do need some help with my business, especially as my phone's broken.' He tried to laugh but it came out a wheeze. 'It never rains but it pours right enough, and thank you again.'

The woman walked off with her message bag and headed for the City Arcade. What a lovely man, she thought. She felt virtuous. It was a good feeling to be able to help someone in need.

She bought a chicken from Imrie's stall in the City Arcade and promptly forgot about the man.

Dolly had kept a discreet eye on the shops across from her house but the man didn't come back. Maybe she had been wrong about him. Perhaps he was just some man waiting for a girlfriend or wife.

Today was Friday and she was going in to say cheerio to Edna as she was leaving again after her week's work was finished. The dreadful Nancy would be back on Monday, but how long for?

Edna was sorry to be leaving again. She enjoyed the camaraderie of this shop and she was going to miss everyone. She thought Eddie might ask her out to the pictures but he didn't.

He was worrying about her because Dolly had mentioned the man and he had also seen him standing in the doorway watching the shop.

'What're your plans now, Edna?' he asked, as she was taking off her overall.

'I've got a week's work at an office in Dura Street on Monday. I start at nine o'clock.' She dug the memo out of her handbag. 'Steven's Scrap Metal Company. It's probably a small company. It usually is. Molly gets work from people who can't employ a lot of staff and if one or two go off ill, or for whatever reason, then they ask us to help and we then ride to the rescue.'

'I wish you would consider coming here to work all the time, Edna. I dread the thought of Nancy coming back.'

'Surely she can't be that bad.'

'She is. She can't count and she gets the customers' change all wrong. Then she won't admit it and gets cheeky with the poor customers. We've had people who say they won't be back but, thanks to Albert, they always are.'

'Well, maybe I'll be back soon if Nancy goes off ill again.'

'If she's ill then I'm a monkey's uncle,' said Eddie and they both laughed.

Molly was also dreading going in to work. She was normally off on a Friday but because there had been so much work with the house sale items, she had said she would help out. That had been a couple of weeks ago, before all this domestic tension had built up. The house had an oppressive feel about it, which wasn't helped by the heat. The past week had seen record temperatures and yesterday's thunderstorm had done little to freshen the air.

There had been no sign of Lena and while Joe, Mike and Christie were still working hard in the sheds, the house was quiet. At dinnertime, she went upstairs to the bathroom to wash her face in cool water. She tried to be as quiet as possible in order not to waken Lena. As she left the bathroom, she thought she heard quiet sobbing. Then she heard Kenneth's voice. It was quiet and subdued and she couldn't make out what was said so she hurried downstairs.

An hour later, Kenneth appeared and she couldn't get over the change in him. Gone were the dapper good looks and he looked gaunt and ashen-faced. Molly couldn't help wondering if the letter had been the cause of this. That and the engagement to Nelly.

All this tension had started the night the engagement had been announced. Still, after next week she wouldn't have to think about Lamont Antiques any more.

When he came into the office, she said, 'Kenneth, can I have a word with you?'

He gave her a blank eyed stare before focusing on her. 'Yes, of course, Molly.'

Molly hesitated. She didn't know how he would take it. After all, they were very busy and Lena was no help at the moment. She hoped he wouldn't be very disappointed at her decision.

'I would like to finish here next week if that's all right with you and Lena.'

A muscle twitched in his jaw but he was calm. 'Yes, I think that's for the best, Molly. Shall we say next Thursday?'

Molly was dumbstruck. She knew she wasn't indispensable but she had thought he would at least have made a show of regret at her leaving. She hadn't expected this blank-eyed comment.

Well it all goes to show how wrong you can be with people. She had liked him a lot and she thought he felt the same. They had become friends.

When she got home, Marigold was waiting for her. She had taken a pot of tea and a jug of orange squash out to the garden.

'Molly, Would you like a drink?' she called over.

Molly opened the gate and sank down on the wicker hair with the squashy cushion. She was annoyed at herself because all the way home, she had been on the verge of tears. How professional is that she thought as she wiped her eyes with her hand?

Marigold sat down beside her. 'I was talking to Peggy again today and she's been making enquiries about old Mr Abbott. She was speaking to Bunty who's ninety-one and who used to be a sort of a housekeeper to him. She didn't live in or anything like that but she went in every day and did his cleaning, cooking and shopping. Now she says that he did have a daughter called Elizabeth who ran away and got married when she was seventeen. She had a son but the husband died. When the lad was about ten, they came to visit Mr Abbott and she told her father she was going abroad to marry a widower who had two children.'

'Do you know where she went, Marigold?'

'Bunty thought it was Belgium. She wasn't sure but Mr Abbott told her it was in Europe.'

'When he died, who would have inherited the house and farm?'

Marigold took a sip of her orange squash. 'I suppose it must have been his daughter or the grandson. Bunty said she never set eyes on the two of them again and neither did Mr Abbott.'

Molly told Marigold about leaving Cliff Top Farm. 'I think there's been some sort of family crisis or maybe a bereavement. Kenneth was quite cold when I told him. Maybe they've been trying to get rid of me for a while and didn't want to tell me.'

Later, back home, she made plans to go to the office tomorrow and see what was on the books. Edna would also be finishing today so Molly hoped some work had come in.

There was a letter from her parents and Molly read it without taking it in. Nell was keeping well and her parents were enjoying the new scenery and the weather. Her father had signed off with. 'Hope you've got lots of work in the agency.'

Edna and Irene took Billy to Broughty Ferry beach on the Sunday. It was still warm and sunny and she thought the outing would do them all a world of good.

204

She had enjoyed her two weeks at the Albert's Store but now she had to get used to going where she was sent. The scrap metal business in Dura Street would be a challenge. What kind of office would they have there she wondered?

The large family sitting a few yards away were squabbling. Someone had bought ice cream cones and they were melting in the heat. Then two of children lost theirs as the ice cream fell onto the sand. They let out a wail of disappointment and their mum had to intervene.

'Will you stop howling. Look you can have mine and your auntie will give you hers.'

This satisfied the two youngsters but it annoyed the auntie.

Although she wouldn't admit it, Edna was nervous about this new appointment because of the two hoaxes, but Mary had assured her that a woman had made the call so everything was all right. Wasn't it?

It was still hot the following morning and Edna decided to wear a dress instead of her suit She reckoned a scrap metal yard was hardly Buckingham Palace so she set off. She was really nervous and, when she got to Dura Street, she had to look for the address. She had the piece of paper in her hand but had to go quite a bit along the street before she found it.

There was a double wooden door with 'Steven's Scrap Metal and Rags' written on it. The door looked weatherbeaten and could have done with a new coat of paint. She tried to open this door but it was firmly closed. Her heart sank. Not another wild goose job.

She surveyed the property and found a smaller door a few yards away and when she pushed it, the door opened. The yard was quite small but filled with piles of old metal objects and long lengths of piping laid out on the concrete surface.

I really do get the best of jobs, she thought. There was a small building at the rear of the yard and although its window was covered with old cobwebs and grime, the door was open. She walked towards it and called out, 'I've come from McQueen's Agency.'

There was silence and she suddenly wanted to turn and run back through the gate. But Mary had said it was a woman who had ordered some temporary help so she forced herself through the door.

The tiny office was dingy. A desk and a chair lay against the back wall and the desk was littered with piles of paper. Edna glanced at them and saw they were bills and invoices. 'They certainly need some help here,' she said out loud.

'That's why I sent for you,' said a voice from the past and Edna nearly fainted with fright. 'Hello, Reg. I thought we would meet up again.'

Reg emerged from a door at the rear of the office. 'I've had a bit of bother getting to see you, Edna. You've been gallivanting around with different men, and I don't like it.'

Reg was tall and heavily built. He was wearing a white shirt and dark-coloured trousers but the last time she had seen him he had been dressed in an army uniform.

Edna decided she wasn't going to be cowed by him. 'If you mean gallivanting with men during my working day then you're right. And it's got nothing to do with you.'

His face filled with fury and he pushed her down onto the dusty chair. 'What do you mean, it's got nothing to do with me?'

Edna was frightened. She knew what he was like when he got angry. She had to placate him . . . for Billy's sake.

'You've been gone a long time. What have you been doing?'

He lit a cigarette and blew smoke into the already airless room. It hung like a blue curtain between the two of them.

He pushed his face close to hers. 'I'll tell you what I've been doing, shall I. I've been fighting for King . . . no, for Queen and country in Korea. Three years of hell with thousands of Communists rushing at me. I was one of the lucky ones who survived. I was wounded but twenty of my comrades died right beside me. Oh yes, it was hell on earth I can tell you, Edna. But do you know what kept me going? The thought of seeing you again.'

'Oh, I see.' She knew she sounded banal but what else could she say?

'And what do I find when I get home? My girlfriend seeing other men.'

'Reg, I was never your girlfriend and you know it. I'm sorry you were wounded in Korea but you chose this life, just as Will did. Boy's own adventurers, the pair of you. You both loved the army and all the danger and excitement of being in strange lands and in the thick of battles. As a result, I lost Will and Billy has grown up without a father.'

'I always looked on Billy as my son,' said Reg.

Edna was infuriated. 'But Billy isn't yours . . . and neither am I.'

Reg's face became red with anger. 'When I pulled your husband out of that shattered hotel in Jaffa, I tried to save his life. We were having a quiet drink when those murderous terrorists, The Stern Gang, blew it up. We had a terrible time in Palestine. Soldiers were being murdered by the Jews and the Arabs. Do you know what they did? They kidnapped two soldiers and hanged them from eucalyptus trees. What kind of people do that?'

Edna's face softened. 'I know you both had a hard time in the army and I'm sorry, Reg. I'm grateful you tried to save Will's life and I always will be. And, thankfully, I have Billy who'll always be a part of my husband.'

'I've tried to look after you, Edna, and you know I asked you to marry me after I came home. But you said no, that you didn't love me. But a lot of time has passed since Will died and I hoped you had changed your mind.'

'I haven't. As I said, I'm grateful for all the kindness and help you gave me after Will's death but I don't love you.'

'I suppose you've fallen in love with one of your men friends from your work?'

'No, I haven't. Like you, they are just friends.'

Reg lit another cigarette and Edna felt sick. The room was quickly filling up with smoke.

'Well I'm going to be honest with you, Edna. I don't care if you love me or not. I want to get married before I leave this country again.' He saw her astonished face. 'Oh no, I'm not in the army any more but I've got a good job with a security agency that goes overseas. I'll be leaving in a week's time and I want you and Billy to come with me. Just think, Billy will love being in another country and a different culture.'

'Why all this cloak and dagger stuff, Reg? Why didn't you just come to see us at the house?'

He laughed but it was without humour and it frightened her. 'And meet up with that dragon of a mother of yours again? No, I don't think so.'

'My mum objected to you because you hit me, not to mention your remark about using discipline on Billy when he was a toddler. You're right, my mum doesn't like you and she's right.'

'I said I was sorry for hitting you, didn't I? In fact, I got fed up always having to apologise when you annoyed me and Billy was screaming the house down at night. A bit of discipline wouldn't have hurt him.'

Edna stood up to leave. 'Goodbye, Reg. Don't contact me again and don't approach Billy or I'll go to the police.'

She was almost at the door when he pulled her back and shoved her onto the chair.

'Are you not listening to me, you stupid woman? I said we are getting married before I leave. And you'll give up that job at that agency.'

Edna's head hurt. She had banged it against the wall when he pushed her and she put her hand up to see if it was bleeding.

'I should have finished you off at the park gate that morning,' he said, his face an inch away from hers.

So it had been him, she thought.

'Well, Reg, are you going to beat me up and then hope I'll agree to what you want? If that's what you want then go ahead because I'm not going to change my mind.'

Although her voice sounded quite calm, she was frantic with worry. How was she going to escape from him?

He sounded peeved. 'I don't know what you've got against me. Loads of women have fancied me but I always wanted you.'

'I'll tell you why I don't want to marry you, Reg. As I said I was grateful at the time, but you always had to be in control. I would never have had a life of my own. You're ruthless, vindictive and cruel. You sent me out on hoax calls two weeks ago because you like to be in charge. I would always be worried about Billy as well.'

'It was just a joke, those hoax calls. Can't you take a bit of a laugh?'

Edna couldn't believe her ears. 'A bit of a laugh? Are you mad? This is my job and I need it to look after my son. It's a blessing that I have an understanding boss otherwise I would now be unemployed.'

She knew she had to get away. The room was small and apart from the door at the rear, the only other means of escape was the main door and he was blocking it. She wondered where the other door led to. If she could reach it, maybe she could get out and run.

She jumped up but he was too quick for her. He gave her a slap across the face and this time she screamed. Edna could feel blood seeping down her cheeks. Or maybe it was tears, she wasn't sure.

She thought, he's going to kill me and there's nothing I can do.

He was lighting another cigarette when the door opened. Edna couldn't believe her eyes when she saw Eddie standing there.

Reg let out a loud laugh. 'Well, well, well. If it isn't lover boy from the grocer's shop. The skinny guy.'

Eddie came over to the chair and told Edna to leave but she pleaded with him, 'Just go, Eddie. He'll hit you and I don't want you hurt.'

Eddie said, 'Oh, I don't think so. His kind only hit women.'

Enraged by this remark, Reg put his head down and charged at the young man. Later, when Edna recalled the incident, she couldn't believe her eyes. As he lunged at Eddie, the lad seemed to grab him and Reg landed on the floor with a loud thud. Huge mounds of dust flew up and mingled with the cigarette smoke.

Picking himself up, Reg gave another charge and once more he hit the floor, but this time he banged his head against the wall.

Eddie grabbed Edna's hand and they both ran out of the door. 'He'll come after us,' said Edna.

'No, he won't. Anyway I've got the van.' As they drove away, she felt so relieved that she had escaped relatively unharmed. The blood had seeped onto her frock but it was just a superficial cut she thought

'What did you do to him, Eddie? He's a big man.'

'I go to martial arts class every week. We learn self-defence.'

'He'll be enraged and come looking for you. He's got a very nasty temper.'

Eddie said nothing and concentrated on his driving.

'How did you know where I was?'

'You showed me the address, just as I hoped you would. Do you know he's been watching you for days? Dolly alerted me about him and I've been keeping an eye on him.' He looked at her stained frock. 'I'd better take you home.'

Edna didn't want Billy to see her like this. 'Can you go in ahead of me and warn my mum?' she asked.

When they reached Paradise Road, Eddie went up the stairs while she remained in the van. Then he came down again with Irene in tow. Her mum was upset and angry.

'I've sent Billy downstairs to play with his pal.' She leant inside the van and helped Edna out on to the pavement. 'Look at the state of you.' She tried to smile but her eyes were full of rage.

'Here, son, help me up to the house,' she said to Eddie and he put a strong arm around Edna's waist and half carried her to the house.

Edna's cut wasn't too bad. It had bled a lot but it was superficial and Irene bathed it in warm water.

Irene said, 'I have to thank you for helping Edna. That Reg is a bad lot and I've never liked him. I think you should go the police about him, Edna.'

Edna said no. 'I have to remember how good he was to Billy and me after Will died. It was when he wanted the relationship to go further that he turned nasty.' She twisted her handkerchief in her hands as if remembering that time. She smiled at Eddie. 'The ironic thing is I almost married him when Billy was eighteen months old. Then one night we were coming out of the La Scala picture house when this young lad with a rucksack on his back came up to me. He wanted directions to Victoria Road so I told him where to go. Reg said nothing at the time but further up the road he accused me of flirting with the lad. He gave me a hard slap but immediately apologised for it. Then it happened again on another occasion followed by the same apologies. Then he threatened to smack Billy and that was the end for me. I told him I didn't want to see him again and although he hung around for a couple of months, I haven't heard anything from him for the last three and a half years. He's been fighting in Korea, he said, and now he's off to a job overseas, so I hope he's gone for good.'

Edna walked down the stairs with Eddie. 'I know you said I showed you the address of this job today but why aren't you at work, Eddie?'

'I asked Albert for the day off. I said I had to go to the dentist so no one knows about any of this.'

'Thanks again.'

'Oh, before I forget, Dolly is coming to see you tonight. I hope you don't mind but she was worried about you.'

'She'll get on well with Mum and I'll be pleased to see her.'

After he left, she went back upstairs and burst into tears. Irene let her cry, as she needed to get all this out of her mind and she was furious at Reg for causing all this mayhem. Edna said he was going abroad but Irene was worried he could cause trouble before then.

Dolly arrived not long after teatime. She brought a Dinky car and a comic for Billy who immediately started playing with the car, putting it in his little garage.

Dolly told Irene that Edna was being missed already. 'Nancy turned up this morning, late as usual and scowling. I think that lassie has seen too many gangsters' molls in the pictures and likes to think she looks like them. She says she has a smouldering look but she has a pained expression, like she's lost a half crown and found a tanner.'

'There was a wee queue waiting to pay for their messages and what do you think wee madam was doing?'

Edna and Irene said they didn't know.

'Filing her nails and putting on her lipstick. Totally ignoring us all. Well Albert shouted at her and told her to get her backside off the chair and start manning the till. She just gave him her usual snooty look and ignored him. He was heard muttering, "I'm going to get Edna back." Well, what do you think of that, Edna? We all want you back.'

Edna was touched but he said. 'I'm not sure what I want to do, Dolly. I might have to give up my job and look for something else but I'm not sure. My head's in a mess.'

Dolly patted her hand. 'Just you get back to normal, lass, and take as long as you like. You've had a terrible shock with that awful man, but don't let him ruin your life.'

Irene said, 'I've said the same thing, Dolly. If she lets him ruin her life then he's won.'

'I've got Eddie to thank for helping me. I didn't know he did martial arts.'

Dolly said, 'He's been a member of the club since he was a laddie. I always used to tell him it would come in handy one day and it has.'

Edna knew she would have to go to the office and explain everything to Molly but she had made up her mind to leave the agency. She had brought nothing but trouble and worry in her wake.

She was also worried what Reg's next move would be. She knew he wouldn't be happy at Eddie for showing him up in front of her. He was a proud man and she knew he would get his own back in some way.

She hoped this job he was boasting about was imminent. If that happened then he would be away and life would become normal again. Wouldn't it?

# 28

At the moment when Edna was worrying about his reaction, Reg was in his dingy bedsit flat in Ann Street, seething with anger at Edna and the skinny guy who had made such a fool of him.

He stubbed out his cigarette into an overflowing ashtray. Who would have thought a skinny guy like that could put him on the floor? And as for Edna's rejection . . . well, he would leave that for now.

He was going back to Palestine with a firm who dealt with security for businesses abroad. Back to the Holy Land. Or, as he and Will had called it, the 'Unholy Land', where there had been so much carnage between the Jews and the Arabs.

He tried to forget about his time in Korea and the horrors of war over there. He had been injured with shrapnel before the ceasefire and had spent two months in hospital. But he was over that now and all he had on his mind now was revenge.

His small bag was packed, his rent paid up to the end of the week and he had returned the key for the scrapyard. He had decided not to rent it after all, he told the young lass on the desk; a pretty girl who looked at him admiringly. This had boosted his confidence and he almost asked her out to the pictures, but no, there would be time enough for that later.

Molly was still dealing with the country house sale. Kenneth and Joe must have bought the entire contents she thought but it was good to be busy. Kenneth didn't go over to the shop that afternoon and as far as she knew neither did Lena.

Molly hadn't seen Lena for a few days and was worried that something was badly wrong with her but Kenneth had said she was in bed with the 'flu.

Christie, Joe and Mike were kept busy delivering items to customers. but Kenneth never left the house. He spent most of the day upstairs and Molly saw him carrying trays of food and pots of coffee to Lena's room.

When the phone rang, she thought it was for Lamont Antiques but it was Mary on the other end of the line. 'I've got Edna here. She wants to speak to you.'

Molly knew there must be something wrong and when she heard Edna's voice she was proved right.

'I'm sorry to bother you at your work, Molly, but there's been a bit of trouble again.' She went on to tell her the entire sorry tale. When she was finished she said,

'I'll finish at the end of the week, Molly, as you have enough to cope with without all this hassle.'

Molly told her to wait at the office and she would be over as soon as she could get away. She thought Kenneth wouldn't mind her going a couple of hours early.

Leaving the office, she stood at the foot of the stairs and called up,

'Kenneth, can I have a word?' There was no reply and everything was silent. She knew he was there because he had passed the door a short while earlier. She called out again but there was still no answer.

She decided to go out to the sheds and speak to Joe. Christie was alone and busy stacking paintings against the far wall.

'Is Joe here?' she asked

'No, you've just missed him. He's gone out in the van with Mike.'

'Listen Christie, something has come up at the agency and I have to leave early. I've tried calling up to Kenneth but there's no answer, so can you give him a message and tell him I'll be back tomorrow?'

Christie said he would pass it on when he saw either Joe or Kenneth.

'I hope it's nothing serious, Molly,' he said.

'No it's one of my workers. Something has happened with her assignment and I have to be there to sort it out. I'll see you tomorrow.'

She didn't want to elaborate to Christie about the problems she was having with hoax calls and, judging by Edna's story, this was more serious.

As she drove along the narrow road towards the ferry, she was considering her future with the agency. She would have to look at the financial statement and see if it was worth carrying on. The job she had was a good payer but now she had burnt her bridges by leaving. And all because of some domestic situation that was no concern of hers.

When she reached the agency, Edna was sitting with a tearful Mary. When she saw her, Edna jumped up but Molly said,

'Can you please make a pot of tea for us all, Mary?'

Mary scuttled upstairs, glad to be out of the firing line. She was worried she would get the blame about this latest fiasco but it had been a woman who had called about the job. She wondered if it could have a man who disguised his voice but no, she was adamant it was a woman.

Downstairs, Edna was telling Molly the entire story. 'I know him from years ago, Molly, and I had my suspicions this was all his doing. but he hadn't been in touch for over three years.'

'What do you think he'll do now, Edna?

'Well, he'll want his own back if I know him, but he did say he was going to a job overseas so with a bit of luck he'll be away again.'

Mary put down the tray with the tea and three cups. 'It was a woman who phoned, Edna, I'll swear to that.'

'It's not your fault, Mary. He got a stranger, a woman, to call from a phone box to fool you. He was quite proud of his deception, but he is devious.'

'Do you want to take a holiday and get away with Billy, until you're sure he's away?' asked Molly.

'I thought you would want me to leave.'

'No, I don't. All this isn't your fault.'

'Well I'd rather keep working, Molly, if you don't mind. Billy starts school again next week so I want his routine to stay the same.'

'Well, leave it with me and I'll go over the diary with Mary and let you know what's available.'

Mary showed her the diary. There were some small jobs booked but nothing more than a week at a time.

'I'll put Edna on this one,' said Molly; a vacancy in a small office in Tay Street, initially for one week.

Molly was quite worried, as the diary didn't show enough work for everyone. She would be finished on Thursday and now felt stupid for saying she was leaving. Maybe by Thursday, Lena would be feeling better and she might ask her to stay on, but she couldn't rely on that happening.

It didn't matter so much if Jean and Betty were laid off until something else turned up and Molly could tackle the other two vacancies. What she needed were other clients like John Knox and Lamont Antiques.

Mary was twiddling her pen, looking at Molly, a bright expectant look on her face. Molly's heart sank.

'I know I said I was going to advertise for another school leaver to do the reception work, Mary, and let you go out on agency work, but after this awful affair with Edna I would be worried about your safety. We don't know if this man, Reg, is still around.'

Mary said she understood. After all, she didn't relish going into some deserted building with a maniac and she shivered slightly at the thought. It was one thing going to the pictures and seeing Frankenstein terrorising everyone and being in the same situation for real.

'As soon as all this blows over and when we get a lot more bookings, then you'll be going out and about.'

Molly decided to go home. Mary was dealing with anything that turned up at this end and there was lots of work she could do at in the house.

Marigold was sitting in the garden when she arrived home and she called over the fence.

When Marigold saw her face, she said. 'What's happened, Molly? You look terrible.'

Molly sank back in the roomy garden chair and found herself telling her neighbour about the trials and tribulations of the agency. Marigold was horrified when she heard about Edna.

'And she says she knows this man?' she said.

Molly nodded. 'He's some army pal of her late husband and quite a controlling person by the sound of it. I hope he goes away and doesn't come back as I think Edna is frightened of him.'

Marigold was sympathetic. 'I had a good friend once, when I was young. Her name was Bella. She fell in love with a young man from a good family and her parents were delighted when they got married. He was the perfect man in their eyes, but her life was a hell on earth with him. He tried to control everything she did but her mother wouldn't believe her when she told her. Said she just had to put up with it.'

'What happened to her?'

'She went out one night and disappeared. Her shoes were found on the shore but she was never seen again. The verdict was an accidental death, but I knew she had come to the end of her tether with her so called perfect man.'

Marigold picked up her cup and drained the last of the tea from it. 'Let me tell you Molly, it's amazing how many dark secrets can be hidden from prying eyes.'

Molly didn't realise she was shivering until she went into the house. Don't be silly, she thought. You're just cold because the sun went in and a cold breeze blew in from the river.

Charlie had been busy. There had been a spate of burglaries and some trouble with kids who had been running around the Howff graveyard, knocking over headstones and trampling on the bushes.

Then there were the kids who played regularly on the tops of air raid shelters. People who lived in the surrounding houses were forever complaining to the constable on the beat. As a result, he had made the trip to warn the kids away from this dangerous ploy.

One of the women who had been complaining had given a statement. 'One of these nights somebody is going to fall off and break their neck.'

Ina Kidd was in the house when he arrived at Tam's door.

'Come in,' she said, 'Tam and Jock are out walking with Rover, but they'll not be long.'

She went over to the sink and started to wash the dishes. 'Tam thinks he'll be able to take Rover out now. He says he can't hide away for ever.'

Charlie wasn't very happy with this because he hadn't managed to solve this case but he understood Tam's need for independence. He would wait another five minutes and if he wasn't back by then he would come back in a day or two.

But Tam and Jock arrived back within a couple of minutes and Rover ran ahead of them into the small kitchen. Tam looked pleased to see Charlie.

'Any news?' he asked

'I think I've come to the end of my enquiries, Tam, and I've not been able to connect anyone to Harry. It's turned into a dead end, I'm afraid, but I'll still keep trying. In the meantime, just watch out when you're out of the house. The man who attacked you is still out there so be careful. I wish you would get Jock to walk Rover.'

Tam shook his head. 'They've been so good to me and I can't keep playing on their good nature. I'll watch out and if that man comes near me again, well I'll have Rover to warn me, like last time.'

Charlie walked away down the stairs. It was a lovely night and loads of people were out on the streets. The City Centre Bar on the corner of Dock Street was busy. The door was open and he was able to see people enjoying a drink and a gossip. Tam's assailant could be mingling amongst these crowds.

The Empress Ballroom was open and a large queue had formed at the door, waiting for admission to a night's dancing and merriment, while couples strolled through the Victoria Arch after a walk around the wharves. This was a popular evening's entertainment; strolling over the little swing bridges that connected the various docks and looking at the boats that were berthed.

He was still sure that Harry hadn't died a natural death but proving it was going to be almost impossible. He hated to lose a case but this one was a lost cause, which was a pity, he thought. Still he had given it his best shot but wished he had solved the crime.

# 29

It was Molly's last day at Cliff Top House and she was full of mixed emotions about it. On one hand, she was glad to be leaving all the tension behind but she would miss this place and the wage it brought in. Although she tried not to think about him, she also knew she would miss Kenneth. She liked his company very much and she had thought they had become friends, even though he had been cool with her these last few days.

She was clearing her desk, putting all the completed invoices in the filing cabinet, ready to go when Kenneth appeared.

'Are you finished up here, Molly?' he said, looking at some vague spot over her right shoulder. Molly said she was and picked up her handbag.

'Lena doesn't want to give you this 'flu she's suffering from, but she says to tell you what a great help you've been to the business.' He handed her an envelope. 'This is the payment for last week, plus a bit extra for all your help . . . and thank you.'

Molly took the envelope and put it in her bag.

'Say goodbye to Lena for me. I've enjoyed working here very much.' She held out her hand. 'Goodbye, Kenneth.'

She didn't go into the sheds to see Joe, Mike or Christie. After all, she was an employee and not some guest of the family. She was getting into her car when Christie came over.

'Joe told me you're leaving. Is that right?'

Molly said she was and this was her last day.

'Can I come and see you some time? Maybe go out for an evening together?'

Molly was surprised by this. She wasn't sure if she wanted to see him again but she nodded. 'I'll look forward to that,' she said.

As she drove up the twisting drive to the main road, she wondered why she had said that. Was she really looking forward to meeting him?

Kenneth watched as she left the room and went to the kitchen window to see her get into the car. He wanted to run out and tell her how he felt about her; to ask her to run away with him to some place where they could live their lives without people like Nelly poking their noses into his business.

He had his hand on the window latch, ready to call her name, when he saw Christie approach the car. What did he want, he wondered?

He quietly opened the window, thankful that it opened smoothly and overheard the conversation. He waited with bated breath to hear what her reply would be and was upset to hear her say she would look forward to seeing him.

He went into the lounge, poured out a large whisky and slumped down on the chair.

Molly was taking it badly, having nothing to do. On Saturday she went over to the office in the morning and made a pretence of organising the files. She had given Mary the day off.

Edna had finished with her week's work and there was very little in the diary. Jean and Betty could have some time to themselves now and she and Edna would share the remaining jobs. Hopefully, things would pick up soon.

It was the summer holidays that were to blame she told herself. At this time of year firms weren't hiring temporary staff.

She had been surprised by the generous cheque from Kenneth, money that would tide her over for a few weeks. After that, well it was anyone's guess what would happen. She was depressed that her business wasn't the success she had hoped for. All the planning since coming back from Australia had amounted to very little, but most of all she dreaded having to tell Edna and Mary that they could be out of a job.

She was busy checking the bookkeeping ledger, glad to note that it was kept meticulously up to date by Mary, when the door opened.

John Knox stood on the doorstep, looking uncertain.

Molly smiled. 'Mr Knox, how lovely to see you.' And she meant it.

John sat down. He looked unsure.

Then he spoke, 'I'm needing someone to help me tidy up my book and file away my notes. I wondered if you had anyone available, Miss McQueen?'

Molly almost blurted out, 'Take your pick.'

'I know Mrs McGill didn't seem happy about coming back but if Mary is available, that would be fine.'

Molly made a great show of studying the diary. 'I think I have both Edna and Mary available. When do you want one of them to start?

He looked sheepish. 'On Monday, if possible. I know I should have given you some warning, but I've been trying to do it all myself and it's a proper muddle I can tell you.'

'I'll have someone round at nine o'clock on Monday morning,' she promised and he left, still looking unsure if he had done the right thing.

Edna arrived later and Molly told her of the new job. 'I don't know if you want to take it, Edna,' she said. 'If not I can ask Mary.'

'No, I'll go,' she said. 'I was warned off this job by Reg, but I can't live my life in fear all the time. Anyway I'm hoping he's gone overseas.'

'Well, it's initially for one week but hopefully it'll last a wee bit longer,' said Molly.

Edna stood up. 'I'd better get my messages done. Mum has asked Eddie to the house tomorrow for his tea, to thank him for all his help with Reg.'

'How do you feel about that?'

Edna hesitated. 'Eddie did ask me out to the pictures when I worked in the shop before but I told him I had to look after Billy. But I'm really so grateful to him for all his help. I would probably have taken a good beating from Reg if he hadn't shown up. I'm going to tell him that I value him as a good friend.'

After she left, Molly sat for ages, watching all the pedestrians walking down the Wellgate, but there were no more clients beating the door down for her help so at five o'clock she closed up.

She didn't feel like going home so she wandered along the Murraygate, looking in the shop windows. Before she realised where she was, she was standing outside Lamont Antiques. The shop looked deserted and when she tried the door, it was locked.

She hadn't thought what she would say if the shop had been open but she would have gone in and spoke to Kenneth, saying she was just passing and wanted to say hello.

She stood and looked in the window. As usual, it was a simple display of a tapestry and a vase of flowers. Unlike the first time when she had stood outside this shop, the tapestry only partially covered the back of the window and she was able to see a small area inside the shop, She had the strangest feeling that someone was watching her from the dark interior, but she told herself not to be foolish and walked away.

The figure sat in the dim back shop, watching Molly standing there. Now why was she here? they wondered. However, there was a lot of work to be done and not enough time to do it in.

The figure moved towards a stack of packing cases and dismissed Molly from their minds. At least for the moment.

# 30

Edna approached the house with uncertainty. The last time she had seen John Knox, he had walked away, annoyance written clearly on his face. Now she was about to do some more work for him.

Molly had left it up to herself if she wanted this post. She had been willing to send Mary but Edna said she had to explain to him about her reluctance to finish the initial work.

The house looked the same. The garden still had that neglected look and the rose bushes were hanging over the path.

She rang the bell and he answered the door, delight clearly visible on his face. 'Edna, how lovely to see you, do come in.'

The house still had the warm, homely feel and she was glad she had come.

'Miss McQueen said you wanted another week's work done on your book.'

He decided to be as business-like as she was. 'Yes. It needs tidying up and then I would like all my notes to be filed away.'

They worked away all morning, both being pleasant and polite but nothing more. At dinnertime he said, 'I've made some soup and sandwiches if you would like to join me.'

She smiled and laid down the pile of files she was arranging into some sort of order.

It was so good to be back in this house, she thought. It felt safe and comfortable, a bit like a well-loved pair of comfortable shoes.

They were sitting at the kitchen table with two bowls of hot broth and thick slices of bread when she said, 'I have to apologise to you, John. About the way I suddenly stopped working for you, especially after you were so kind to me in Arbroath.'

'You don't have to explain to me Edna. If you don't want to.'

'But I do,' she insisted.

She told him the story of Reg and his threats. 'He said he would harm Billy if I kept working for you.'

John had stayed silent throughout the story but now he looked furious. 'I'd like to get my hands on him.'

Edna told him he was probably abroad by now but even if he wasn't, she couldn't live her life always looking over her shoulder and, if Reg threatened her again, she would report him to the police.

John nodded. 'That's the best thing to do with a scoundrel like that. Threatening a woman and child like that, he should be in jail.'

Suddenly he smiled and took her hand. 'I'm glad you're back working here. I've missed you very much.'

'Oh John, I've missed you as well. You've no idea how rotten I felt when I stopped coming here to work. I love your company and this warm and homely house but I had to protect Billy, you do understand don't you?

John was overcome with emotion. 'Oh I do understand Edna, but you're here now and nothing can change that. That horrible man is in the past and he won't bother you again. Not if I have any say in it.'

Edna suddenly felt so protected and loved by this man.

At four o'clock he said he would walk her home. When she protested, he said, 'Just in case he's still around. I don't want him bothering you again.'

Molly decided to stay in the office and send Mary out to a job in Rough and Fraser's bakery in Kinghorne Road. The clerk had taken ill again and this was the second time they had used the agency. Mary was delighted to be out and about and this job would give her some experience.

It was also near her house so she could walk to work every morning.

Jean had come in a few days previously and said she could no longer work. She had heard of the trouble that Edna had experienced and her husband wasn't keen on her going out to strange places where anybody could be lurking. Those were her exact words and Molly had to agree with her, so she paid her out of the petty cash box and she left.

'That's one down, only the rest to go,' she said to herself.

She planned to put another advert in the *Courier* and *Evening Telegraph* that week to see if that would bring in some more work. If that failed, well she would have to seriously review the entire business.

The phone rang. 'McQueen's agency,' said Molly in her best confident and business-like voice.

There was silence on the other end and Molly repeated herself.

'Is that you, Molly?' said a quavering voice.

It was now Molly's turn to be hesitant. 'Yes, it is.'

'It's Lena here.'

Lena, what did she want? Molly wondered.

'Hello, Lena. How are you?'

'I'm a lot better now, but I'm phoning to ask if you could work on Saturday afternoon and evening. We're putting on another party and I need some help.'

Molly wasn't sure what to say but she needed the work and Saturday was available. But then so were Tuesday, Wednesday, Thursday and Friday come to that.

'Yes, that will be fine, Lena. What time do you want me to come?'

Lena seemed to give this some thought as the line went silent. After a few moments, she said, 'About three o'clock and then on to the evening.'

When Molly put the phone down, she realised she would see Kenneth again and she felt a mixture of emotions at the thought. He had seemed so friendly to begin with but had suddenly turned cool. Almost as if she had done something to displease him.

However she had no idea what had caused the rift. She suddenly felt sad that the friendship had faltered.

She decided to reorganise the office. Having something to do would fill the day while she waited for any clients to ring in. She moved the two armchairs nearer to the window and dusted the desk and telephone. She was looking around for some more housekeeping jobs when Mary appeared.

'The manager of the bakery has asked if I could do some extra time, Molly. The office girl will be off for another week at least, as the doctor has signed her off from work.'

Mary looked apprehensive. A look that was noticed by Molly

'Is something wrong, Mary?'

'Oh no, I love the job. It's just that I wondered if you wanted to take it over seeing it's going to last longer than planned.'

Molly assured her that she had no intention of taking over. 'This will give you valuable experience, Mary. I'm actually thinking of keeping you on as an agency worker. I can stay in reception until I get someone else to look after the office.'

Mary looked as if Christmas had arrived and hurried out with a smile.

On Saturday, Molly chose her outfit with care. She thought her grey suit was professional-looking, especially teamed with the red spotted blouse she had bought from Grafton's fashion shop on the corner of Church Street and the Wellgate.

She decided to wear flat shoes instead of her usual high heels as Lena's parties could last well into the evening.

She had been watching the weather from the window and the mist was so thick it was impossible to see the end of the garden. It was a thick haar that had drifted in from the North Sea.

At last, she gathered up her handbag and gloves and went towards the garage to drive the Anglia to Cliff Top House.

Molly was reminded of the first day she had taken this assignment. The mist had been just as thick on that day as well. She drove slowly, watching the edges of the road, frightened she would land in a ditch or maybe scrape one of the drystane dykes that bordered the fields.

The mist hid the opening to the drive but Molly was familiar with the run now. She turned off the road and drove slowly along the rutted track. The house seemed to loom out of the mist like an apparition and soon Molly was parked safely in the courtyard.

There was no sign of the van or any of the men. Everything seemed to be deserted but Molly reckoned it was the weather that had deadened all the usual sounds of the place.

She walked towards the back door, her heels making clicking noises on the paving stones. The kitchen was empty but everything was cosy and there was a pot of coffee on the stove. She saw the note as she took off her jacket.

*I'll be down in a few minutes. Have a cup of coffee while you wait. I won't be long.*
*Lena*

She picked up a cup from the dresser. The aroma from the coffee was tempting but she had not long had a hot drink so she filled the cup with cold water and drank that. There was another cup and saucer on the draining board so she rinsed it out and placed her cup beside it.

It was such a murky day that the kitchen lights were on but there was no sign of any activity for tonight's party. Perhaps Kenneth and Christie were in Dundee, collecting the food, she thought.

She wandered into the office and was surprised to see a film of dust over the typewriter cover and the surface of the desk. It seemed as if no one had been in here since she left. Maybe the invoices were being typed in the sheds because Lena still had her plaster cast on. Molly didn't know how long a broken arm took to heal but Lena seemed to have had her cast for weeks.

After drinking the water, Molly needed to use the bathroom so she quietly climbed the stairs. All the doors were closed and everything was silent. She opened the bathroom door and was almost overcome with a strong antiseptic smell. A large opened bottle of Dettol had landed in the washbasin and most of its contents had spilled down the plughole. She was surprised by this show of sloppiness in this pristine house but she replaced the cap and put the bottle on the glass shelf.

As she made her way downstairs, she wondered if she should let Lena know she was here. Perhaps she was still sleeping. Molly glanced at her watch. It was after three o'clock. Surely Lena wasn't still in her bed.

Although she didn't relish the thought of meeting Mike in this mist, she decided to go out to the sheds. It was like *The Marie Celeste*. The kettle had been boiling because the steam had misted up the window and there was a cup with milk and sugar in it.

She called out, 'Joe, are you there? Mike? Christie?'

She had turned to leave when she heard an agonised groan. It came from the back of the shed and she made her way warily towards the sound. It came again only louder.

'Help me. I'm trapped.'

Molly ran to the rear of the shed and almost fainted when she saw Mike lying under a huge metal rack. There was blood on the floor and his leg was lying at an unnatural angle.

'What happened?' she said, trying to move the rack but it was too heavy. 'I'm going to phone for an ambulance. I'll be back as soon as I can'

She hurried into the office and dialled 999, explaining the accident and giving the address. 'I think his leg is broken and there's a lot of blood coming from a cut on his head.'

The cool, professional voice at the other end of the line said an ambulance would be on its way as soon as possible.

She glanced up the stairs again but there was no sign of Lena. Where was she? Molly wondered. She called out loudly, 'Lena, are you there?'

Silence.

Not wanting to leave Mike alone, she darted back to the sheds. He seemed to be semi-conscious. She had grabbed a towel from the kitchen, which she placed under his head. He tried to focus on her. 'It's going to be all right, Mike. I've sent for the ambulance. It'll be here soon. I can't find Lena, do you know where she is?'

Mike grabbed her arm. 'Look out for Joe.' His voice was weak.

'Joe's not here, Mike.'

'Watch out for him'

Molly didn't know what to think about this warning. There was no sign of Joe or any of the others. She hurried to the door so that the ambulance men would see where to come.

The mist swirled around like a wet blanket, soaking her blouse and her hair.

It was then she heard the scream. Paralysed by the shrill sound for a brief moment she tried to figure out the direction it had come from. She ruled out the house because she was sure it had come from the river.

Then she remembered the boat. Oh my God, she thought. Lena's fallen in the river.

She ran down the length of the lawn, struggling to keep from slipping on the wet grass. The lawn ended abruptly and she almost fell down onto the beach. Gingerly stepping down the set of steps that were cut into the cliff face, she landed at the foot of the drop and saw the boat at the end of the wooden jetty.

The scream came again and she almost skidded along the slimy surface and landed in the boat, which rocked violently with the momentum of her landing on its deck.

There was no sign of Lena and she called out, 'Where are you?'

It was like a scene from a nightmare with the swirling mist blotting out all the surrounding scenery.

Molly made her way towards the back of the boat. A dark shape lay on the deck and she realised it was Joe. The wet deck was slippy but she managed to reach him.

She shook his shoulder. 'Joe, are you hurt? What's happened?'

He looked dead and she tried to check for a pulse. No, he was alive but she had to get help for him. Where was Lena?

She had risen to her feet when she saw a blur of movement by the wheel then the coughing sound of someone trying to start the engine up. It was Lena. The sound came again and Molly ran to the side to escape back onto the jetty. She had one leg over the side when the engine fired up and the boat began to move.

Thrown off-balance she landed with a heavy thud back onto the deck. Then she heard men shouting as they ran down the jetty. It was Kenneth and Christie.

Kenneth threw himself almost at her feet and the boat rocked violently again.

Kenneth called out. 'Stay with Mike, Christie, and call an ambulance.'

'I've already called one, Kenneth, but Joe is injured and Lena is steering the boat.'

'Yes I am,' she said, 'so come and sit over here where I can keep an eye on you.'

Kenneth moved towards her. 'Lena, take this boat back to the jetty.'

'Don't tell me what to do, Kenneth,' she said, stressing his name into two long syllables.

Lena was dressed in a warm jumper and cardigan with a thick tweed skirt while Molly was freezing in her short-sleeved blouse. The boat picked up speed. Lena must be mad she thought, to head into the mist like this.

She remembered her father telling her of the treacherous sandbanks on the river. 'Lena, you'd better slow down. You don't want to hit a sandbank at this speed.' Molly's teeth had started to chatter but she tried to control it. It wouldn't do to make Lena think she was afraid. But she was very frightened and puzzled at this turn of events. She had been hired to help with a party and now she had landed in the middle of another domestic scene.

Kenneth had made his way to look at Joe and he came back to stand in front of his sister.

'What did you do to, Joe?'

Lena laughed. 'Oh he just drank a couple of cups of my coffee then fell asleep.' She looked at Molly. 'And very soon you'll be asleep yourself, my dear. You see I put strong sleeping pills in the jug of coffee and when I checked the kitchen and saw your cup on the draining board, along with Joe's cup. Now I want you to hand over the key, Molly. The one you stole from my room.'

Molly opened her mouth to say she hadn't drunk any coffee but then decided to remain silent. What was all this about a key?

'I don't have any key. I don't know what you're talking about.'

Lena gave a high-pitched laugh. 'Of course you've got the key. I searched your house and your office but it wasn't there. So where is it?'

Molly remembered the night she thought someone had been in the house. The night she had almost had the accident because she was so tired.

Kenneth grabbed Lena's hand. 'Turn this boat around at once. What do you think you are doing? You're insane Lena. Stop all this now.'

'I'm sorting everything out, that's what I'm doing. I've worked it all out. This is our chance to get away from Nelly and the business. When the bodies of Joe and Molly are found, or maybe not found, the police will think it's us, Kenneth. We can then make a new start . . . a new life like we planned years ago. That's why I had to kill the sailor and shut the old man up and I should have killed his stupid dog when I had the chance.' She faced Molly and started to shout at her 'I want my key, the one you stole. Give me my key.'

Molly couldn't believe her ears. Lena was planning to drown both her and Joe. Lena probably thought she was drugged and that it would be easy to topple both bodies over the side, but she hadn't drunk the coffee and she wasn't going to sit in this freezing wet boat and let herself be killed. Also, she had no idea what key Lena was talking about. She had never seen any of the house keys let alone steal one.

She stood up and marched over to Lena, grabbing her arms and trying to pull her away from the wheel.

Taken aback, Lena gasped and realised she had miscalculated her foe. Molly grabbed at her arms again while Kenneth came over and helped. There was a strong smell of antiseptic and Molly saw that Lena was no longer wearing her plaster cast.

Kenneth grabbed his sister by the shoulders and her cardigan came off to reveal a large suppurating wound on her lower arm, which looked as if it hadn't had any medical attention. Molly was almost overcome by the pungent smell of Dettol.

Lena suddenly twisted the wheel and the boat slewed sharply to the left, throwing Molly and Kenneth off-balance. Getting back up was a painful process but she had to stop Lena carrying out her murderous plan.

Molly launched herself at Lena again, trying to force her towards the little cabin. Hopefully, she and Kenneth could lock this door if they succeeded in her plan.

Because of Lena's injured arm, Molly had the advantage. She was also younger than her adversary and much stronger.

Kenneth came towards them but before he could reach the two women, the boat gave a violent lurch and they both fell overboard.

Molly hit the water with a feeling of shock. It was freezing cold and strong currents tugged at her body. She began to sink, but with an almighty struggle, managed to keep her head above the water.

She was a good swimmer, but that was in a swimming pool or at the beach, not in the cold grey waters of the River Tay. Molly looked around her but because of the mist she felt she was alone a world of water and fog. She couldn't see any landmarks, not even the boat.

Lena's voice carried over the water and Molly heard splashing like someone trying to keep afloat. The noise got louder and suddenly Molly felt herself being dragged down under the water. She felt Lena's sharp fingernails grab the back of her neck as she held onto the collar of Molly's blouse.

Molly tried to hold her breath but the woman kept pulling her under and because Lena was holding onto the back of her neck, she couldn't prise Lena's hand away In desperation she suddenly jerked her elbows backwards and was gratified to know they had struck Lena a sharp blow. She let go of Molly's collar and began wheezing in the cold water. It looked as if Molly had winded her.

Turning in the direction of the noise, Molly tried to aim a kick at Lena but only managed a half hearted blow. Later on, after it was all over, Molly suddenly remembered that she should have swam downwards as the other person wouldn't follow. This was how it was taught in Australia but at this particular time all reasonable thought had deserted Molly's brain and she was acting on sheer survival mode. Her first thought was to push Lena away and escape.

She went under the water again and panicked when she tried to think ahead.

Molly felt her arms and legs go numb and she knew she had to get away from Lena. She swam up to the surface and gasped for breath, her lungs on fire and her head throbbing. She was also so cold that she knew she couldn't last much longer. The struggle with Lena had left her weak and breathless but she knew she had to swim as far away as possible from Lena. She couldn't make out any landmarks but Lena was making a great deal of noise and splashing about in the water so Molly swam in the opposite direction. Lena began to shout and call out and Molly wondered if she had lost all sense of direction like herself. There was no way she was going anywhere near her because she had deliberately tried to drown her.

She tried to remember if the tide was in or out. If it was ebbing then there was the chance of being swept out to the North Sea. The strong currents tugged at her body and she decided to swim. But in what direction?

She heard a voice calling. 'Molly, where are you?'

It was Kenneth.

'I'm over here.' Her voice was weak but she hoped he had heard her. She tried calling more loudly, 'Kenneth, I'm over here.'

She heard the sound of someone swimming but was afraid it was Lena, but she almost cried with relief when Kenneth's strong arm encircled her waist.

Molly still couldn't see the boat and was afraid they would swim in the wrong direction and perhaps miss it altogether. Then through a break in the fog she saw the vague outline of the boat and within a minute Kenneth was pushing her on board where she landed with a heavy thud and a lot of water.

For a minute she lay still but then felt sick, having swallowed so much of the mucky river water. She hung over the side, trying to pull Kenneth on board and retching at the same time.

Kenneth was almost on board when Lena's voice called out. She was screaming. 'Kurt, Kurt. Help me. I'm drowning. Help me please.' The scream carried over the quiet stillness and was all the more disturbing by its intensity.

Kenneth hesitated then slipped back in the water. Molly tried to hold his hand. 'No, Kenneth. Come back in the boat.'

Lena screamed again but not so loudly this time. Kenneth turned his anguished face to Molly one last time, then began to swim away in the direction of the scream.

Molly tried to shout. 'Kenneth, come back.'

She heard him call out. 'I can't, Molly. I'm sorry.'

Molly fell back on the deck. She tried to stand and managed to reach the wheel. But how did it start? Her head was throbbing and she couldn't think.

She remembered Joe and made her way to where he was lying. She tried to wake him up but all she got for her frantic efforts was a loud snore.

She shook him again 'Joe, wake up. Joe, please wake up.' But there was no reaction. Lena had done a good job with he sleeping pills and once again Molly was glad she hadn't drunk any of the coffee.

She called out Kenneth's name over and over again but there was no reply and Lena had stopped screaming. There was a silence from the river with only the waves lapping against the boat.

She knew that they had drowned and began to cry. Then this thought was replaced by the idea that they had both made it to the shore but she knew she was clutching at a false hope.

The boat was drifting but Molly had no idea whether it was heading for the shore or out to sea. The water lapped against the side and in the distance she heard the screech of seagulls but there were no other sounds.

She suddenly felt very, very tired and slumped down beside Joe. She was shivering violently now as her wet clothes clung to her body. She knew she should go into the cabin to look for a warm blanket but she was too tired. All she wanted to do was go to sleep.

She would never see Nell and Terry and the new baby or her parents again. Or Marigold and Sabby. And the strange thing was . . . she didn't care. She was at peace as she settled down beside Joe.

The sound of a foghorn brought her back from a deep sleep. Then there was a ray of orange light sweeping over the river. She heard voices calling and tried to shout back.

The dark shape of a boat came into view and Molly rose stiffly to her knees to peer over the side.

It was a lifeboat and its crew were soon on board. She was wrapped quickly in a survival blanket as was Joe, and taken into the lifeboat.

She said in a whisper. 'There are two people in the river. Kenneth and his sister.'

They searched for quarter of an hour but there was no sign of Lena or Kenneth.

'We have to get you back,' said one of the men and the boat headed towards land.

Christie had sprung into action the minute Kenneth had sprinted down the jetty and leapt onto the boat. He heard the engine splutter before chugging off into the mist. Going to the sheds, he saw Mike lying with the rack over his leg. It was clear that his leg was broken but Christie was worried about the bad head wound. There was a pool of blood on the concrete floor.

Mike was still conscious but groaning loudly. Christie knelt down beside him and said, 'The ambulance is on its way, Mike. It won't be long.' He didn't want to touch or move him in case he did more damage to his injuries. He did, however, try and lift the rack and, after a great deal of effort, managed to set it upright.

He heard the sound of the ambulance coming into the court-yard and he hurried out to meet it. It took the two medics quite a while to set his leg and look at his head wound, but soon Mike was on a stretcher and being lifted in to the vehicle and away to the hospital.

Christie hurried down to the edge of the jetty, but there was no sound of an engine. Suddenly he heard screams and shouting although he couldn't judge how far out the boat was. Then he heard splashing and more screaming.

He ran back to the house and dialled the emergency services. The operator put him through to the police.

Then he went upstairs and went into Lena's room.

# 31

Molly woke up in a warm bed, although she was still shivering. The nurse came in with two hot water bottles and tucked them under the covers. 'These will keep you warm,' she said. 'I'll be back later to change them when they get cold.'

To start with, Molly was disorientated and wondered where she was. Then realisation dawned and she tried to sit up. She was in a large ward and some of the other patients were gazing over at her.

The elderly woman in the next bed leaned over.

'How are you now, dearie? Feeling any better?'

Molly tried to speak but her voice seemed to have deserted her. The entire dreadful incident flashed into her mind and her body shook with an intense bout of shivering. Kenneth and Lena were both dead. She was sure about that because no one could last long in the cold waters of the river.

'There's been a policeman sitting by your bedside but I think he's gone off to get a cup of tea.' said the woman. Her shrewd grey eyes alive with interest.

Molly was alarmed. 'A policeman?; Her voice came out in a whisper 'Did he say what he wanted?'

The woman thought for a moment then said. 'He didn't speak to me. In fact I don't think he spoke to anyone except the doctor and nurses, dearie, but I did hear him tell the doctor that he had to question you over the accident.' She pulled her bed jacket closer to her body, as if she had also been in the river and was suffering from hypothermia.

Joe was also awake but feeling terrible. He had been sick again and his brain felt woozy, like a lump of cotton wool. There was no sign of Kenneth or Lena but he hoped they would hold their tongue over whatever had happened. If only he could remember. No one in the hospital had mentioned the accident, so there was no way he was going to tell the police anything.

Hopefully he would get home soon from the hospital and he would warn Mike to keep quiet as well. He lay back on his pillow, feeling totally drained of energy and sweating heavily. These hospitals were always so hot.

Christie made the hospital visiting time with twenty minutes to spare. He had three patients to see. He decided to see Molly first.

She was sitting up in bed and feeling a lot better. Although she still looked pale and tired, she had managed to eat something and was looking forward to going home. The policeman hadn't stayed long, much to her neighbour's dismay, but he would be coming to see her when she got home.

Christie arrived at her bedside with a bunch of flowers and sat down in the chair by the bed. 'How are you feeling, Molly?'

Molly said she was well on the road to recovery and asked after Joe and Mike.

'I'm just going to see them both after I leave here.'

Suddenly, Molly gripped his hand, and she began to cry. 'They both drowned, didn't they, Christie? Lena and Kenneth. Why?'

Christie said he didn't know, but perhaps it was an accident.

'No, it wasn't. Lena was acting like she was deranged and then we fell into the water. Kenneth saved me first but then he went to try and rescue his sister.'

'Look, Molly, I have to go and see the other two patients, but I'll come and see you soon, at your house when you get home. I promise.'

Molly wiped her tears and tried to avoid the scrutiny of the woman in the next bed.

Christie found Mike and Joe in the same ward but while Mike was near the door, Joe was further up on the left-hand side.

Mike's bed had screens around it and when he asked the nurse on duty, she said he couldn't have any visitors because he was recovering from an operation on his leg and his head wound had also been treated.

'I'm a work colleague,' said Christie. 'Is he very ill?'

'He's got a badly broken leg but there is no skull fracture. Just a very bad cut where the metal rack hit the side of his head and he's had quite a few stitches in the wound. He's got concussion and will be in hospital for some time, but he's young and fit and he'll recover. It'll just take time.'

Christie thanked her and went in search of Joe. He also had screens around the bed but he could have visitors. He looked terrible. He was unshaven and his eyes still looked a bit dazed. However, he recognised his visitor.

'Thank goodness you've come,' he said, as soon as Christie had sat down. He sounded upset and worried. 'Tell Mike not to say a word about Lena and Kenneth. Tell the police it was a domestic argument, and I'll sort it out with them when I get home.'

Christie was taken aback by this.

'Joe, you know that Lena and Kenneth are both dead. You were all out on the boat and they drowned in the river. Mike is in this ward too, with a broken leg and head injuries. He's not allowed any visitors and won't be speaking to anyone for some time. Molly almost drowned as well, but Kenneth saved her. She's also in this hospital.'

Joe turned his head away.

The bell sounded, heralding the end of visiting time and Christie was relieved to be leaving.

Edna and Mary arrived in the evening to see Molly. They had heard the dreadful news about the event but were both under the impression it was an accident. Molly didn't want to alarm them so she let them keep that assumption.

After asking her how she was feeling Edna said, 'The agency is working away fine, Molly.' She turned to her companion. 'Mary has been a gem and is still working at Rough and Fraser's bakery while I'm doing two jobs; helping John Knox with his book and back at the grocer's shop. Nancy has taken another cold seemingly.

'Jean is holding the fort on reception. Her husband doesn't mind her being in the office. It was going out and meeting homicidal maniacs he was worried about.'

After they left, Molly sank down on her pillows and tried to sleep. Perhaps if she managed that, the dreadful memories would vanish.

Still, she was getting home tomorrow and thankfully would be in her own house and able to grieve properly for the dead.

Marigold arrived in the late morning, after the doctors had done their rounds. She looked so healthy and sensible that Molly began to feel better. She had brought a small brown attaché case with clean clothes.

'Right then,' she said. 'Let's get you home.'

Molly could have cried with relief at her no-nonsense attitude.

'I've got a taxi waiting to take us to the station and I've ordered another one at Wormit to take us home.'

Molly was a bit slow at putting on her clothes, as if she had aged ten years in the last few days. Her arms and legs were still weak, but the doctor had said she would recover fully; it would just take time. He had wanted her to stay another day or two in hospital but she had persuaded him to let her go home and recover there.

The sun was shining as they got into the taxi and the journey over the Tay Bridge wasn't as bad as she thought it would be. She sat in the middle seat so she couldn't see the river. However, it was a different matter when she got home.

Marigold had pulled the blinds down in the living room and that helped. She had been taken aback to see the Anglia parked in the drive.

'I forgot all about the car,' she said. 'How did it get back here?'

'That nice man, Christie, brought it back. He was on his way to the ferry so he drove it from Cliff Top House.'

She sat beside Molly and took her hand. 'Try and forget all what's happened.'

'I wish I could Marigold but I can't. I keep seeing Lena and Kenneth's faces and Joe lying there. If Kenneth hadn't saved me I would have drowned as well.' Then without warning, she burst into tears. Marigold made sympathetic noises and told her to cry for as long as she wanted. 'Better to get the grief out than store it up Molly.' Then Marigold went to get a clean handkerchief for her tears.

Sabby, who had been sitting in the window seat, suddenly jumped up on Molly's lap, before flopping down and purring.

Both women were so taken aback and Molly burst into tears again as her hand stroked the cat's warm fur.

# 32

Charlie Jones was on duty when news came in about the fatalities in the boating accident.

'More inexperienced people messing about in boats,' he said, as he looked at the list of he people involved, but he caught his breath when he saw a name he recognised . . . Molly McQueen. Now there's a coincidence he thought. He, however, was a man who didn't believe in coincidences.

He had gone to see her briefly in hospital but she wasn't in a fit state to be interviewed, nor was the other survivor, Joe Lamont. That was another strange thing. Molly McQueen had almost drowned along with Joe's wife, Lena, and her brother Kenneth, but Joe had taken a large dose of barbiturates and had been unconscious when admitted to hospital.

He hoped he would get the entire story from Miss McQueen now that she was she was back home.

Driving the black police car was Constable Williams and they made their way to Craig Pier and waited in the queue. It was a grey, overcast day with a strong breeze and the river looked turbulent.

'A bit of a strange case this, Sir,' Constable Williams said as they waited in the queue.

Charlie agreed. There was something about this McQueen woman he couldn't fathom. First, she had admitted knowing Harry Hawkins and now she was involved in a boating accident that had resulted in another two deaths. Events certainly seemed to happen around her . . . and all to do with water.

The weather had worsened during the crossing and by the time they reached Newport, the rain was torrential. The windscreen wipers could hardly cope with the amount of water.

Marigold was in the house with Molly when the two policemen arrived and she showed them into the living room where Molly was sitting in an armchair, a rug over her knees. There was a cosy fire burning in the grate and Marigold was in the kitchen.

Marigold said she would leave them alone but Molly asked if she could stay. Charlie said he had no objections so the older woman went and sat down on the window seat with a very handsome striped cat.

'Just tell me in your own words how it happened,' Charlie said.

Molly's hands were clasped on her lap but she seemed composed. She began by saying she had been employed initially by Lena, Mrs Lamont, because of Lena's broken arm and how much she had enjoyed the work.

'How did you get on with the other members of the firm?'

'I didn't have too much to do with Joe, Mike or Christie. Most of my work was with Lena and Kenneth, her brother. I liked them both very much. The work wasn't too hard and they paid well.'

'But you left your employment suddenly, didn't you?'

Molly said she had. 'I got the impression things weren't going too well with the family. There was a lot of tension in the house and I thought I should give them some notice of my leaving.'

'Were they worried they wouldn't cope when you left? You said Lena had a broken arm. Was she annoyed that you were leaving?'

Molly was silent for a moment or two. 'Actually, I think Kenneth was relieved that I was going. I said I would stay on until they could maybe get someone else or when Lena's arm was better but he became very cool and curt. He said . . .'

'Yes, Miss McQueen? What did he say?'

'I've just remembered something. When Lena was in the water, she kept screaming for Kurt to come and help her.'

'Do you know who she meant?

Molly said she didn't.

'Can you tell us what happened on the day of the accident?'

'I was asked to go back that Saturday, to help with the monthly party.' She explained how this event was held, with valued clients coming to view the paintings and furniture. 'There was a pot of coffee on the stove with a note to help myself, but I had not long had tea with Marigold and, anyway, I don't like coffee.

I went to the sheds and that's where I found Mike, lying injured under a rack. I went back to the house to phone for an ambulance and then I heard the scream which I thought had come from the boat. I ran to the jetty and into the boat. Lena was screaming and Joe was lying on the deck. I thought he was dead, but I now know he'd been drugged.

Kenneth and Christie arrived back in the van and Kenneth jumped onto the boat just as Lena was trying to start the engine. He kept telling her to go back but she wouldn't listen. She kept accusing me of stealing her key, but I never had a house key. There was always someone there when I arrived for work. Well, she wouldn't believe me and kept saying I had her key. She said she had searched my house and office but I had hidden her key and she couldn't find it.

'I noticed her plaster cast was off and thought she had been back to the hospital but then I saw the horrific wound on her arm. It had gone all septic and I realised she had been cleaning it with Dettol. She said she wished she had killed the dog that did it.' Charlie interrupted sharply, 'What dog?'

'She didn't say. She just said some dog had bitten her and she wished she had killed it at the time. Then she told Kenneth that she was planning to kill Joe and me and that the bodies would never be found. Then they could go away and start new life away from Nelly.'

Charlie asked about Nelly.

'She's a rich widow, who announced her engagement to Kenneth one night at a party. I think the family were shocked, especially Kenneth. The only one who seemed amused was Joe.'

Charlie then took her through the time in the water but she was becoming distressed. Marigold went and sat beside her.

'I think that's all, Miss McQueen. Thank you for all your help.'

When the two men were back in the car, Charlie asked the Constable what he thought. Dave Williams was pleased to be asked for his input and he gave it some thought. 'Well, Sir, I think the girl is telling the truth. It's a strange story if you ask me, but that's why I think it's true.'

Charlie said. 'I agree. Now let's go and interview Joe Lamont.'

The car swished through deep puddles and they almost missed the opening to Cliff Top House. It was Charlie who noticed the small sign and the driver had to reverse the car.

'Not a very wide drive, is it sir?'

Charlie said it wasn't. The view wasn't good today because of the wet weather but the house was impressive.

'Must be lots of money to be made in the antique business,' said Charlie, stepping out of the car and dodging the puddles in the courtyard.

Joe came out of the kitchen door and said to come in. The kitchen was warm but there was no welcoming cup of tea here. They sat on the wooden chairs around a large table.

Charlie asked about the boating accident.

Joe leaned back in his seat and lit a cigarette. 'It was an accident. Lena and I had had a row that morning and she was upset. She went onto the boat to get away from the house, as she often did when we fell out over some trivial matter.'

'What happened to your workman, Mike? Did he pull the rack on top of himself?'

'He must have. I think he stretched too far and the rack tumbled on top of him.'

Charlie changed tactics. 'How did you manage to get on board when you had taken all those sleeping pills?

Joe didn't hesitate. 'I took them before I went to see Lena. Then I must have passed out.'

'Do you normally take such a large dose of barbiturates? The hospital had to pump out your stomach or else you could have died. Was that intentional? Were you trying to kill yourself?'

Joe tried to laugh. 'No, not at all. I must have taken more than I meant to. It was an accident.'

'Seems there were a lot of accidents that day. What if I tell you that I have a witness who tells me your wife was planning to put you and the witness overboard and pretend the two bodies were your wife and her brother? And that she was planning to run away to start a new life with her brother . . . away from someone called Nelly?'

Joe's face went white. However, he recovered quite well.

'If that witness is Molly McQueen then she's a liar. I never liked her. Lena thought she had stolen her key, she couldn't find it. Lena was really upset at that.'

Charlie stood up. 'Thank you for your time, Sir. We'll be in touch.'

Outside, he asked PC Williams what his impressions were.

'Well, he's certainly not grieving for his wife or her brother.'

Charlie had thought the same thing.

'Now let's go and see Christie, the man who raised the alarm. He'll be in the sheds, which I think are over there.'

Christie had been waiting all morning for the police to arrive. When he saw them approaching the sheds, he went out.

Before Charlie could speak, Christie handed him a sheet of paper. 'I think you should read this letter first,' he said.

# 33

Charlie and PC Williams sat in two luxurious armchairs in Nelly Marten's lounge. The first floor flat in Magdelen Road had a large window with a panoramic view of the river and the Tay Bridge.

The room was furnished with good taste. The expensive furniture and curtains and the paintings on the wall spoke of wealth.

Nelly sat opposite them and Charlie thought she was one of the plainest women he had ever met. She was wearing a black dress, which did nothing for her complexion and her dark hair, which was sprinkled with grey, had a coarse look. The one and only bright spot about her was the red necklace she wore. It sparkled in the light and Charlie thought something so vulgar must be a cheap piece of jewellery.

She seemed composed but her eyes looked red, as if she had been crying. 'What can I do for you?'

Charlie handed her the letter. She put on her spectacles and began to read it. Afterwards, she placed it on the low coffee table in front of her.

'Did you write that letter?' asked Charlie.

Nelly sighed and gazed out of the window. 'It would be stupid of me to deny it, wouldn't it? But I'm really sorry I did. It's brought nothing but grief. I thought it would bring Kenneth to me but it's led to his death.' She took a small hankie from her pocket and dabbed at her eyes.

'Can you tell us the background to its contents?' Charlie settled back in his chair. He had an idea the story would take some time. 'You mention Lizzy and Benjamin. Who are they?'

Nelly gave a deep sigh.

'The story goes back years and years, when Lena and I were children. She was my sister. I think I always resented her because she was beautiful with blonde hair and she took after our mother, while I inherited my father's looks.

'In 1925, our mother died. She was Scottish but my father was born in Holland, and was a distant cousin of my late husband, Hans Marten. They were in business together, along with a Jewish family called Rosenberg, who were diamond and jewel merchants, as well as antique dealers. Their business was in Rotterdam.

'In 1930, my father remarried another Scottish woman; a widow with a sixteen-year-old son. That son was called Joe Lamont and, because of our Scottish connections, we were all educated in Edinburgh.

'Then Hitler came to power and the Jewish people became afraid because they had heard about the restrictions on their businesses and on travel. Mr Rosenberg decided to sell out his share of the business to Hans, just as a temporary measure until Hitler and his cohorts fell from power.

'The Rosenbergs had a son called Benjamin; a lovely gentle lad who was a writer and a poet. Lena had gone to work for them as a secretary where she fell in love with Ben. He didn't want anything to do with her. In fact, he told me once that she repulsed him. She must have overheard because she looked shattered that day.

'Then Ben went off to university where he met Lizzy, another dreamy, gentle soul and they were married in 1939. Lena was incandescent with rage and she said she would sort him out somehow.

'Kenneth, or to give him his real name, Kurt Deitrich, also worked with the firm and had always been in love with Lena. I think she got engaged to him to spite Ben. She knew I was in love with him, but Lena never loved anyone but herself. Although Kurt had a German name he was a Dutch citizen as his great grandfather had settled in the Netherlands.

'At the end of 1939, the Jews were being rounded up and Hans and my father made a plan to get the Rosenbergs away to Britain. The Rosenbergs owned a seaside house on the French/Belgian border and they managed to get there. By now Lizzy was expecting a baby but she was a delicate creature and was ill most of the time.

'By this time, I was married to Hans. He was much older than me but we had a fairly happy marriage until he died just after the war ended. Joe's mother had also died in 1939.

'Hans knew a ship's captain. They were great friends and went on regular fishing trips together. He asked him if he could get the Rosenberg family to Britain and he agreed. It was decided that Joe and Kenneth would go and take them over on the ship but Lena announced that she wanted to go as well.

'So they all set off from Rotterdam one night and made their way to the town where the family were staying. Hans had emptied their house of all the valuables because he didn't want the Nazis to confiscate everything. They owned some fabulous jewels and diamonds as well as beautiful antique furniture and paintings. Their house was a real treasure trove.

'The jewels were all in a strongbox and Lena demanded that she should look after it. I was wary of her motives so, before she left, I took out the most valuable things and just left some of the diamonds and other less valuable jewellery.'

Her hand went to her neck and she stroked the red glass necklace.

'Well, it all went wrong. The British army had landed in France and were in retreat and all hell broke loose. Kenneth and Joe reached the town all right but when they got there, a neighbour told them the Rosenbergs had been rounded up by the Germans and taken away. She said they hadn't come back.

'Kenneth tried to make some enquiries in the town, but time was against them so they had to come over to Britain on their own. Joe said the best plan was to pretend to get married to Lena and pass Kenneth off as Lena's brother. It was just a marriage of convenience because Kenneth and Lena had been living together as a cohabiting couple. Kenneth and Joe tried to find out what happened to the Rosenbergs after the war and it turned out that Lizzy had died on route to the concentration camp. Mr and Mrs Rosenberg were separated from Ben and he was put into a work party. He never saw his parents again and died a couple of years later. Kenneth found a survivor from Auschwitz, who had worked with Ben. He told him the whole tragic story, but said he died of a broken heart.'

She stopped talking and gazed out the window at the peaceful scene beyond, her mind back in those terrible days.

'One day, just after the end of the war, Lena came here in tears. She said her relationship with Kenneth had broken down and he had told her he no longer loved her. She then said she wished she hadn't betrayed Ben because he might have married her once Lizzy had died.

'I was shocked. We had all thought it was a tragic turn of events that had led the Rosenbergs to their deaths and here was Lena, saying she was the one who had informed the Germans about their whereabouts.

'Well, I decided my turn had come to marry Kenneth after all these years and I announced our engagement. I thought that Lena couldn't open her mouth and protest. What I didn't realise was Kenneth's reaction to my proposal. He was shocked and that's why I sent the letter; to let him know what Lena had done. Lena was always mentally fragile but she became worse as the years went on and Kenneth was afraid that she was becoming deranged. I didn't know the full story of his attraction to Molly. I guessed a bit of it but I didn't realise how much.'

She stood up. 'That's the whole sordid story and I'm really sorry for my part in it. I should have kept quiet about Lena but, as I said earlier, I really resented her.' Her hand went up to the necklace again. 'I wear this all the time. I wanted Lena to see it every time I came to the house. I never wanted her to forget what she had done.'

Charlie asked, 'Isn't it a glass necklace?'

Nelly laughed but it wasn't a humorous sound. 'This was Ben's wedding gift to Lizzy. A necklace of perfectly matched rubies.' She undid the clasp and put it on the coffee table.

'But you're right . . . by wearing it I've managed to make it look cheap and it's just red glass as you say. One thing I will say is that something happened on that journey that changed all their lives forever. I never found out what, but I do know Kenneth was never the same with Lena after that.' Charlie thanked her and the two policemen emerged into the street. Nelly was standing at the window. She looked a pathetic sight.

'Well, what do you make of that, Sir?' said PC Williams.

Charlie was quiet for a moment then he said, 'I remember when I was at school we all went to see a play; a tragedy full of death and mayhem. That's what this story sounds like. People's lives wasted in the search for love, revenge, money and power.'

'Where do we go from here, Sir?'

'We're going back to see Joe Lamont. If he won't answer our questions then I'll take him to the station and see how he likes it there. Telling us this whole sorry affair was the result of a domestic tiff!'

Joe was sitting in the sheds. He had just come back from the hospital. Mike was in a good deal of pain and it would take ages for his broken leg to heal.

Joe clenched his hands into two fists. If Lena had still been alive he would have lost his temper with her. She had deliberately pushed the rack onto Mike as he tried to stop her from dragging him into the boat. Mike had told him he must have been groggy from the pills and he had seen her half carrying Joe aboard the boat.

Memories, he thought, and all of them bad.

He was still sitting there when Christie arrived, carrying a clip-board. It looked as if business was going on as usual.

'How's Mike?' he asked.

Joe said he was as well as could be expected. 'Do you know, Christie, Mike saved my life a few years ago.'

Christie was surprised by this statement but he stayed silent.

'I was fishing one evening in the river. Not here, but further upstream, nearer Perth. I slipped in the water and my waders filled up. I almost drowned. Mike had been fishing as well, and he jumped in and pulled me out. He was just out of the army after the War and was in a job he hated, so I asked him to join the firm and he's been here ever since. Oh, I know he doesn't have a great way with women, he doesn't know how to handle them, but he's been a good friend to me.'

Christie said, 'What will happen to the business now, Joe? Will you continue to run it?'

Joe gave a hollow sounding laugh. 'I expect Nelly will take over. She's always been the boss, but she's been more of a silent partner. She inherited the business from her husband Hans.

'Maybe I'll stay on. It all depends on how well Mike does. If he wants to stay on then I will as well.'

The two men were still sitting there when the policemen arrived.

'I've got some more questions that need answering, Mr Lamont,' said Charlie.

Joe nodded. He seemed a different man from the one who had been interviewed the day before.

'First of all, we have talked to Mrs Marten and she has told us all about the Rosenberg family and how you, Kenneth and Lena all came to Britain.'

Joe gave a deep sigh and slumped down in his chair.

'Yes, she phoned me. It happened so long ago. Yes, the story Nelly told you is true. We went to get the Rosenbergs out of France, but they had been taken away by the German SS officers.

'Because I was a British subject I had to escape as well and the other two joined me. I remembered this place from my childhood, it belonged to my grandfather. My mother always told me she had inherited it and that it would be mine one day. So we decided to come here. He had to keep our heads down and try not to attract much notice but after the war ended, Nelly came up with the idea of an antique business.

'When my mother was seventeen she gave birth to an illegitimate son called Kenneth Drummond. He died when he was six months old but I found his birth certificate amongst my mother's effects when she died. So we thought up the idea of Lena and I pretending to be married and passing Kurt off as her brother Kenneth. My mother had married my father, Arthur Lamont, but he disappeared. She later found out he was dead and when she met Wilhelm Marten in a hotel in Dundee, they fell in love and got married. Because Nelly's husband was a second cousin of her father, she didn't have to change her name when she married.

'That's how I went to Holland with her and became stepbrother to Nelly and Lena. The business did very well, mostly because of the furniture and paintings from the Rosenberg house, plus all the jewellery. Nelly's husband, Hans, had taken it over legally and, in the eyes of the law, it all belonged to him. Of course, it was all supposed to go back to the Rosenbergs after the war, but they all perished in Auschwitz.'

Joe looked at Charlie. 'And that's the whole story. Everything would have gone on as before if Nelly hadn't made that stupid proposal to Kenneth.'

But Charlie knew there was more. 'Tell me about the wound on your wife's arm.'

Joe looked astonished. 'How did you know about that?'

'Never mind how, just tell us how she came to have such a bad, septic wound.'

'It was all so stupid. Lena and I were at the docks one day, at the shipping office when this man appeared. "How are you keeping?" he said. Lena looked at him and asked "Do I know you?" The man, who looked as if he was a seaman, said he had worked on the boat that brought us all over here, in 1940.

'Well I thought Lena would faint, she went white. I told her to just say hello and thank him. I don't think he was trying to be anything other than friendly, but she ran after him and I heard her ask him to meet her that night at the docks. She wanted to repay his kindness, but she had to go to the bank to get some money.

'She said afterwards that he had tripped and fallen into the water; that she had had nothing to do with it. The next morning she was back at the shipping office when she saw this old man and his dog sniffing about, she said, and asking questions about his disappearance.

'Well, Lena being the way she was, followed him. She told us afterwards that she kept following him and tried to stop him going on about the sailor. One day, she followed him to a graveyard and saw that the man's name was Harry Hawkins. She got it onto her head that this Harry Hawkins had told this old man everything; She said she just wanted to stop him poking his nose in, but the man's dog went for her and gave her a very nasty bite.

'Of course, she wouldn't go to the doctor to see about it and began treating it herself and cleaning the wound with Dettol'

Charlie was puzzled. 'But your wife had her arm in a plaster. How could the dog have bitten her. For the first time, Joe laughed. 'Oh yes, her plaster. She went around telling everyone that someone had tried to murder her. The truth was she fell down the stairs and sprained her arm, but she went around telling everyone, including Kenneth, that her arm was broken. She would never have told me but I caught her one morning winding the bandage around her arm. It was never a plaster but a thick white bandage. She always wore long-sleeved dresses to hide it. When it suited her, she removed the bandage and her arm was perfectly all right. She liked to think she was the injured party here and even hired that McQueen woman to come and work for her. Well, it backfired, didn't it? Kenneth fell in love with her and Lena was furious. I was suspicious of Molly McQueen. I couldn't understand what game Lena was playing because I knew her arm was all right so I asked Mike to check up on her but as usual Mike's macho way with women spoiled our chances of discovering that agency woman's motives. He even stole a handbag from a stranger on the ferry. He said he thought it was Molly and seemingly they both looked similar, at least from the back.'

'Miss McQueen had no ulterior motive. She was hired by your so called wife to come and work here. And another thing Mr Lamont, why didn't you tell Kenneth about Lena's deception?'

'I wish I had now but Lena begged me not to tell him and I stupidly listened to her. Quite honestly I had had enough of Lena and all her dramas.'

Charlie looked over to PC Williams who was writing everything down in his notebook, his eyes like saucers at all the revelations.

Joe crossed his arms and it looked like the interview was over. Charlie could almost hear his sigh of relief. Although he had no evidence he decided to make one last stab at getting the whole truth. Nelly had said that something had gone seriously wrong on that journey thirteen years ago. But what?

'Mr Lamont, what went wrong when you went to rescue the Rosenbergs? Nelly said you were all in a panic according to the captain of the ship, but he had no idea why.'

Joe glared at him. 'I don't know what you're talking about.'

Charlie leaned forward. 'Oh I think you do. Don't you think this all has to end here? Something happened and I think you should get it off your chest. Then you can make a new life for yourself and start again.'

Joe hesitated. Then it all came out.

'We made our way to the town to pick up the Rosenbergs and found an abandoned house just outside the town. Kenneth told Lena to stay there while we went to fetch them. Of course, when they weren't there, we were confused and as we didn't have a lot of time, became a bit panic-stricken. Then, some neighbours of the Rosenbergs told us that SS officers had picked them up. They had been taken away and hadn't come back.

'So we hurried back to the house but when we got there we found a young soldier, a sergeant who had left some injured men in the forest and was looking for medical attention for them. Stupidly, Lena had locked him in a bedroom. She said he had tried to question her and she didn't know what to do.

'We gave him a meal and some tea from our stores and Kenneth and I decided to slip the key under the door as we left, so he could let himself out. We were on the verge of leaving when Lena said she would take the man some tea. Then we heard a shot.

'She had brought a little pistol that she owned, but we didn't know she had it. She said he had tried to escape but that was a lie. He was still on the bed and still alive. Kenneth said we could carry him to the doctor in the town and say we found him on the road, but we hadn't reckoned with the retreat at Dunkirk. There were soldiers everywhere, but we managed to get the poor man to the doctor and we left him there. I don't know if he survived or not.'

'He didn't.'

They all turned in astonishment to see Christie standing in the doorway. He walked over and handed a sheet of paper to Charlie. It was creased and written in pencil. On the reverse side was a drawing of a clown, obviously done by a small child.

Dear Mum,

I've been taken prisoner by a woman and two men. From the snatches of conversation I've overheard it seems they are on a mission to rescue some people called Rosenberg but they failed. They are leaving on a boat tonight. I trust the two men but the woman scares the life out of me. The men say they will release me when they leave. I'm hoping to make my way into the small town and get medical aid for my four wounded comrades. If I survive this then I'll destroy this note.

Your loving son, Colin.

Charlie said. 'Who is this Colin?'

'He was my brother.'

Joe stood up Astonishment written all over his face. 'But the soldier was Scottish.'

'My father and mother separated when we were small. I went to Canada with him and Colin stayed with Mum.'

'Where did you get this note?' asked Charlie

'The doctor who treated him found it in his boot. It was addressed to my mother and after the war, he posted it on to her. He was buried in a small cemetery in the town.'

'How did you end up here?' Charlie asked.

'It was the name Rosenberg. My father is an antique dealer and when the jewellery first came on sale it was marketed as theirs. I came over to Scotland when my mother was ill and she begged me to find these people and get closure for Colin. When she died last year I decided to stay on and try and trace the people and my enquiries led here.'

He turned to Joe. 'I've been investigating you all for ages and I was almost ready to confront Lena with the death of my brother. I found the strongbox with the jewellery in it and Nelly's letter.' 'Although the letter was written to Kenneth, he gave it to Lena. It was in the same drawer as the strongbox.

Joe said, 'So you've spying on us?'

Christie admitted that he had.

'Where's this strongbox now?' asked Charlie.

Joe said, 'It's upstairs in Lena's room but she lost the key. Lena was frantic, she said the key had been stolen.'

Charlie suddenly remembered Molly's statement. 'Miss McQueen said your wife accused her of stealing a key but she had no idea what she meant.'

'She searched Molly's house but she didn't find anything, She even got a copy of Molly's office key made so she could search her office.' said Joe.

Christie went upstairs and reappeared with an oblong box about twelve inches by fourteen. There were a lot of scratches around the lock where someone had tried to open it.

'That was Lena, 'said Joe. 'She was frantic trying to open it without the key, but now it's lost'

'I know where the key is,' said Christie. They looked at him with astonishment.

Molly was surprised when the men turned up at her door. Christie said, 'Have you got that five-year diary, Molly, that was delivered to you a few weeks ago?'

Molly was confused. 'The one I got from my sister in Australia?'

'No, I sent it. Could you go and get it please?'

Molly went to the bookcase and brought it out. The key was hanging from a cord tied to the cover.

Christie held it up. 'One key for one strongbox.'

Charlie opened it up to reveal a parcel of diamonds and other assorted necklaces and brooches within.

Nelly had said she had taken out the most valuable items but judging from the contents of the box, there was a fortune still lying inside it.

PC Williams had never seen anything like this. He was used to road traffic accidents or driving around to burglaries and drunken rabbles in the pubs at closing time. Now he was involved with all this drama.

Charlie locked the box and they left for the police station with Christie and Joe. They had to make statements, said Charlie.

Marigold came in and Molly, who was still confused, told her the story of the diary and the key.

'To think I had the key to all those diamonds,' she said.

Marigold shook her head. 'They haven't brought very much joy or luck for the owner, have they?

Molly had to agree.

# 34

Charlie was sitting in Tam's kitchen. Rover was curled up by the fire.

'I can't believe all that evil could come from a woman,' said Tam.

Charlie had to agree. 'Still, if you hadn't insisted that Harry had been pushed into the river maybe all this wouldn't have come out. The deaths of Lena and Kenneth may have been treated as an accident and Miss McQueen's statement regarded as over-dramatic. Still it's queer that the Canadian fellow managed to investigate his brother's death. He must have put a lot of work and time into it.'

'I'll go to Balgay cemetery tomorrow and put some more flowers on Harry's grave.' said Tam. 'Poor man, he just met with the wrong person at the wrong time.'

Molly was back at work. Things were looking up and work was coming in on a regular basis. Edna, Mary, Jean and Betty were all out on various jobs. Molly was hoping to interview another school leaver for the job as receptionist, as Mary had done a great job at Rough and Fraser's bakery.

She was sitting in Edna's house and the two women were discussing the business. 'Is everything going well for you now, Edna?' asked Molly. 'I mean that bother with Reg?'

'I haven't had any more word, thank goodness. I assume he's gone abroad and hope that he stays there. I'm hoping to keep seeing John and he feels the same way about me. I'll always be grateful to Eddie for saving me when Reg threatened me but I've told him about my feelings for John and he wished me good luck with whatever I do. I'm going out to dinner with John tomorrow.'

'Well, good for you, Edna' said Molly. Although not envious of her, she did feel a little sad. There was no man in her background and she was missing Kenneth. Or Kurt, as he was called, but Molly would always remember him as Kenneth.

# 35

The sun was beating down and the small town looked deserted. Reg sat in his car, waiting for Anya to finish work. He had met her in the local hotel and was quite smitten with her dark Arabic looks. He had a week off work as his boss was on holiday.

He was due back in a week's time, so that would give Reg lots of time to see Anya. Mind you, he thought, she was a bit of a firebrand, but he would soon knock that out of her. He would show her who was boss. Like last night when she tried to leave him behind. Well, he let her know he wasn't going to let a woman treat him like that so he had given her a slap.

He was going to see Edna when this job was over. He had some unfinished business with her . . . and with that skinny lad who had managed to humiliate him. The thought of revenge was sweet and he settled back in the car seat.

This was the life he loved. The heat and the danger. He missed his army days but this was the next best thing. People had to pay him respect out here and he didn't take any nonsense from the natives.

He noticed the dark-haired man walking along the street but he was just a kid. However, his training kicked in and he kept his eyes on him, which was a pity because he never noticed the other man coming up behind the car. He heard the explosion before it registered in his brain.

From the hotel doorway, Anya glanced at the dead body in the car, then walked away in the opposite direction with the two men.

# 36

Marigold had baked a Victoria sponge cake filled with home made raspberry jam. She had set the table very carefully as it wasn't every day Molly had a visitor.

Christie sat in the chair by the window and looked at the two women. He thought Molly looked tired and there were still dark shadows under her eyes as if she wasn't sleeping very well. He was glad that Marigold was near at hand to keep an eye on her. Not that there was any danger now but she had suffered an emotional shock which would take a long time to recover from.

The two women were eager to hear his story.

'What I can't understand,' said Molly, 'is how you managed to trace them to this part of the world.'

Marigold said she was wondering the same thing. 'It's just like a detective novel.'

'When I came over to see my mother during her illness, she showed me the letter. She had spent years agonising over Colin's death and begged me to try and find out the what had happened to him. I started to investigate, but she died before I really got started. My father came over for the funeral and I showed him the letter and told him I was going to stay on and search for the truth.'

'But where did you start? asked Marigold.

'I had a rough idea of where he was when the retreat of Dunkirk happened. The letter mentioned a town but no name so I went over to France and did a bit of digging around. In a small seaside town near Dunkirk I struck lucky and found the doctor who had treated Colin. He remembered him very well and he had even managed to treat the other four injured soldiers, because Colin had told him roughly where they were.

'They all survived and were sent to a hospital when the German soldiers entered the town three days later, but sadly Colin had already died. The doctor was puzzled by his bullet wound. He said he didn't think it had been caused by a soldier's weapon. Colin was buried in a small cemetery on the outskirts of the town.

'The doctor mentioned the two men who had brought him in that night. The entire area was in the midst of the fighting between British Forces and the German Army. He said it had been a terrible night of wind and rain and they had both been soaked and covered in mud but he recognised them as the same men who had been making enquiries about the Rosenberg family who owned a house in the town and were well-known in the area as they used to spend summer holidays there in the days before the war.

'He also said there was a rumour that the men had arrived by boat along with a woman and planned to leave the same way.'

Christie stopped and gazed out of the window.

'I just get a bit emotional about the way Colin died. He managed to save his four comrades but not himself,' Christie said.

'I came to a halt with my enquiries then. The four British soldiers were all sent to prisoner of war camps after being discharged from the hospital and I couldn't trace them. The doctor who told me that, said he had no idea where they had been held and, after the war, when all the prisoners were repatriated, it was a dead end.'

Molly said. 'How did you manage to find out more?'

'It was my father who came up with the idea of getting someone to investigate it for me. He said he knew someone who was a retired policeman who had opened up a small detective agency. I hired him and he was great. He managed to trace the ship's captain who had brought Joe, Kenneth and Lena over to Britain. He told him that their destination had been Scotland, possibly somewhere near the coast, although he had dropped them off near Hull.

'He also gave me the names of the three of them, Joe Lamont who was the stepson of Wilhelm Marten, Kurt Deitrich and Lena Marten and that they were in the antique trade. So, armed with this knowledge, I scoured the antique shops and looked up the names in the telephone directory. I came across Lamont Antiques in Dundee and arrived one morning, a year ago.

'I went into the shop in the Nethergate and met Kenneth. We got chatting and I told him I was also in the antique trade, but wanted to spend a working holiday in Scotland . . . and the rest is history. I knew right away when I arrived here that I had the right people but I couldn't prove anything.'

He looked at Molly. 'That was when you almost caught me in the house. I was looking for evidence to see what had happened at that farmhouse in 1940. I had found the strongbox with jewels and I also found the key. The key, which I sent to you, Molly. I'm sorry I implicated you in this, but I didn't know where else to hide it.

'There was a hue and cry on the day it went missing. I thought Lena would explode with anger and she demanded that a search be made of all the rooms. Fortunately, I had to go to Dundee with you that day so I took the key with me, bought the diary and left it at your door.'

Marigold was puzzled. 'But it had an Australian stamp on it.'

Christie laughed. 'It was a Canadian stamp but I smudged it with some ink to make it look foreign and hoped you wouldn't notice it. A week ago I was on the verge of confronting Lena with my information when everything blew up and that's the whole sad story.'

Molly said, 'I remember the day Lena came to the agency. She looked so elegant and lovely and I really liked her.'

'Well that's the face she put on but underneath she was wicked through and through. Joe and Kenneth have turned out to be the two good guys in this whole tragic mess, and even Nelly has turned out to be a decent woman. Nelly has said that Joe and

Kenneth have been watching out for Lena all these years as they both knew she was mentally unbalanced but Kenneth had no intention of marrying Lena after Colin's death.'

Marigold wanted to know, 'What will happen to the business now?'

'It all belongs to Nelly. She inherited it from her husband Hans and he bought out the Rosenbergs in good faith, so everything they owned is also Nelly's. That was why she was always invited to the parties because it looked good if this rich woman was buying expensive pictures. Of course she never really bought them, it was just a front.'

Molly wanted to know what his plans were. 'Will you stay on here or will you go home?'

'I've booked my passage to Canada next week. Will you come and see me off from the station, Molly?'

'All right Christie. . .. I don't know your surname.'

'McCulloch, Christie McCulloch.'

# 37

Nelly was leaving. She had put her flat up for sale and was going back to Rotterdam. She had spoken to Joe and he said that Mike was still willing to work with him, so that is what she would do. Joe would look after the sale of the flat and that would be the end for her in this country.

They would also look after this end of the business as before while she remained in Holland. She had plans to hand the business over to Joe as she had lost all enthusiasm for it now.

She recalled Lena as a child, a beautiful, blonde vindictive child. Her father had doted on his lovely daughter and he gave her everything she asked for. Then, when she couldn't have Ben, the one person she really wanted and loved, she became hell bent on revenge. Now all this destruction, unhappiness and death had all come about.

She was honest enough to admit her part in this because of her impulsive proposal to Kenneth. How could she have got it all so wrong? To misread the signs. She had honestly thought Kenneth cared deeply for her and that love would have grown over time.

He had always been so charming to her and, foolish woman that she was, she thought she stood a chance with him.

All the plans had gone horribly wrong. Joe, Kenneth and Lena were meant to stay quietly until the war ended and then, when they had all made their fortune with the Rosenberg's jewellery and furnishings, plus all her inheritance from Hans. Afterwards they could all go back to the Netherlands and live happily ever after.

Nelly smiled in spite of her grief. Happy endings only ever happened in fairy tales.

She took one last look at the house, picked up her suitcases and left.

# 38

Charlie Jones had typed up his report and it was now with the Procurator Fiscal. There wouldn't be a case as the main suspect was dead. No bodies had washed up and, although that situation could change, Charlie had a gut feeling Lena and Kenneth would both remain undiscovered.

What a tragic case it had turned out to be, from the initial report of Harry Hawkins' death and the dogged determination of one old man, who firmly believed that he hadn't died a natural death, to this terrible conclusion.

From that Shakespeare play all those years ago, one quotation remained in his mind: 'A tale told by an idiot, full of sound and fury, signifying nothing.'

This had been such a tale, not told by an idiot but by a vengeful woman and it had signified a lot. There had been nine deaths, if one included Lizzy's unborn child, but it could have been much worse if Molly McQueen and Tam had also died.

The telephone on his desk rang. 'DS Johns,' he said. It was a report of a burglary in Broughty Ferry.

PC Williams was on the stairs as Charlie made for the door.

'Ah, just the man I need. Drive me to this address, would you? They've had a burglary.' He gave PC Williams the address.

As they both went downstairs, a look of dismay crossed the

constable's face. After all the excitement of the Lamont case with its echoes of wartime betrayal and fabulous jewels, this burglary was taking him back to the drudgery of a policeman's lot.

He gave a deep sigh then slipped behind the wheel of the car.

# 39

Molly stood on the platform of the railway station. Christie was late and she hoped he wouldn't miss his train. The station was busy with people coming back from day excursions and shopping trips.

Small children, tired from a day out, were whining and needing their beds. Molly glanced at the large railway clock. It said six o'clock. Christie would have to hurry as his train would be arriving in fifteen minutes. She saw him hurrying down the stairs with two large suitcases. She waved and he saw her.

'I thought I would miss the train,' he said. He sounded out of breath as if he had been running. 'Joe asked me to go with him to see Mike and I didn't like to refuse. I just wanted to say goodbye to them both.'

'Well, you're here at last.'

'I'm really pleased you came to see me off, Molly. I'll miss you.'

Molly looked surprised. 'Will you?'

'Don't look so astonished. Of course I'll miss you. I liked you from the very first day you came to Cliff Top House.'

Molly didn't know what to say. When he had asked her to come and see him off, she hadn't realised how he felt about her. She had seen so little of him during her time at the house.

'I've got a great idea. Why don't you come over to Canada? You would do well there with your agency and I could open a detective agency next door to you. Then I could do all the investigative work while you do the office stuff. We could become partners in crime.'

Molly laughed. 'You sound like someone from an Agatha Christie novel. Was that why your parents called you that?'

'I've no idea. Maybe my mother was a fan of hers. But I'm serious about the Canadian offer. Will you think about it?'

The train arrived, sending great belches of steam over the roof and the platform. Christie shook her hand.

'I hope this isn't goodbye. Will you keep in touch?'

'Yes I will. I'll write to you with all my news.'

The train slowly pulled away and Christie leaned out of the window. 'Remember my offer. Canada is only a few thousand miles away.'

Then he was gone.

Molly felt dispirited. After all the drama of the past couple of weeks she now felt she was in the doldrums. She had prayed that Kenneth would be found but, as time went on, it seemed highly unlikely.

She didn't feel like going home so she made her way to the Wellgate and the agency. The street was busy with people all heading for a night out at the pictures or maybe just for a walk on this fine summer night.

When she got near the agency she was surprised to see Edna and Mary standing at the door.

'We thought you might be a bit down in the dumps, Molly, so we thought we would come here and see you,' said Edna.

Mary had a small white box in her hand. 'We've bought some cakes from Nicoll and Smibert to have a cup of tea.'

Molly took her key from her bag. 'Well, what are we waiting for? Put the kettle on, Mary, and we can drown our sorrows with tea and cakes.'

When they were all sitting down, Molly said. 'Christie asked me to go to Canada with him.'

Edna looked at her. 'And? Are you thinking of going?'

'No' said Molly. 'What I am going to do is convert the rooms upstairs into a flat for myself. I don't want to stay with my parents when they come back from Australia.'

Edna gave her a shrewd glance. 'Why's that, Molly?'

272

For a moment, Molly didn't answer, then she said, 'I can't bear looking at the river from the window in the house. It brings back horrible memories.'

Mary went over and gave her a hug. 'You've still got us working for you and the business is getting busier. You've still got your friends.' She stopped. 'I remember where I saw Mike. Do you remember I said I thought his face was familiar? Well, the night Rita and I went to the Palais, I'm sure he was standing near us at the tram stop earlier that day.'

Molly was embarrassed when tears came into her eyes. 'It's all over now, Mary, and yes, I'm very lucky with you both. You're friends as well as work colleagues.'

Later as they all left to go home, Edna touched the letter in her pocket. She had been shocked to hear of Reg's death. There had an old letter from her in his pocket when he was shot and the authorities had written to inform her.

She had never wanted him to die, just to go away and leave her alone. Now, of course, he wouldn't ever bother her again. She was glad she hadn't mentioned it. Molly had suffered enough bad memories. She could do without hearing about her troubles just now.

Molly caught the train to Wormit. She had left the car there and as she slowly made her way home, her mind was full of confusing thoughts, mainly about Kenneth. Joe had told her that Kenneth was falling in love with her and she now realised she felt the same about him. He was far older than her but he had been a lovely man and she knew she would have had a great life with him. But like Tom, he was also dead so what was the good in thinking like this? She felt like there was some kind of jinx.

Marigold was waiting at the gate when she arrived. Sabby was sitting at her feet. Molly could tell she had been gardening because she was wearing her enormous canvas gloves, which had been the death of many a weed and thistle.

She was holding up a small yellow square. 'Molly, a telegram came for you about an hour ago.'

Molly always associated a telegram with bad news. She took it and quickly opened it.

'Nell had a baby girl yesterday, She's to be called Molly. Both well and asking for you.'

Marigold was dancing with joy, much to Sabby's displeasure. 'Oh that's wonderful news. A wee girl and called after you, Molly.'

Molly said, 'There's a bit more. "What a pity you couldn't be here. You've missed all the excitement. Mum and Dad."'

'Missed all the excitement indeed,' said Marigold.

Molly laughed so hard that she cried.